NARASIMHA

Kevin Missal wrote his first book at the age of 14, and at 22, the St Stephens graduate is a bestselling author and a full-time writer, with the first two books in his *Kalki* series being runaway successes. *Dharmayoddha Kalki: Avatar of Vishnu* and its sequel *Satyayoddha Kalki: Eye of Brahma* have sold one lakh copies in under a year. Kevin loves fantasy fiction and has always been a fan of mythology. His books have been featured in publications like *The Sunday Guardian*, *The New Indian Express* and *Millennium Post*. He lives in Gurugram and he can be contacted at kevin.s.missal@gmail.com

BOOK 1

NARASIMHA

THE MAHAAVATAR TRILOGY

KEVIN MISSAL

HarperCollins *Publishers* India

First published in India by
HarperCollins *Publishers* in 2019
A-75, Sector 57, Noida, Uttar Pradesh 201301, India
www.harpercollins.co.in

2 4 6 8 10 9 7 5 3 1

P-ISBN: 978-93-5357-076-7
E-ISBN: 978-93-5357-077-4

Typeset in 11/14.7 Minion Pro at
Manipal Digital Systems, Manipal

Printed and bound at
Thomson Press (India) Ltd

This book is produced from independently certified FSC® paper to ensure responsible forest management.

To all my readers – you have been awesome.
To all aspiring writers – keep writing and don't give up.

NOTE TO THE READER

Before you begin this novel, I have the responsibility of telling you the truth: this is not an accurate tale of Lord Narasimha. This is only my interpretation of it; my reimagining of him.

This is the story of Narasimha, a warrior who is half-man, half-lion, from the world of Illavarti (a fictionalized, fantastical version of the Vedic Age) where I take different analyses of religious texts and create a coherent narrative around them. For example, Lord Narasimha is worshipped as a physician in some villages of India, so I added that part in the book. Also, some texts depict Prahlad not just as a Vishnu Bhakt, but also as a soldier in Hiranyakashyap's army. So I put both depictions together and included them in the story.

The overarching tale, though, is similar to the mythology. I have only stitched different stories together for narrative consistency.

THE TRIBES

DEVAS

The Devas are foreigners who come from the island of Swarg, which lies to the north of Illavarti. They usurped the northern part of the country and gained control of major cities. Their ruler is called Indra. They worship various elements of nature, like fire, water and ice. They have long lifespans – two to three hundred years. They are really fair and are often associated with the colour white. They are the creators of Somas, which is a blue medicinal liquid derived from the Somalia plants found in Swarg. They believe in Dharma as well as the Trinity Gods—Vishnu, Mahadev and Brahma.

ASURAS

The Asuras are foreigners from the island of Pataal, which is to the east of Illavarti, across the Black Ocean. They are brown-skinned, golden-eyed and worship attributes like strength and valour, rather than the elements like the Devas. They rule the southern lands of Illavarti and their capital is Kashyapuri. They are often associated with evil because they do not have a religion and don't believe in one. They do not partake of the Somas. They have a strong exoskeleton and are competent in battle.

DANAVS

The Danavs are divided into Poulomas and Kalakeyas. The Poulomas are short giants, often ranging from ten to fifteen feet, while the Kalakeyas are over twenty feet tall. They live in large towers that are specially constructed for them. They eat large amounts of food and water. They are historically blood brothers of the Asuras and live in Hiranyapur. Other than the need for constant sleep and food, they do not have a purpose in life.

SIMHAS

According to mythology prevalent in Illavarti, the Simhas were created by Lord Vishnu in his first battle against evil. The Simhas are half-lion and half-human in spirit. They wear the skin of a deceased lion. They live in Vaikuntha, the forgotten religious city of Lord Vishnu. Since the Devas are close to being on the side of Dharma, the Simhas fight the battle on the side of the Devas. They are against practices looked at as being related to Adharm. They have strong claws and their skin is pale yellowish. They have reddish beards. This Yug's Avatar is destined to be from the Tribe of the Simhas.

PROLOGUE

KAYADHU

Death was close.

Kayadhu saw the balls of fire falling and exploding against the ground, the parks and fields, the huts in the kingdom. A volley of flaming arrows struck close to the heart of her palace, striking her Asura guards who fell back, bleeding.

She watched from her window before evading an arrow, which missed her by a hair's breadth.

What is happening?

Before she could comprehend the situation, she saw guards in black armour enter her room, with the Manav Guru Narada close behind them.

'My lady, we need to escort you out of the kingdom,' he pleaded.

'Who is behind this attack?' she asked, the curls on her temple dancing in the wind.

Before Narada could answer, another arrow flew into the room and struck close to the cradle. The baby began to cry.

'Where is Anuhrad?' she asked as she rushed to the cradle, grabbing hold of the infant.

'He's … uh … he's in the underground passage,' Narada whimpered. He was a bald man, wearing a white dhoti with a long white muffler across his chest. 'Hidden. The enemies will not find him.'

'That's good.' She picked up the infant from his cradle and handed him to Narada. 'Let them not find Prahlad either.'

Narada took the child and looked up at Kayadhu in anguish. 'What about you?' he asked.

Kayadhu swallowed a nervous lump. She didn't know what to do. She couldn't hide. She had come all the way from the island of Pataal for a better future, for hope … to not be burdened by the evils of society.

'Where are the Kalakeyas and Poulamas?' Kayadhu asked, referring to the Danav forces that resided in Kashyapuri.

'Most of them left with your husband, my lady,' Narada said.

She cursed. *How foolish was Hiranya to leave the kingdom isolated with a reduced army*? She knew her husband had gone to scatter the ashes of his brother over the holy river in Pataal.

And she knew that he would not be returning for a while.

'Bana is here, though,' Narada said, reading Kayadhu's mind and referring to the Danav lord who was in the palace. 'As is Holika. She's holding them off at the southern gates.'

So there was some hope, Kayadhu thought to herself and smiled. But then she looked at the infant in Narada's arms; innocent, confused and crying, and her brow furrowed. She leaned over and kissed the child's forehead. 'Take him to safety.'

'But what about you, my lady?' Narada asked.

Kayadhu grabbed her sword and unsheathed it. She took two daggers and a breastplate from the guards, who had come with Narada. 'I need to be out there, fighting for my kingdom. I just want to know … whom do the banners belong to?'

Narada lowered his eyes. 'Thunder.'

That bloody warmonger! she cursed to herself.

'He agreed to the truce! Why is he attacking now?'

'My lady,' Narada nodded apologetically, 'he's an opportunist. Seeing Lord Hiranya leave, he decided to attack and conquer Kashyapuri.'

I shall not let him do that, Kayadhu vowed to herself.

As the queen bid farewell to her son, she held his tiny, dimpled hands and realized that despite the war outside, there was a lot of beauty in the world.

Everything had seemed unreal until my sons were born.

As she tried to pull away, the infant Prahlad held on, as if he knew something that she didn't. Kayadhu pulled out her locket and handed it to her son, whose chubby fingers closed around it.

'I shall always be with you. Don't worry.' She kissed the infant once more before parting ways. Narada reluctantly left with Prahlad in his arms, followed by the guards.

As Kayadhu walked further, the corridors of her palace were strewn with corpses – handmaidens pierced with arrows, soldiers with their throats slashed. And just as she was taking in the horror of the scene before her, she was accosted by the sight of the Vanars, who had been waiting to pounce on her.

So the monkey tribe is involved too, she thought, preparing herself.

The Vanar Sena, in their white armour, attacked the instant they spotted her. Using her sword and deflecting their attack with ease, she smashed and slashed the skin and bones of the monkey men, and they fell back.

As she ran down the stairs, she stopped short on seeing that one of her Asura handmaiden's clothes were being torn apart by a Naga, blue-eyed and black-haired. She brought her sword down upon the Naga, splitting its head in two as the handmaiden cried out.

'Leave for the underground immediately, and take as many women and children with you as you can,' Kayadhu instructed the girl.

The handmaiden nodded and ran off.

Kayadhu opened the gates of her palace and saw the field up front – the sheer size of her men fighting against the Tribal army was enough to frighten her. Both sides were using swords, clubs and tridents, hitting and smashing at each other as anger boiled within them and spilled over.

Kayadhu drew her sword and began to tear at the Tribals, stabbing and piercing as she pushed forward.

Perhaps all was not lost. After all, there were not only Asura soldiers in her fort. The black-skinned Rakshasas and the fair-skinned Manavs were on her side too.

That was the thing. Ever since Devas and Asuras had begun ruling the country of Illavarti, the Tribals and Manavs who were separate races had begun to side with them. Though it's fair to say that the number of Manavs was higher towards Indra's side while Asuras had more Tribals.

For a split second, she'd been lost in thought, and she just managed to evade an arrow that flew past her head, missing her by merely an inch.

Curse you, mortal! She cursed as she spotted the bowmen targeting her and charged at them, deflecting the arrows with ease.

She had learnt sword fighting from the powerful women gurus in Pataal, and now, after years of training, her skills were finally being put to good use.

As she got closer to the bowmen, they instantly began to scamper. But they were no match for her speed, and with a quick swing, she cut off one's head and stabbed the other. She then saw the fort walls crumbling as a giant fell to the ground with a thunderous crash.

It was Bana.

He was a Poulamo, a kind of Danav – fifteen feet tall, which was short for a Danav. He had greasy long hair, a big snout for a nose, and gray, pallid skin. They were considered blood brothers of the Asuras, but while the Asuras were beautiful, with golden eyes and luminescent skin, the Danavs looked like abominations.

Kayadhu saw Bana being pulverized by two Simhas – a golden-haired Tribe that wore lion pelts instead of armour. They had tough claws that could break through any hard surface. As Bana finally began fighting them off, Kayadhu came forward, calling out, 'Hey, you!'

A Simha looked up – the human face shadowed under the hide of the lion skin. The Simha, ignoring Bana, lurched towards Kayadhu who deflected his claws with her sword.

'Now even savages are part of the war,' she mocked.

The Simha didn't respond. He was feral, clawing at and attacking her continuously until her arms began weakening from blocking his blows. The Simha pounced, but before he could get to her, a huge hand picked him up.

It was Bana, who had managed to kill the other Simha. He then took the one in his hand and ripped him apart.

'My lady,' he sighed as he knelt before the queen, exhausted. 'We are winning. Do not worry.'

Kayadhu smiled at him. 'Thank you so much for saving …'

And then it happened. The ground shuddered – even Bana noticed. Before Kayadhu could comprehend what was going on, a lightning-shaped arrow, about ten feet long, flew past her and struck Bana's chest, piercing through it and electrocuting him to death.

She knew this arrow. It was a Vajra.

Kayadhu turned her head and saw that the ground had shaken because, from the main gates, a huge elephant had entered the battleground, surrounded by roaring Simhas. Mounted on the elephant was a large weapon, a sort of arrow launcher.

The man who rode the elephant whistled. Slowly, the elephant raised his trunk, and the man climbed on it. The elephant then lowered him to the ground, next to Kayadhu. He was brown-skinned and adorned in gold, with white hair on the sides of his bald head and grayish eyes that mirrored the skies.

Kayadhu moved to attack him, but when she turned, she saw that her guards had been killed. The Simhas facing her stood in wait, their postures suggesting that they were ready to attack her.

'Devendra,' she breathed. 'You are wrong if you think you can take over this kingdom in the king's absence.'

The man shrugged, grinning as if the war pleased him. 'Do you really think I care about this kingdom? Well, actually I do, but I didn't come here today just to conquer it.'

Kayadhu sighed. She was beginning to feel battleworn.

'I came here for you, my dear,' Devendra said.

'Why me? We agreed to the truce. And you broke it. We could have lived together peacefully, supporting each other. But you had to show your supremacy. My husband ...' she broke off as tears swelled in her eyes. The amount of convincing she had done to bring about this truce was boundless. 'I had tried my best so that we could finally live in the age of peace, but you ... you started a war. A war that might not end. You broke the truce, again! Just like last time, when you didn't give us the Somas and decided to put it in nature.'

'Because you would have used the Somas to kill me!' the man exclaimed. 'Please, my dear, do not think of me as a fool. I know why your husband has gone to Pataal. He wants to convince the Council to give him more soldiers, so that he can attack me.'

Kayadhu shook her head. 'He's not a backstabber like you. He genuinely went to Pataal to scatter the ashes of his brother over the holy river.' She arched her brows. 'Did you really attack Kashyapuri because you were scared that he might break the truce, just like you did before, and are doing again?' She chuckled. 'A thief can only see a thief in an innocent man's heart.'

For a moment, there was a flicker of uncertainty in the man's eyes, and then he grew stern. 'All right, even if you are right, and I am being a fool by breaking the truce, I don't want to take a chance and get attacked, however small the possibility. So this beautiful disaster I created today, an invasion of sorts, is a reminder to him.'

'Reminder of what?' Kayadhu asked.

'To not do things – like going to Pataal – that will make me question his integrity. To remind him, that even though there is a truce, I am the ruler of Illavarti and he shall always be the vermin under my feet,' Devendra announced.

'You are an idiot,' Kayadhu spat at the Lord of Devas. '*Lord Indra*,' she mocked him.

Indra wiped the spit from his face and grinned. 'Well, see you soon. Hope he learns his lesson and so do you, to not mess with me.'

The elephant lowered his trunk again, and Indra had just stepped on it when suddenly, Kayadhu lunged forward towards him. Instantly, a figure stepped before Indra, blocking him from Kayadhu's blow, and the sword struck the figure across his chest. The Simha returned Kayadhu's attack, and with his gigantic claws, slashed Kayadhu's abdomen and pushed her to the ground, stabbing her in the back as she tried to crawl away.

Pain began to shoot down her spine and she cried out. As she turned, trying to get hold of the sword that had fallen from her grip because of the surprise attack, the figure stepped on her palm and instantly clawed her right shoulder, until she dropped her weapon.

She felt … *nothing*.

And then there was a burning sensation, and she touched her throat from where it originated. She realized that her throat had been slit, and the blood slowly oozing from it wet her fingers and turned warm. Her skin grew pale, as life ebbed away from her body.

No.

'Fool!' Indra shot an angry glance at the figure. 'We were not supposed to kill her. We were just supposed to scare her!'

A crimson thread trickled from her mouth when she smiled. Even though he acted nonchalant, she could hear the fright in his voice. She loved the sound of it; of the beating fear in Indra's heart.

'You …' she looked at the Simha whose sword had killed her; from whose weapon her blood dripped.

'He will return … he will kill you …' she coughed.

And then her vision blurred, and she was finally enveloped in the darkness of her enemy's making.

FOURTEEN YEARS LATER

1
NARASIMHA

I have a bad feeling about today.

He didn't know why he felt the way he did, but there it was. He was usually not an instinctive person, but for some reason, something about today felt off. *It must be the weather*, he told himself.

Trying to shrug off the feeling, Nara concentrated on the vegetables on his plate. He was famished. And no matter how much of the green stuff he ate, it never made him feel full. He wanted meat; needed it. *Just like I used to before …*

But no, he had promised himself that he would never again hurt another living being to fill his stomach. Not after everything he had done in the past.

I have too much to bear.

As he stuffed the beans and the juicy tendrils in his mouth, he noticed how the tavern was filled with drunkards. Nara believed in keeping his body disciplined, and he had always stayed away from these sins. Music played in the background and his feet tapped to the beat, for it was a catchy tune composed of flutes and drums. There was a smell of drinks and meat in the air. The loud chatter of men and women enjoying each other's company filled the tavern.

They were Manavs. And judging by his looks, Nara seemed like a Manav too.

Because I am not wearing my skin.

He was drinking water from a terracotta jug when he heard it – a loud cry.

Suddenly, silence fell, and everyone in the tavern looked around, trying to see where the noise had originated from.

Nara sniffed and then concentrated, closing his eyes. His ears pricked, picking up the softest sounds in the dull silence. And then he realized where the cry had come from.

Outside!

He instantly got up and walked out with the rest of the civilians to see the scene outside. The brawlers from the tavern were already there, taking in the action.

The cry had been a woman's. She was bruised. There was a large wound around her eyes and a man, most likely her husband, was beating her as she cried.

'How dare you!' he slapped the ill-fated woman and she fell down.

'Please, please!' she wept.

'How dare you!' he said again and slapped her harder than before.

Nara closed his eyes at the horror of the scene. No one interfered. For them, it was a usual occurrence – a man beating his wife.

'She wanted him to come home,' one of the villagers said to the other as they stood next to Nara. 'He didn't. She forced him and well, she's paying the price.'

Most of the people went inside after the scene became an ordeal to watch. It was a personal matter, anyway. After a while, leaving his wife weeping on the muddy ground outside, the husband, square-shouldered and long-haired, walked into the tavern to get himself more drinks. As he passed him, Nara could smell the man – he reeked of alcohol. In disgust, the Simha eyed the man.

'What ya lookin' at, man!' the abuser scowled at Nara, who stood tall and firm at the door of the tavern. 'This isn't a public party!'

Nara didn't speak. He felt his anger grow, but he didn't say anything. Taking a deep breath, he nodded, letting himself calm down.

'That's good, man. Don't ya dare look at me …' the drunk hiccupped. 'Otherwise, I shall do worse to you than I did to her. Mess up that pretty face of yours, heh!' And he hiccupped again before entering the tavern.

Nara sighed and went forward, his eyes fixed on the woman. 'Are you okay, ma'am?' he asked.

She looked up, venom in her eyes. 'What do you care?'

'I am a physician. I can treat your bruises.'

Her eyes softened. Doctors in this village were scarce and they were very well-respected. 'I apologize … I just …' her voice drowned in fresh tears.

Nara nodded, kneeling on the ground next to her and patting her on the shoulder.

'What's your name?' he asked.

'Sandhya.'

'Let me bring my things, Sandhya.'

'All right.'

Nara walked to his horse, which was hitched next to the tavern ledges. He had satchels and bags hanging from his brown stallion. From one of them, he pulled out cotton and some ointment, as well as a painkilling syrup.

He walked up to the woman and helped her sit on the stairs of the tavern. Then he began tending to her bruises.

'My husband, Shantanu, was never like that,' she began, as he rubbed the tulsi ointment on her wounds. She hissed in displeasure as it burned, but continued, 'It's because of the company he's keeping. They are all drunkards and they are spoiling him too.'

'I have always believed alcohol makes a man foolish,' Nara responded.

She chuckled, and then groaned as pain shot through the side of her mouth, which was blackened with a bruise. 'What really surprises me is that no one came forward to help me,' she said.

'We live in the age of cowards,' Nara said, realizing that her words were aimed at him too.

I am an escapist. Far worse than any other coward out there.

He wrapped the bandage and used a pin to tie it up. 'There, you should be fine. You just stay away from him. Don't you have a family to go to?'

'My parents made me marry him at a young age. They live in Dakshini,' she said, and Nara wondered how young she had been, since she was most likely in her late twenties now. Her husband looked like he was the same age as her too. They were kids, while Nara was … oh, he was old.

Dakshini was a long distance away. Nara looked at the snow-capped hills of Mandara, which stood tall, piercing the skies with their needle-like peaks. The village he stood on was one of the many small settlements in the foothills of Mandara, one of the tallest ranges in Udaiyas, along with the Mahendragiri Mountains.

'Were you always a doctor?' she asked.

Nara pursed his lips. 'Time made me one.' He managed a smile.

'How does time make one a master of medicine?'

'Erm,' he thoughtfully mused, clenching his jaw, 'when you see too much bloodshed, you realize it's better to save people instead of killing them.'

'You were a warrior? A soldier?' She narrowed her gaze. 'You are awfully golden for a Manav, you know.'

Nara shook his head. 'Oh, I am a Manav,' he lied. He knew he was golden. All the people in his Tribe were – golden, with gold hair and reddish beards.

Just then, the door slammed open. Before Nara could turn, there was a sudden blow on his back that threw him to the ground. As Nara came to his senses, he saw who his assailant was – the woman-beater, Shantanu. And this time, two of his friends were standing behind him with angry faces. One of them was scarred at the forehead and Nara knew him for some reason.

'What ya doin' with my wife out here?' Shantanu grabbed hold of her hand and pulled her up, slapping her again. 'If I needed her to go to a bloody doctor, I would have taken her myself.' He slapped her again.

Nara didn't say anything. He remained calm.

But then, he saw Shantanu pull out his knife.

'Please, no, my love, not the knife again!' Sandhya cried. 'He was just trying to help, my love!'

So he's used it on her before. Fury boiled in Nara's chest.

'Shut up, whore! I k-k-know what you were doing. Flirting with this pretty face!' his bloodshot eyes revealed he was out of his senses. Even his speech was slurred.

Nara looked at the ground, hoping that the guards from the tavern would come and break up the scene, or someone, anyone, would intervene. But no one cared.

No one but him.

At this moment, he regretted choosing to stay in a backward village where there was no superior protection from a lord, a king or a chief. It was an independent village, too small and insignificant to even be noticed by the nobles of the country.

I have to do this. I can't ... I can't just let it happen. Because if I don't stop it, it will continue.

'For that, your punishment should match the crime,' Shantanu laughed as he began to graze his knife on her skin, slowly inching closer to her chest—

And then he stopped.

Shantanu looked up and saw that Narasimha was gripping his hand with his gloved fists. 'I would suggest you leave,' Nara said in a cold voice.

Shantanu blinked for a moment and then tried to punch Nara with his free hand. But his punch had no effect – not a single bit.

'Who … are … you?' he gasped.

Nara twisted his hand and broke Shantanu's wrist. He fell to the ground, yelling in agony. At that moment, Nara saw Shantanu's two friends come forward, pulling out their daggers.

'Leave him!' one of them yelled to Nara.

Nara stepped back and Shantanu scampered away.

'Who the hell do you think you are?' the scarred friend asked.

'Are you the company that's spoiling him?' Nara asked, cracking his knuckles.

'I am Virata,' the scarred one responded. Nara knew him. He was the village headman's son, a landlord himself and an infamous man. 'Shantanu is my friend. You have no right to interfere in his personal business. When you mess with him, you mess with us.'

Nara smirked. 'One must understand that friendships are meant to help a person grow, not support them when they are going on the wrong path.'

'Don't give us philosophical lessons, doc. We have heard about you – a shaman who has no home, no identity and nowhere to go. How dare you speak like this to a person like me, you lowlife.' Virata was quite eloquent for a person who was drunk. 'I could get you killed and no one would know or care.'

Nara shrugged. 'I don't want trouble, son. I just helped a woman …'

Virata didn't let him finish. He came forward and pointed his dagger towards Nara's chest. Nara pulled back, dodging the blow, and grabbed Virata's arm. With a jolt, he lifted the Manav and tossed him down, dust swirling around him as he hit the ground. Virata yelled, and Nara grabbed his arm, twisting it so far back that he knew the other man wouldn't be able to use it for at least a month.

The other so-called friend of Shantanu didn't say anything. In fact, he threw his dagger, whimpered and ran away. Virata cried for him, but he didn't look back.

I didn't want to do this. But he was really annoying.

'ARGH ... I shall not spare you ...' Virata rasped. 'I shall find you and kill you!'

Nara shrugged, ignoring the headman's son, as he walked towards his horse. He could hear the crowd that had gathered muttering about his strength, and discussing whether he was even human. But he decided to let it be. He felt sad about hurting two kids, but then they did deserve it.

And it had felt right. To punish those who deserved it.

Lord Vishnu knows, how many innocents I have killed; those who were undeserving of the punishment of death.

The guilt still clung to him – the guilt of the wars he had been part of, where he had murdered those who had families, those who were good people.

I had to leave all of that. I had to.

And yet here he was, hurting more people. Despite the promise he had made to himself that he would never do it again. But then, this was different. He had punished those who deserved it, and he hadn't spilled any blood. Only bones were broken.

And this was for the right reasons.

He sat on his horse, as the crowd still stood there, watching him in awe. He walked his stallion next to Sandhya. She was now tending to her husband Shantanu, who had fallen unconscious. 'I hope you take care of yourself. You are much stronger and more important than any man who wants to hurt you. Do not settle for a man who hits you and doesn't respect you,' he said to her, and then looked at Shantanu. He pulled out a vial filled with blue syrup. 'Give him this twice a day. His pain will lessen.'

'I thought you weren't a soldier,' she responded, taking the vial.

'I am not.' Nara looked ahead. But that didn't mean he could tolerate injustice. He hated it and he would always try to prevent it.

He kicked the horse on the side and rode away. Sighing, he realized that he had been right all along. He needed to trust his instincts.

No wonder I had a bad feeling about today.

2

PRAHLAD

Death was all around him.

He was in his battle fort, watching his men, thousands of them, dying at the hands of the Tribals – Vanars, Yakshas and Nagas. Blood was spilled, heads were severed and limbs were torn off.

Prahlad knew that, at fifteen, he was too young for this.

He cursed under his breath. Despite his age, he was tall, with short hair and scars already adorning his body. Scars from battles and fights, and from his father.

His father was always merciless when it came to battle training, even to the point of hurting his sons. After all, strength defines a person in the Asura culture.

The Asura war captain appeared next to Prahlad, sweating profusely. 'What should we do, your highness?'

Your highness … he was a prince of the capital of Dakshina, Kashyapuri. But he always felt odd when someone reminded him of his title. It didn't matter that he was a prince. He had always been humble.

Prahlad narrowed his gaze and looked at the battlefield – red, dusty and swirling with blood as the two armies, the black-armoured one of the Asuras and the many-coloured one of Agni, fought each other.

This was one of the many battles fought against Agni, who was serving Lord Indra as his General. And with each battle, Agni inched closer. Kashyapuri was just two hundred kilometres away from this battleground. In the last battle, it had been four hundred kilometres away.

The next fight will probably happen in Kashyapuri itself!

Prahlad had been sent by his father Hiranya to use his strategies against Agni's battalion.

'Use the catapults,' he told the captain now. 'Use flaming balls of fire against the enemy,'

'That'll take time, your highness,'

Prahlad pursed his lips. Catapults were certainly time-consuming. He saw how Agni's army was using wide shields against the Asuras. They were made of bronze, had spikes on their outer surface, and had to be carried by ten men.

Agni is smart. Protecting himself as he kills.

'Why don't you just scamper away to your toys and let me handle it?' said a familiar voice from the back.

Prahlad turned to face his older brother, Anuhrad. He was a handsome man, but his voice was venomous and abrasive, the opposite of Prahlad, who was quiet and gentle. Anuhrad had long hair he kept tied back, and his eyes were lined with kohl. He wore the Asura battle gear made of obsidian.

'What are you doing here?' Prahlad asked.

'Helping you, as always.' Anuhrad walked in, taller and firmer than his brother. 'Father got a pigeon from the captain that you were losing.'

Prahlad felt betrayed, and instantly glanced at the captain, who lowered his head.

'I'm fine. *We* are fine,' Prahlad emphasized, but he was pushed away by his brother, who took position at the lookout from the fort.

'Doesn't seem like it,' Anuhrad smirked as he looked at the battlefield, and then turned to the captain. 'Bring the fire arrows, distract the enemy while you still have the backup army.'

Prahlad didn't want to use the backup army. They were mercenaries – untrustworthy Tribals – the cannibalistic, hungry and absolutely evil Pishach. He hoped to refrain from using them, but Anuhrad … no … Anuhrad didn't care.

'All right, my lord.' The captain was beaming now.

Was Auhrad showing the signs of a true king, a true leader? A pang of jealousy stung Prahlad, but as always, he stayed silent.

'Send them out. Also, the volley of the arrows needs to hit beyond the rams they are using. If possible, build up the catapults while you are using the arrows. Also charge at them with war elephants. How many do we have?' Anuhrad confidently asked.

'Erm, my lord, four,' the captain replied.

'What about the Danavs?'

'Two have already been sent out. One of them is injured.'

Anuhrad grew thoughtful. 'Get your best bowmen on it and hit the ones beyond the ram. The ram is our enemy for today, my man!' he said, and the captain rushed to follow his instructions.

Prahlad eyed Anuhrad. 'You do realize the Pishach are not our safest bet? They can turn on us.'

'We pay them enough, brother. Do not worry.'

'And the elephants? We will be losing most of our resources on the first few days of the war. We need to keep enough so we can sustain ourselves till the end of the war.'

Anuhrad squared up next to Prahlad, his golden Asura eyes watching his younger brother. 'What makes you think this isn't the end? Going by the number of people we are losing, brother, we will end up massacred by tonight. I fight like there's no tomorrow because the best form of defence is offence.'

He turned and left the room. Prahlad followed him, and they went down the tower. They reached the ground where the soldiers were preparing to return to battle. Food was being supplied, quivers were refilled, nurses were tending to the injured.

Prahlad began, 'Father should have trusted me.'

Anuhrad walked to the gigantic stables where more than a hundred reserve stallions were kept. 'He did and then you shook his trust when you lost on the first day of the battle.' Anuhrad grabbed the black stallion and saddled it up, mounting it and examining his sword.

Prahlad felt disappointed and betrayed. Most of all, he was angry with Hiranya. But he stayed calm. 'Where are you going?' he asked his brother.

'Out there!' Anuhrad pointed his sword towards the main gates of the fort, which were now barricaded. 'If the prince doesn't go and spill his blood, no one will take him seriously.' He grinned. 'Sip your wine and enjoy the triumph from your tower.' He winked and rode towards the gate, followed by the Pishach, who had geared up and were battle-ready.

Prahlad looked at their frightening visages – they had dark, peeling skin, big, gruesome eyes, and a strange inky pattern that ran across their entire body. The Pishach were the most frightening of Tribals and Hiranya had teamed up with them. The king believed that other Tribals were too noble and the Pishach were savage. So he had paid them well and promised that all the bodies from the war would be given to them for dinner. More than the money, it was this promise of human flesh that had interested the Pishach.

The very image of them eating humans made Prahlad sick, but he shrugged off the thought.

What should I do now?

He looked at how the captain was handling the entire situation with the bowmen, and he even told his men to get the elephants out into the battle. Cavalry was dispatched, but Prahlad could only focus on the wounded – all the soldiers who were dying, or getting bruised, or losing their limbs. They were paid handsomely for serving the crown, but was gold more important than life?

In the beginning, Prahlad's father had fought for nobility for his clan, and then for the protection and survival of his race. But now, he fought for vengeance against the evil of Lord Indra, who had attacked Kashyapuri and killed Prahlad's mother Kayadhu.

This war was *personal*.

In the beginning, as his guru Narada explained to him, Indra was ready to work with the Asuras and even invited them to share the Somas – the celestial drink that gives one strength to full capacity. But rather than giving the Somas to the Asuras, Indra betrayed them and spread it in the world. This led to continuous wars between Indra and the Asuras.

And then Lord Hiranyaksha had been killed.

Things changed. Peace was offered by the Asuras since they realized the futility of a war that would end up killing millions. Hiranyakashyap didn't want any more war and agreed to the truce where the north, where Devlok stood, was given to the Devas, and the South, with Kashyapuri, to the Asuras.

The truce was thought to herald a new beginning …

But once again, Indra had struck Kashyapuri, and this time, he'd done so when Hiranyakashyap had left to scatter the ashes of his brother over the holy river of Pataal. Indra had brought the battle to the heart of the kingdom, killing Prahlad's mother and breaking the truce.

When he returned, Hiranya's rage had known no bounds.

He wanted to destroy every single part of Indra and he was mostly successful, with the help of Andhaka in the north, Anuhrad in battle wherever he was sent, which was mostly everywhere, Holika in the city to defeat spies, and Vigyasa in the east, where Yakshalok stood.

Indra, meanwhile, worked from Devlok, protected by barriers and ordering his lieutenants – Varuna in Naglok, Agni in Yakshlok and Bhairav in the north where the Mandara hills were. Indra had his only son Jayant lead most of these lieutenants and their armies. Jayant did not work strategies like the other senior Devas; he was a warrior through and through, ready to get his hands dirty on the battlefield.

And even now, Jayant was helping Agni. According to reports, he was a sadistic man.

This had been going on for fourteen years now.

War is complicated, and often, all over the place. For as long as he'd been alive, Prahlad could remember the war, and how challenging it had been.

And for Hiranyakashyap, this war had meaning. It was a war for revenge, and that meant the king was at his most aggressive.

And Prahlad knew, because of Indra's betrayal, that there was no scope left for a truce any more.

Prahlad thought of his mother. He hadn't known her; never had the opportunity. And he was angry about it, every day. He didn't like war, but he fought it … for her. And he knew that this same sentiment fuelled his brother Anuhrad in battle too.

Prahlad knew that his mother would be proud if Indra's empire fell and his head was on a spike.

I must make you proud, mother. And I must make my father proud.

Prahlad grabbed the nearest weapon, a solid sword which he sheathed before mounting one of the stallions. He then made his way to the gates.

'What are you doing, your highness?' the captain called from above.

Prahlad didn't respond. He ordered the Asura gatekeepers to open the doors. He rode out, the horse's hooves hitting the bloody ground. A short distance ahead, the battle raged.

I must do it.

'Here we go,' he breathed. As he rode into the heart of the war, the last question that haunted Prahlad was, *by doing this, am I making myself proud?*

3

NARASIMHA

Look at you. You were born to kill.

Nara woke up to the hooting of the owls. He blinked. It was night and the incessant chirping of the crickets was annoying him.

Struggling to his feet, he staggered across the cave and, picking up the jug of water from a small handcrafted wooden basin, splashed some of it on his face, drenching his uneven beard.

Suddenly, Nara recalled the time he had been told his future – what he would end up doing. He held on to the grave truth, and so far, had revealed it to no one.

If what I was told is true … then it is better for me to live in isolation.

There were many reasons why Nara had left the war, why he'd left Indra's Simha army. And one of them was his fate. He knew where he was going to end up, and he saw no point in continuing what he was doing.

But most of all, he knew who he was.

There had been signs, early on. When he had ingested the Soma stones, created by the thunder king himself and engineered to enhance one's ability to fight the war for Indra, Nara saw the changes. While other Simhas had grown to their full capacity, the stones had done more for him – given him more strength, more durability.

The Soma stones didn't have adverse effects on the Simhas, as the Simhas were a disciplined Tribe. Other Tribes, in comparison, were not given the Somas since most of them were driven mad from it. The Soma stones were like fire. If one knows how to tame it, it can be used as a weapon. But if not, it'll burn your hand.

Nara recalled the conversation he'd had with Lord Indra after he had single-handedly defeated twenty men during one of Hiranyakashyap's attacks.

Nara entered the war room, where most of the planning happened. He had lion skin draped over his majestic, royal body. But instead of feeling proud, Nara felt weak in front of Lord Indra, whose appearance was firm and muscular. He had a clean face and broad shoulders.

'My lord.' Nara knelt.

Indra gestured him to stand. 'Do you know what you did today?'

Nara knew. Other Simhas had watched him in awe and he felt proud of himself.

'Yes, my lord.'

'Do you know why I gave the Soma stones to your Tribe?'

'No, my lord.'

Indra smiled. He picked up an old scripture page from the table in front of him and looked at Nara.

'On the island of Swarg, there is a prophecy. Every Yug, there will be a Dharm and an Adharm. Good and bad. They will fight for the survival of the world. Whoever wins will decide the fate of the universe. These prophecies were written by seers called Saptarishis. Some call them sons of Lord Vishnu, up in Mount Meru, and I have got an illustration of the prophecy.'

He handed the page to Nara, who glanced at it. On the page, he saw the inscriptions and designs of a lion-faced warrior holding a demon-like man and breaking his spine.

'This is the prophecy of this Yug. A warrior, half-lion and half-man, shall fight Adharm, who is an Asura. It's always the Asuras that are portrayed as evil in the Saptarishis' prophecies,' Indra explained. 'I was keen on finding out more, so I went to Mount Meru in search of these Rishis, to ask how I would know if a man is a Dharm. And they said, I will know when the Somas works "perfectly" on them,' Indra emphasized. 'The Somas were originally called Somalata, and were plants that grew in Swarg. I learnt my father Dyaeus had brought the seeds to Illavarti, where the First Dharm, an Avatar of Lord Vishnu, was born due to the Somas – Lord Matsya. Then Lady Mohini and then, of course … Lord Varaha.'

Nara hadn't known much about Matsya, but he had heard about Mohini. She was the reason the Churning happened – it was the manual creation of the Somas in large quantities to be shared in abundance.

'A Dharm or an Adharm will become active once they ingest the Soma stones. And then they will become Avatars once they define their role in this prophecy,' he said. 'I already knew that by giving the Somas to Simhas, I would be churning out a hero, a Dharm, as Simhas are equivalent to half-man and half-lion. I wanted to churn the Dharm so I could do exactly what I did in the last Yug – kill the Adharm. Hiranyaksha was a tyrant, just like his brother is now. And like Varaha killed Hiranyaksha, I want you to kill Hiranyakashyap.'

Nara blinked in confusion. 'But my lord, are you sure I'm an Avatar?'

'No, you are not an Avatar. An Avatar is a soldier of Lord Vishnu, and he's chosen when he gets the Symbol of Shrivatsa, when he does something that defines him as a Lord Vishnu bhakt. You are the Dharm. You show all the qualities of it, and you have more power than your colleagues.' Indra stood up and came forward. 'Think of being Dharm as a test. If you pass this test, you shall get the symbol of Lord Vishnu to carry the emblem of his name and become the Avatar. An Avatar is a title, but Dharm is a choice.'

'A choice for what? I was chosen for this fate, rather than me choosing it,' Nara argued.

Indra smiled. 'You are Dharm. You have the qualities, but imagine if you spent your life committing atrocities. Would you become an Avatar then?'

'No, because then I'll be Adharm.'

'Absolutely. So isn't that a choice? Your choice defines whether you will become an Avatar or Adharm. And in this Yug,' he explained, holding the paper in his hand, 'you will kill

Hiranyakashyap, most likely the Adharm of this Age, since his brother was one in the earlier Yug.'

'If I don't get a symbol, then what'll happen?'

Indra clenched his jaw. 'Then you would have failed. And another Simha will be chosen as Dharm, so he may pass the test and become an Avatar or perhaps there will not be any Dharm at all, since it is a once-in-a-lifetime opportunity, and only Adharm will prevail in this Yug. That is what I fear the most,' he paused, looking at the page. 'All of this is so vague and so complicated, with every symbol having a different meaning.'

It had been fifteen years since that night and Nara had no symbol. *Perhaps I didn't succeed in being an Avatar.* And he was happy about it – content.

Because I know what will happen to me if I become one.

Nara splashed more water on his face. *If only Indra had known the full story, things would have been different.*

Nara wondered – who was the other Simha chosen as a Dharm now? He could only wonder though. Perhaps the Yug hadn't even started or perhaps … Adharm would win after all.

He didn't like that thought. He had been trying to run away from these suppositions, from these questions for so long now.

I know something about the prophecy that no one else does.

Suddenly, he heard something and his ears perked up. *Footsteps*. He sniffed – he could smell sweat, the fragrance of a *Manav!* Someone was coming towards his hideout.

Nara pulled out the club from his bag and went outside the cave. He looked at the forest that lay before him. A chill ran through the air and he shivered, for he wore no upper clothing, and was only clad in a green dhoti.

'Who's there?' he called out.

No response.

He closed his eyes. And heard it – a *heartbeat.* Several heartbeats. He concentrated more and realized that there were five men hiding in the forest.

No. Six.

He sniffed again and noticed that he could smell the hint of steel.

It's an arrow, an unused one.

Before he could think anything more, an arrow came flying towards him and struck him on the chest, piercing his skin. As the wound bled, another arrow struck his arm.

And then, with loud yells, five men draped in black clothing and black masks to hide their faces, came charging towards Nara with swords drawn. One of them stayed behind and shot rocks at him from a sling, hitting Nara on the head.

The masked men began to stab him on the chest. Pain engulfed Nara, as he fell on the ground. He tried to deflect the attacks, but it was in vain, since he was almost blinded by the pain.

'You wanted to be a hero, didn't you? Well, how are you enjoying being one now?' scoffed one of the masked men. The voice was familiar. Nara realized that it was Virata, wielding the sword with his left hand as the right had been twisted by Nara. 'Now you shall find death because of it,' Virata roared.

Anger began to boil inside Nara. He could feel his sharp incisors, and his hands tightened into fists. He rose and swung his club against one of the masked men's feet, tossing him in the air. The man landed on the ground with a thud, and stayed still.

Nara then rolled away and pulled his gloves off to reveal his claws. Instead of nails, he had the claws of a Simha – sharp blades that could tear through anything.

'What the …' one masked man, Virata, exclaimed. 'You are a Simha!'

Nara grimaced. He was wounded and felt weak. But he was also angry. And when he was angry – *well, things happened.*

He roared, and the sound reverberated through the woods. The men cowered as Nara lunged from his place, jumping at one of them and clawing his face. The boy scurried away, staggering and falling as he fled.

Nara roared again and two more of the masked idiots ran for their lives.

Now, only two were left. One of them was Virata.

Virata moved back and pushed his companion in front of him, who just dropped his weapon and began pleading with Nara. Nara grabbed him by the throat and lifted him up, the claws sinking into the skin of the man until he tossed him on the ground. The boy grabbed his neck and instantly made a run for it.

Nara then turned his attention to Virata, who attacked the Simha with his sword, slashing his skin.

Nara stood still, letting the attack go on for a few moments.

And then, just when Virata swung the sword again, Nara grabbed the blade with his hand and moved his free hand to claw Virata … only to stop himself. Nara sighed, horror in his eyes as he pushed the boy to the ground.

'Run!' he roared at Virata.

The man scampered away, vanishing into the darkness like his friends.

Nara dropped his weapon and smashed his chest in horror and anger, roaring. Fury had got hold of him, though he had tried his best not to let it.

It was self defence, he said to himself.

As the anger began to subside, guilt cast a dark shadow over him. He fell to the ground, realizing what he had done.

No. This is what I was running from. My anger …

Suddenly, he heard another heartbeat. *There had been six of them …*

Who is this now? He wanted to roar but controlled his anger.

A figure came from the forest, wearing a thick set of clothes. He was an old man, bald, except for white hair on the sides of his head, and a thick beard on a wrinkled face. Nara knew him. He knew him very well.

'Don't feel bad, Nar. They had it coming. You taught them a lesson, and the next time, they will know better,' Lord Indra, the king of Devas and Devlok, said with a smile. 'After all, my dear warrior, you were born to kill.'

4

PRAHLAD

A few minutes into the battle, and he knew he was not ready for this.

Prahlad rode past the cavalry and the foot soldiers, charging straight into the heart of the battle. Stallions fell; men were sliced through. Some escaped to get medical aid even as archers shot flaming arrows at them from their chariots.

There was so much happening that Prahlad found it hard to keep track of which soldiers belonged to which side.

He approached one of his soldiers to ask about Anuhrad's whereabouts, but before he could say anything, the soldier was hit by an arrow.

Horrified, Prahlad began to shout his brother's name.

'Anuhrad! Anuhrad!' he yelled, but the older boy was nowhere to be seen.

A volley of arrows rained from the sky. Instantly, Prahlad leapt from his horse and scampered to an abandoned shield. He held the shield up, and the arrows struck it. He was safe.

For now.

An enemy soldier appeared out of nowhere and pushed Prahlad's shield, kicking him to the ground. Another soldier, one from Prahlad's army, ran to the prince's side and stood in front of him. Just as he tried to help Prahlad up, he was sliced by the enemy's blade. His bones and flesh torn apart, blood spraying from his wounds.

Prahlad staggered from the scene, moving away from it as soldiers from his army closed in on the enemy and butchered him in revenge.

A little further away, he wiped the dead soldier's blood from his face and held the locket around his neck: the one his mother had given him when he was an infant.

I need to leave. This is too much.

But he was afraid for Anuhrad. And he was afraid of disappointing his parents.

There is so much at stake.

Before he could decide what to do, he realized that he was suddenly flanked by enemy soldiers.

'Isn't this the boy-prince of the demons?' asked one of the Manav soldiers to another.

'Should we gut him like his pawns?' another cackled.

The soldiers lunged at him with their swords. Prahlad ducked, rolled over, and fell back. A blade swung at him but he deflected it with his own. He pushed his sword against the other and rolled back again, dust swirling as he thrust his blade forward, but his arms were weak and the soldier didn't feel a thing.

In return, the soldier punched him with his metal-clad fists.

Gritting his teeth, closing his eyes and letting that anger take control of his arm, Prahlad began slashing and cutting at enemy flesh with his blade, rage and pain suppressing any fear he felt.

Anger is the key.

Prahlad was not accustomed to killing people. But for some reason, in the midst of this war, it felt justified.

Everything felt justified.

Another volley of arrows rained from the sky and he rushed towards his shield … but this time, he was too late.

His leg was caught by one of the soldiers he had wounded and he fell to the ground. Most of the arrows missed him, but one pierced his back.

Prahlad screamed in agony as he swung his sword and severed the hand of the soldier who was writhing on the ground. He pulled the arrow from his back and pain shot through his entire body. He sighed, falling back on the ground and closing his eyes.

The battle raged around him. He was struggling to his feet when suddenly, his ears went numb and he couldn't hear anything. He cried out … he cried for Anuhrad.

'Brother!' he yelled.

Enemies approached him and he deflected their weapons and attacked them, letting blood spill.

Another followed and Prahlad swung his blade, decapitating the man.

But still he couldn't hear anything. The cries of war … the hooves … the rams …

The ram!

He realized the spiked shields were coming close to him. He could see his soldiers being stabbed by them and some of them were even tied to the blade, yelling in pain as they were tortured to death.

Prahlad staggered away from the ram and was thrown onto the path of a soldier in white armour, whose blade he barely missed, falling to the ground with a cut on his face.

When the soldier turned to charge at him again, Prahlad deflected his blade with his own and smacked the hilt of the blade on the horse's head. The horse lost control and neighed loudly, misbalancing the rider, who fell from the saddle.

Sighing, Prahlad watched his soldiers in battle. The Asuras and even the Pishach, diligently fighting, though the latter in a gruesome way. Rather than using weapons, they were jumping on the individual and eating the head or the arms of the enemy.

They were truly monstrous in nature.

Prahlad walked further as he held on to the locket – he usually did this when he felt weak and defeated. But there was no locket there.

Not even the pain from the arrow had hurt him the way this discovery did.

His eyes searched for the locket on the ground, which was muddy with corpses, heads and limbs, blood and sweat. His eyes searched as his breath quickened. That was when someone grabbed him by the throat and held him in a headlock.

Prahlad tried to fight back, but another enemy soldier appeared in front of him.

'A prince amongst real men! What a shame. Lord Jayant would love to see your head delivered to him,' one of them said.

The second soldier moved close to him and Prahlad used the opportunity to kick him with all his might, and using the strength of his legs, he pushed the man who was holding him. They both fell to the ground and Prahlad tried to get rid of him by breaking the headlock, but it was tough.

And so he did what he had to.

He bit the soldier's bare hand, making him scream in pain and loosen the grip. Prahlad grabbed the sword which was on the ground and plunged it inside the mouth of the soldier.

He stared at what he'd done as he got up. He couldn't believe he had ended up killing so many people. His eyes darted across the field only to find something shiny in the midst of it.

He hurried towards the shiny material when a stallion came from behind and stopped next to him. Prahlad looked up to see a beaming, pale warrior with whitish hair sitting comfortably on the horse, not a speck of dirt on him or his armour.

And he noticed the armour – it had a thunderbolt emblem on it. The white-haired soldier got off and studied Prahlad with his light eyes. He looked like a ghost. It was apparent that the death and destruction around him did not bother him, neither did the mayhem.

Prahlad noticed blood at the tip of his sword. The soldier knelt down and picked up Prahlad's locket. 'Aren't you too young to be here, boy?' he laughed.

Prahlad knew who this was – the way he looked, he was not a Tribal. In fact, he seemed royal.

'You are Prince Jayant, aren't you?' Prahlad asked.

'Son of Indra, at your service,' he grinned, studying the locket. 'What is written here?'

'It's in my native language,' Prahlad said, wiping the streak of blood from his mouth. 'Give it to me.'

'What does it say, boy?' Jayant repeated, his voice cold.

Prahlad clenched his jaw, but he responded calmly, 'I will always be there with you.'

'That's quite touching. Who did it belong to?'

'My mother,' Prahlad responded reluctantly.

Jayant pulled a face. 'Jeez, that's kind of sad, since my father, you know ...' and he made a gesture that suggested that Indra had cut off Prahlad's mother's head.

Prahlad felt rage rise within him, but his eyes were fixed on the locket. He had to get back his mother's locket. Prahlad noticed the double-edged weapon Jayant held – long blades on either side.

'Tell you what, you let me keep the locket and I let you live, since I pity a young boy like you.'

'I won't leave without the locket.'

Saying this, Prahlad sprang from his position, sprinting towards Jayant, who evaded the attack with ease, letting Prahlad trip on the ground and hit his chin.

'Oh dear, you seem quite troubled. Is the war not suiting you?' he mocked the boy.

Prahlad gritted his teeth, but then he saw a sword, someone's sword, abandoned just a few paces away from him.

Crawling, he began to move towards it when he felt a heavy foot on his back where he had been previously wounded.

He yelled in agony.

'You can't defeat me, demon prince,' Jayant chided.

Prahlad knew he couldn't defeat Jayant – Jayant was well known for his swift and graceful moves. He was an executioner and it was especially easy for him to kill Prahlad. And he was a Deva, which meant if he wasn't killed, he would live for three hundred years, just like his father had. Asuras enjoyed long lifespans too, but nothing could compare to the long lives of Devas.

Prahlad saw Jayant pulling out a vial from his satchel that dangled at his hip and drinking a blue liquid out of it. 'Do you need it, boy? It's nectar, you know, the Somas; something your kind really wanted but my father knew better than to give it to you. Your weak, pathetic minds would have been corrupted by the drink. The Somas is powerful and Devas as a race can use it to reach our full potential. And a few Tribals, as we learnt, but not many. It has to be in the right hands, otherwise things can go a wee bit crazy,' he muttered to himself, seemingly enjoying the small talk in the middle of battle.

Prahlad knew the story – how the Asuras had wanted the Somas to increase their power, but they couldn't get hold of it. Indra kept it hidden inside his fortress at Devlok, so it could be only used by those he chose.

It was obvious why the Devas lived long: they had Somas to slow the ageing process.

'Anyway, I'm just wasting time. Any final words, boy?' Jayant asked.

Prahlad closed his eyes. He wanted to pray, but he had no idea who to. Asuras didn't worship gods. They worshipped attributes like strength or love or kindness or anger.

And so Prahlad prayed to the idea of a miracle.

Jayant brought down the double-sided spear and was about to plunge it deep inside Prahlad when …

A sudden push out of nowhere jolted him away. Prahlad's back felt free and he opened his eyes to see Jayant had been tossed aside. He turned his head to find Anuhrad, who was grinning at his brother, but his eyes looked worried. 'I didn't expect you to come here, youngling,' he said. 'But I'm glad you did. Though, rush off now. I don't want you to die.'

'Where were you?' Prahlad asked.

'Saving our people.'

Jayant got to his feet. 'Oh, I wish I had such sibling love. My twin sister hates me, so I made sure she never came from Swarg to Illavarti to trouble me.' And then he brought down the spear, moving so fast that Anuhrad had to be extremely cautious as he deflected it.

But Anuhrad was good with his weapon. He knew how to use it and he was focused. He knew where Jayant was going to attack next.

I have to get the locket.

Prahlad staggered forward to pick up the sword, and when he turned again, he saw Anuhrad on the ground and Jayant standing above him with the spear in his hand. Anuhrad with his bloody, scarred hands, was stopping the blades from piercing him.

I need to save him.

He flung his sword at Jayant, and the hilt smacked the Deva on the head. He fell to the other side and in that split second, Anuhrad grabbed his sword and instantly jabbed it into Jayant's shoulder. A scream pierced the air.

Prahlad got to his feet and rushed to get the locket from Jayant, who held on to it. Anuhrad then pulled the blade out of Jayant's shoulder, who screamed again, letting go of the locket.

Prahlad wore the locket, at peace again.

'Don't think you … you have defeated me,' Jayant sighed, his eyes bloodshot. His white tunic had turned dark red.

'From where I stand, boy, I already have.' Anuhrad focused on Jayant's head, moving forward to sever it.

At that moment, Jayant whistled. Prahlad was confused and exchanged glances with Anuhrad, but then he saw a white horse gallop towards them and Jayant grabbed on to its saddle for support, as the horse took him away from the scene.

'See you soon!' Jayant called as he disappeared in the battle scene.

'Father would have been really happy if we had killed him,' Anuhrad sighed, and then turned to look at Prahlad. 'Thank you for saving me. I am sorry that I am so hard on you …'

Before Prahlad could reply, he felt himself go numb again. His heart began racing and his vision blurred.

'Are youuuuu okayyy?' Anuhrad's voice came as if from far away, and Prahlad felt his body slump and fall to the ground, his head hitting the bloodied mud. He realized what was happening.

He was exhausted. He was wounded. And he was now falling unconscious.

As darkness took over him completely, he clutched on to his locket.

5

NARASIMHA

Fire crackled.

Indra was wearing his fur coat as he threw logs into the flames and then sat down, warming his hands.

Nara watched the king with slight distaste. Indra was bringing his past with him, which Nara had been trying to escape for fourteen long years.

After he had learnt he was a Dharm, and after he had found out the secret of this Yug that shocked him to his core, he had escaped, and since then, he'd never looked back.

Until now.

'I am quite disappointed,' Indra said, smiling. 'You haven't become an Avatar till now.'

Nara sighed. He had no symbol and he was grateful for that. 'Perhaps I failed to complete an important task?'

'True. You have instead been scaring young rebels out here.'

Nara winced at that. He hadn't wanted to attack Virata and his worthless friends, but they had left him with no choice.

Nara wiped his wounds with a hot, damp cloth as he looked at Indra. 'Why are you here?' he asked.

'To apologize,' Indra said, his smile growing wider.

'Without your army, your guards, your elephant? You look like a civilian.'

'I had to. I had to disguise myself to reach you and, of course, having Airavata with me would have made me quite conspicuous. My spies have been searching for you for the longest time, and finally, one of them heard about your antics close to a tavern and told me. I was in Mandara, discussing something with Bhairav when I heard, and rushed down here,' Indra explained.

'How is Bhairav?' Nara had known all of these men during his stint back in the army. Now, none of it made sense. Lord Bhairav was a Shiva, just like Lord Rudra had been before him, during Mohini's Yug. Shiva was a war title given down below in the mountainous regions of the Gana tribe.

'Worse. Andhaka has been a nuisance,' Indra sighed. 'You have to hand it to him, though. Even though he's blind, he's quite the man, quite a warrior.'

Nara nodded. He had heard about Andhaka – the famous son of Hiranyaksha, the previous Asura king. The blind prince who was near impossible to kill, so superior were his battle strategies.

'Why are you here to apologize after fourteen years?'

'Because …' Indra stood up, getting a log and then tossing it in the fire, 'I made you do some pretty questionable things. I know. I … uh …' he sighed, 'I am growing old, Nar. I really am. Jayant is going to take my throne soon … if there is a throne to take, otherwise I'll make sure he leaves for Swarg.

All I'm saying is, in the heat of the moment, in the heat of war, I have done some terrible things. I have ordered executions which weren't necessary and I have led wars which were …'

'Wrong,' Nara completed for him. 'I know, they were. I was part of them.'

'Yes, you and your Simha army. Simhas have always supported the Devas and for that I'm grateful.'

'You misused our trust, my lord.' Nara flared his nostrils. 'We thought you would lead us in the right direction.'

'I still am. The other Simhas are still supporting me. They are under Mrigsimha now,' he said, referring to Mrig, who had once been Nara's subordinate. 'Only you left. Why?'

'You know why. I was exhausted, watching you allow deaths in vain. And then …' He shook his head, recalling one of the many incidents in the village where the supposed Asuras lived, only to learn that instead of Asuras, it was a village of Manavs, and that he had been forced to attack Manav women and children. 'I couldn't spill more innocent blood. Simhas were never supposed to kill innocents. Perhaps Mrig is okay with it, but I am not.'

'Every war has casualties, Nar.'

Nara nodded. 'I know. That's why I left it. I can't stop the war, so I decided to leave it.' He paused. 'You have brought such a long war on yourself. You shouldn't have attacked Kashyapuri. That is the reason everything started.'

And the reason my faith in you was shaken.

Indra narrowed his gaze. 'Is that the reason you did it? Is that the reason you left the war? Because I started it by breaking the truce?'

'I had many reasons, and yes, that was one of them.'

'But that war was bound to …' Indra started, then stopped. He sighed and lowered his head. 'All right, I know I am wrong. I knew it the day Kayadhu was killed. I was wrong and I was abrasive. I shouldn't have, but now it's done. The war is a reality and we are in it, fighting it. And losing most of it.'

Nara knew where this was going. 'I'm not going to help you, my lord. Don't expect any assistance.'

'I know that,' Indra nodded. 'But you left us, you left your people, you left the innocents who are dying now. At least help them, if not me.'

Nara contemplated it. As much as he had hated killing innocent people, he had enjoyed the war – fighting behind enemy lines. He missed it, but he had done gruesome things in the name of it.

And after all, it was not only the fear of killing innocents that stopped him from going back into the world of fire, it was also the *secret* that he had learnt, one which even Indra did not know.

The secret told to him by none other than Lord Rudra, the previous Shiva, during his dying declaration.

'Don't let the world swallow you, child. Being Dharm seems nice, but it's more than that. And I know what'll happen at the end of this Yug, what'll happen to you. I just know. You stay hidden and the prophecy shall never be fulfilled. But if you go out, there is a chance it will …'

Nara shrugged these thoughts off. 'What do you want me to do?'

'Andhaka. You have to find a way to defeat him,' Indra said, clapping Nara on the back in an effort to sound friendly. 'Meet with Lord Bhairav in Mandara. Mrig and your people are also there. Andhaka is ruining the local villages, has threatened that he will keep burning them till we give up the Pashupatastra. He's constantly attacking Bhairav's camp too, breaking his defences. He got to know about the weapon from one of the spies. He knows that if he can get his hands on it, the Asuras have as good as won the war.'

Nara had heard about Pashupatastra, the weapon that had belonged to Lord Rudra, who had crafted it with the science and knowledge of Lord Brahma. It was a weapon so strong and powerful that if used, it could decimate an entire village with one attack. And had the potential to create radiations around fifty miles of the attack.

'I've sent most of my army there, but I have to fight in Yakshlok and Naglok too, where Agni and Varuna stand, where I'm going now after our discussion. If by any chance that maniacal blind man gets his hands on the Pashupatastra, he will use it to no end with Hiranya, killing millions of innocent mortals. And Andhaka, unlike Hiranya, doesn't care about sacrificing innocents for the greater cause of hurting us, hurting me.'

Nara knew the consequences of Andhaka getting the nuclear weapon. 'Why can't Bhairav just destroy the Pashupatastra and end the trouble?'

'And risk our lives?' Indra scoffed, his voice hoarse. 'My brother, you have been away from the war for a long time, but you must know every side should have a backup. Pashupatastra is our backup, if we fail totally, we will use it against the Asuras one final time, but only if there's no choice. Trust me, when I say it. I promise to not use it as long as there's a better choice.'

Nar knew that Indra was a strategist who would never put himself in harm's way. 'Simhas are having a problem too. They are ... distracted,' the Deva said.

'Isn't the Somas helping the Simhas fight better?' Nara asked.

'Somas corrupts Simhas too.' Indra shook his head. 'Simha was one of the Tribes I gave the Somas to in abundance, as they could control it just like us Devas can. But I find that they are unable to handle its strength, mainly because they don't have a leader like you. Mrig is ... well ... he's weak,' Indra mused.

'And how would I be able to help you when your entire armies can't?'

Indra rose from his seat. He laughed. 'You out of all people know what you are capable of. Sure, you might not be an Avatar or even a Dharm. I don't care about it any more, my brother. It doesn't matter to me any more whether you are destined to defeat the Adharm, or even whether Hiranya is next in line to be the Adharm. I just want to win this war so that we can all go home. And I do care if the enemy gets his hands on our nuclear weapon. It's safe with us, but in their hands ... So for now, you need to start thinking more about the world than about yourself ... or me, or this pointless war that I foolishly started. I know I did. But be my redemption, my lion brother, and stop Andhaka.' With that, Indra held out his hand to Nara.

Nara thought for a moment, and shook his head. 'No. I won't go back. Andhaka is not that big a threat to pull me back to the war.'

Indra sighed, nodding. 'All right, if that's what you have decided.' The king of the Devas stood up, dusted off his clothes, and smiled to hide his disappointment. 'I should take my leave, then.'

Nara didn't speak, his face impassive.

Indra stepped out and made for the woods, but he stopped and turned back to look at Nara one last time. 'Are you sure?'

Nara nodded.

Indra smiled, his eyes narrowing. 'It was nice meeting you, brother.'

Nara bowed slightly and the king of the Devas stepped into the forest, disappearing against the silvery moonlight.

Am I going to regret this?

6

NARASIMHA

Nara woke up to cries.

He had gone to sleep after Indra left, but the memories wouldn't let him rest.

He could hear the wails and the screams of the people. Grabbing his gloves and putting them on, he walked away from his shack and ran down the slope to where the main village stood. But the village was not enshrined in darkness any more. He saw fire raging across it. He saw the children and their mothers crying at the charred carcasses of the dead men, their blackened hands gripping weapons they were never supposed to carry.

What is happening?

Nara's feet dug into the land as he moved forward only to find the figures of Rakshasas amid the fiery ambience – huge, bulky, dark-skinned human figures with long, matted hair and maroon eyes. Turning to his right, he saw the Asuras who were taller than the Rakshasas, but fair, malicious grins on their faces. Nara could see the Asura archers aiming for the escaping civilians, and the men being rounded up by the Rakshasas, who were lashing and kicking them.

Fire catapults were being used to attack the houses. Huts were being burnt. The smell of explosives and burning flesh engulfed Nara's nostrils. He saw a huddle of Asuras around the villagers as they questioned them.

Nara strained his ears to hear what the Asuras were asking the civilians.

'Where is Indra?' one of the Asuras asked. 'Our spies followed him here and right after, his trail was lost. Where is he?'

'Please, please ...' the voice said in return and Nara recognized it. It was Virata. He had been defeated by Nara and now he was in a worse condition. 'I don't want any trouble. I don't know where Lord Indra is.'

Nara bared his teeth. They were attacking innocent people to find the King of Devas.

In the pursuit of one man, Andhaka was harming hundreds. What was the point of destroying the village?

Nara knew the reason. It was to show superiority, dominance. An age-old claim learned by Andhaka too soon – that the Asuras were supposed to rule this land and no one else.

Nara walked forward as the people scrambled away. Any sign of trepidation had left him by now. His chest was heavy, and his head held high. He had hurt Virata for being a reckless idiot, but now the man needed his help.

Nara roared.

His roar was so thunderous that everyone's head in the vicinity turned towards him. The Asuras looked at him and left Virata right where he was, tossing him to the ground. The other villagers tried to scamper away from the battlefield, but the Rakshasas wouldn't let them go.

'Leave them,' Nara yelled. 'You have no reason to be here.'

'Who the hell are you?' asked a Rakshas, as he placed his blade against a young girl's throat.

Nara had no intention of revealing his identity to them. He grabbed a rock from the ground and flung it towards the Rakshas, scraping off a part of his skull. The blade dropped and so did the dead Rakshas. The impact was so strong that the other Rakshasas fell back, unsure of how to deal with this new threat.

The Asuras were alarmed and left the civilians to charge at Nara, coming towards him with full force.

There were five of them in total.

Nara had to think about how to deflect their attacks all at once. He was not how he used to be when he fought in the war–agile, quick, arrogant, abrasive and strong. Now, his bones had turned heavier, his knees hurt and he felt a strange pain in his chest, which had been pierced earlier by Virata's men.

But he had to do it.

As two of the Asuras came forward, one of them managed to thrust his sword in an attempt to impale him. Nara grabbed hold of the blade and tilted it towards the attacker, jamming the sword into his forehead. He pulled the sword out of the enemy and swung it towards an oncoming Asura, piercing him too in the forehead.

In a quick flash, he rolled over, barely dodging the remaining Asura's sword. He withdrew the sword out of the fallen Asura's forehead and quickly used it to stab the other one in the torso, plunging his blade until the blood sprayed.

He walked to the staggering Asura, clenched his pale face in his grip and swiped his claws across.

He roared his victory. Three down. Two to go.

As Nara held his ground against the two axe-wielding Asuras, he rolled back and scraped some of the sand from the ground and hurled it in the Asuras' faces. They were blinded for a moment, as Nara swung the fallen blade next to an Asura's feet, chopping his limbs away, which was followed by an agonized scream.

One to go.

The last Asura menacingly swung his axe. He rammed it against Nara's shoulder. Nara grimaced for a moment, as he pulled the axe from his flesh and growled. The Asura looked incredulously at Narasimha.

Nara pushed the glove off his free hand and then clawed the Asura's face. The Asura soldier began to bleed as he fell on the ground, blinded, wailing in pain. Nara stomped on his chest again and again until the screams stopped. He pulled the axe away. He saw the other Asuras scampering for safety as he swung the axe at an Asura's back, splitting his spine into two. He collapsed, his mangled body lying lifeless on the ground.

Nara, holding his hand to his wound, which was bleeding profusely, roared loudly. Now the villagers had come with bamboo sticks and swords of their own. The bowmen from the village had appeared as the other Asuras and Rakshasas mounted their horses and tried to escape.

'Our intel was wrong. Indra is not here. Let's just leave before more of us die,' one of the Asuras cried.

Nara knew all of this would be reported, but for now, the surviving Asuras and Rakshasas were retreating. They were afraid.

He could smell their fear.

He didn't pursue them. Instead, Nara walked to Virata, who had his head lowered. 'Assist your father and get medical aid for everyone.'

'Y-yes.'

Nara sighed, seeing the women and men who were hiding in fear. Many of them were injured, many more dead. The corpses of children lay flat on the ground, along with a few women.

The village had suffered casualties for no reason at all.

'I attacked you but you saved my life. Why would you do that?' Virata lowered his eyes.

'Don't dwell on what you have done before. Prepare yourself for what should be done next,' Nara said.

'They shouldn't have attacked us. There was no reason for it,' he said under his breath. 'It's not the first time though. They have been pillaging villages nearby to get information on Lord Indra, who has been hopping from village to village in disguise. It was our turn. With the north being destroyed by Andhaka's army, and with Lord Shiva's forces suppressed, we have no one to protect us.'

Nara thought for a moment. He had turned down Indra's request for aid, but Nara was worried now. If Andhaka could massacre so many innocents with a small force, what would he do with Pashupatastra at his disposal?

I have to do something.

'I have got to go,' Nara said, as he limped away from the headman's son, his hand held against his wounded shoulder as he hobbled forward.

'Where are you going?' Virata called to Nara's retreating figure.

It had been fifteen years. Perhaps the prophecy had been wrong. Perhaps the secret that Nara feared would come true was of no value any more. Perhaps he could come out of hiding.

Lord Rudra would be upset about it, but then … *It has been a long time now.*

Perhaps I'm not even destined to be a Dharm any more.

Perhaps it was over and he could go back again. But this time, it would be to save innocents, rather than to kill them.

'To the north. Andhaka needs to be stopped,' Nara answered Virata's question without turning back.

7

PRAHLAD

Death didn't get him.

He opened his eyes to find that he was lying in a bed, flanked by cushions. Light gleamed from the many pearls that were studded on the ceiling of the room; the air was scented with the smell of incense. The room was silent. He heard nothing. It was peaceful.

Finally.

Prahlad blinked as he sat up, realizing that he was back in his room, in his palace at Kashyapuri.

How long was I knocked out for?

He had bandages all over him, and the smell of ayurvedic ointments irritated him. He was famished. It felt like he hadn't eaten in weeks.

He instantly went for the fruit platter on the side table, biting into an apple.

His back still hurt, but he sighed, lulled by the pleasures of home. He then recalled his locket and clutched it tight.

It's still there.

Prahlad smiled to himself. His heart had sunk when Jayant, that Deva lord, had grabbed it from him. *It was my mother's. It doesn't belong to anyone else.* He was also protective of the locket because of its significance, given that his brother hadn't received any such object from their mother.

She chose me for it.

The door of the room opened and Prahlad directed his attention to the tall figure that had just walked in – Anuhrad. He was in plain clothes now, loose pyjamas and a grey tunic, with a dagger sheathed at his belt.

'How was your beauty sleep?' His brother grinned as he calmly sat on the bed, close to Prahlad's blanket. Prahlad noticed Anuhrad had some bandages on him too.

'How many hours did I sleep?'

'More like how many days.'

Prahlad gasped. 'How many?'

'Three.' Anuhrad shrugged. 'It's all right. It happens. The first time I fought in the war, I was out for a week.'

'I think I've lost some weight.' Prahlad felt his protruding ribs. His body felt numb.

'You need to have weight to lose it in the first place.' Anuhrad stood up, stretching himself.

'Who won?' Prahlad asked earnestly.

'We did. Kind of, I mean. Jayant was wounded so he pulled back Agni's army.'

Prahlad grinned. Not bad for his first time fighting on the battlefield. Usually he aided Anuhrad or his father.

It was the second battle which he had looked over. In the first one, he had won. And even now, with the aid of Anuhrad.

'That's good.'

'Hey, listen …' Anuhrad said.

Prahlad looked up.

'Yeah?'

'Thank you for saving me back there.' He held out his hand as a gesture of peace.

'You want to shake my hand for saving your life?' Prahlad chuckled. 'That's just awkward. Don't be so formal. I'm your brother.'

'I don't know how to do this.'

'Do what?' Prahlad was having a blast annoying his older brother. It was not every day that Anuhrad – his rude, self-centred older brother – expressed his gratitude.

'How to be *nice*,' Anuhrad sighed. 'Screw it. When you are ready, call for a proper breakfast and then come and meet father. He wants to see us and wants to tell us something together.'

'Together?' That made Prahlad uncomfortable. His father could be a little … mysterious.

'Yes.' Anuhrad smiled. 'Let's hope he announces who the next king is.' He winked. 'But then, he isn't retiring anytime soon, not until Indra is defeated.'

'And, of course, it'll be you,' Prahlad sighed. 'You are the older one.'

Anuhrad shrugged. 'I know. But thanks, youngling. You proved useful.'

Prahlad laughed, because he knew Anuhrad did feel grateful, though he couldn't help being rude. Prahlad felt a glow of happiness. The war seemed to have brought them closer.

Anuhrad left, closing the door behind him, and Prahlad began to dress, struggling with his clothes since one of his hands was still sore. While he was wearing his tunic, the cloth got stuck and he tried to pull at it, but it wouldn't budge.

Just then, there was a knock at the door.

Great.

'Who is it?' he called.

'Prince Anuhrad sent breakfast for you, my lord,' a childlike female voice responded.

'Don't ent—'

But the door opened. The girl was about to see his naked torso.

Oh no …

'Oh, I'm sorry!' she shrieked. 'I didn't know you were getting dressed, your highness.'

Prahlad couldn't see the servant because his tunic was stuck halfway down his head. 'Can you help me, since you are here?'

'Uhh … um …'

'Please, I'm stuck. My arm is sore, so I can't do it myself.'

'Yes, of course, my lord.'

Prahlad could feel soft hands brushing his arms as the girl lifted the tunic a little and then pulled it gently back down over him. Now dressed, he looked at her and saw a young face with bouncing curls down to her neck, bright red in colour. He had never seen hair like that before, but it suited her round eyes and oval face, pink lips and perfectly shaped nose.

'You are new,' Prahlad remarked. *And pretty.*

The girl blushed. 'Yes, I am, my lord.'

'Which quarters?'

'Cook. I assist Master Ravneet.'

Master Ravneet? Prahlad had no idea how many cooks worked at the palace. After all, he was a prince and every day, there would be a new servant, a new cook, a new guard around him. But she … she was beautiful and he wished she would stay.

'What's your name?' he asked

'Dhriti, my lord.'

'What does that mean?'

'Strength.'

Prahlad nodded. 'Your parents named you?'

She shook her head. 'I'm an orphan. The nurses at the orphanage gave me my name.'

'I see. Are you a cook yourself?'

'I'm learning.'

'Ah.'

Prahlad smiled as he sat down and began to eat. He watched Dhriti leave, a strange but pleasant sensation lingering from the tunic incident. He liked her; she was sweet and childlike.

But also just a servant.

She was lowborn and seemed like a Manav, for she didn't have any attributes of another Tribe. There weren't many Tribals here in the capital anyway.

Prahlad walked the halls of his palace, carefully descending the steps. The sun was shining outside as he reached the golden fields. His father had always liked gold, in fact the entire palace was adorned with gold from ceiling to floor, punctuated with pearls and crystal.

The garden area was spectacular, with a statue of Hiranyaksha, Prahlad's uncle, standing beside Hiranyakashyap's own image in stone. When the brothers had built this palace, they made sure their statues were erected first, as symbols of their achievements that they could look upon with pride.

The field was surrounded by forest land and there was a small fountain on the side. Walls at the corners had thorns and barricades and guards in black armour stood watch. There were no Danavs here at the palace, and that was good, since it was difficult to accommodate them – imagine twenty-foot creatures just sitting and picking their teeth out of boredom. Just for them, Prahlad's father built the city of Hiranyapur, that lay in the west of Kashyapur, where the Kalakeyas and Poulamos resided in comfort. All the palaces, the gardens, the fortresses there were large enough to almost dwarf the massive Danavs. It was from there that they were summoned for battle.

Prahlad could see two ministers standing in the middle of the field. He knew them. Shand and Amarka. Shand was the minister of finance, the treasurer of the city with a thin moustache, a big round head like a ball, and short hair. Amarka, on the other hand, was the minister of cultural affairs, quite the opposite in appearance to Shand, being tall and very lean, though he too had a pencil-thin moustache.

Anuhrad was standing in between them and they were watching something farther away on the field. Prahlad's vision grew clearer as he approached them and realized what they were focused on.

It was King Hiranyakashyap they were watching, their eyes wide with awe and admiration.

Hiranyakashyap stood seven feet tall, broad-shouldered and with thick, protruding muscles defining arms as big as maces. His hair was oiled and pulled back and his thick moustache spread proudly above his mouth. His golden eyes, the most striking of his features, seemed brown now and were sunken deep with all the suffering they had witnessed.

He was in his royal golden dhoti, standing between two wrestlers in fighting stances.

Prahlad's father had a habit of waking up early in the morning and warming himself up by wrestling with the finest warriors in the city.

The two wrestlers charged at him. Hiranya didn't roll out of their way as Prahlad might have done in that situation. Rather, he grabbed the wrestlers by the throat and lifted them up in the air. And then smacked their heads together before tossing them to the ground.

'What is wrong with you two?' King Hiranya said hoarsely. 'You are not even trying, as far as I can tell.' He went to get a damp cloth from the mat close to the arena and started wiping off his sweat while the two wrestlers massaged their head in confusion.

'Father,' Anuhrad spoke with deep respect, 'if this will continue to be your competition, you might as well fight our cousins, the Danavs.'

Hiranya laughed as he hugged Anuhrad and then looked at Prahlad, who was standing in the corner. 'My son.' He grinned as he embraced him, holding Prahlad's small body against his mighty, perspiring frame.

Prahlad pulled away and wiped his face. 'You need to bathe, Dad.'

'And I shall,' he chuckled, ruffling Prahlad's hair. 'But I need to discuss something with you and Anuhrad. Shand, Amarka,' he turned to the Asura ministers, 'give me a moment to speak with my sons.'

The pair nodded and stepped aside.

'What is it, father?' asked Anuhrad.

Hiranya sighed, as, instead of answering, he began to check Prahlad's wound and then Anuhrad's. 'I love the scars, boys. You have made me proud.' He grinned. But Prahlad found it unsettling that a father could take pleasure in seeing his child hurt. He had seen fathers making sure their children were safe, and he had seen it most often during his childhood, between his servants and their children. 'Prahlad, I'm glad you survived the ordeal. Every time I send you out, I can feel my heart in my throat. Anuhrad can take care of himself, but you, you were always the weaker one. But it's a sign of strength how you won this battle. I won't be afraid any more,' the king said.

That's my father – appreciative and condescending at the same time.

'I have some bad news, though,' he added.

For Hiranyakashyap to describe something as bad surely meant terrible news. He seldom exaggerated.

'I have to leave for the outskirts of Yakshlok,' he said, arching his brows. 'Vigyasa is close to defeating Agni, and he needs me and my men. I have to go and support him.'

Prahlad had never met Vigyasa, since he was stationed at the outskirts, though he was said to be cunning and ruthless – perfect for this war.

'Why do you have to leave? I'll go,' Anuhrad volunteered. 'I defeated Agni's army here.' And then he glanced at Prahlad. 'With Prahlad, of course. We wounded Jayant too.'

'Yes, and as reports mention, Jayant has left for Devlok to recover. Even the stupid, useless Somas couldn't help him.' Hiranya paused. 'I knew that more than some magic blue liquid, it would be our will and resolve that would lead us to victory. Just a few more days of hard work and we will have avenged your mother.' He kept his bulky hands on Prahlad and Anuhrad. 'Also,' he said, looking at Prahlad's older brother, 'you can't go to Yakshlok because you are needed somewhere else.'

At Kashyapuri – as acting king. Of course.

Prahlad wanted to be happy for Anuhrad, but felt a pang of jealousy. And who wouldn't be jealous of Anuhrad? Apart from his arrogance, he was a good man.

'I am just not sure you can handle it.'

Anuhrad pleaded, 'No, father. I can. I know I can.'

'You and Andhaka never see eye to eye,' Hiranya mused.

At that, Prahlad exchanged confused glances with Anuhrad.

'How is …' Anuhrad began, slowly, as if trying to put two and two together, '… how is Andhaka in the picture?'

Hiranya looked up, widening his gaze. 'Oh, I didn't explain the context. I want you to go to the Mandara Hills, to Sonitpur to be precise.'

'Sonitpur?' Prahlad raised his brows. That was where Andhaka had his army stationed.

'Anuhrad, I know you don't like Andhaka, but he needs support and he has asked for you specifically.' Hiranya emphasized that last word.

Prahlad knew why Anuhrad was chosen. He was a better warrior and a strategist.

'Take some of the mercenaries with you, especially the Pishach. You know how to tame them and support Andhaka in the north. The Simhas are overpowering him. And we need to get Pashupatastra. It will give us a huge advantage if we have to attack Devlok and steal Somas from them, while we stab the bloody Devendra. That is one of the only ways to do it. Andhaka has been kind enough to help us for he avenges his father, your uncle. He's diligently held the north for years fighting the forces of Bhairav.' He paused. 'Anuhrad, don't you return empty-handed. I want you to fight in the north as long as you have to, to get Pashupatastra, and I know you are capable of success. Promise me, will you?'

'Yes, father, I promise,' Anuhrad said in a softer voice than usual.

'Andhaka can really use your strength. He has been working really hard, poor boy.'

And enjoying his freedom as acting ruler of Sonitpur too.

'Help him.' He patted Anuhrad's shoulder. Anuhrad nodded without saying a word. Prahlad could see he was disappointed. Not only was he not getting the throne of Kashyapuri anytime soon, but he was being sent to a deserted, snow-capped kingdom ruled by a tyrant. 'And you, Prahlad, you are not ready to help anyone in the war now. You are weak ... for now. You showed bravery, but you are more brains than brawn. And I know where to use it best.' Hiranya turned and called out to his ministers, who were discussing a matter between themselves.

The ministers scurried over and stood next to Hiranya's towering frame as he said to them, in front of Anuhrad, 'My dear councilmen, I would like to formally introduce you to the acting ruler of Kashyapuri … Prince Prahlad. He will be your king until my return from Yakshlok. You will serve him now.'

Prahlad's heart began to sink … No. Not *his* heart.

He turned to look at Anuhrad.

His brother's.

8
NARASIMHA

Nara rode up to the creek.

I've been travelling for a week now.

He had reached the curving path of the Mandara hills from where he could see part of Illavarti – and it was majestic. Harsh wind blew against his face, most of which was covered with a muffler. He wasn't as immune to the weather as he used to be, since the power from the Somas, ingested a long time ago, had somewhat waned. He watched the land in front of him, its valleys, rivers and mountains, the forests and the volcanoes. It was a tapestry of bright colours, and the sun was hiding behind a shroud of mist.

Nara rode down the undulating path that led to the golden city of Sonitpur. Even from the distance, it shone brightly. According to Indra, it had been claimed by Andhaka's army and was an impenetrable fortress. From his saddle, Nara could see walls of iron and steel, along with bronze towers. Andhaka's men would spot any approaching threat, and the archers on the walls looked prepared to defend it against any enemy.

Andhaka has made the place absolutely impregnable.

Nara turned his steed in the opposite direction, away from Sonitpur, and began descending the rocky terrain. He soon reached the familiar land where the first Shiva had made a home for himself. There stood the tall, hulking fort of Lord Bhairav, a mini kingdom, and one could easily locate the fort, for the flag was hoisted from one of the watchtowers – a flag with the trident symbol on it. This was the defining symbol of all Shivas.

A Shiva was not part of Manavs or Tribals, though people of both groups often served Shiva – his followers were diverse in nature. The first Shiva, Lord Nataraj, had started this practice during the time of Lord Matsya, the First Vishnu Avatar. The Shiva and his army were warriors who followed Dharma. Lord Bhairav sided with the Devas because they were closer to the idea of Dharma in comparison to the Asuras, who followed the practices of evil.

A Shiva was a leader, popular and much respected. He was not under anyone, not even Indra, but he followed Lord Mahadev. In fact, Indra was under him because, if angered, a Shiva's followers could lead a revolt.

But right now, by the state of the fort, Nara could see the faded image of the Shiva – defeated, almost dying. The walls showed cracks, the snow was grey and bloody, the flag scorched. When Nara was here before, during Rudra's time, the place had been a thing of beauty.

And now, it was a thing of horror.

But it wasn't Lord Bhairav's fault. Andhaka had come too close to home, built his own castle and continuously attacked them. Anyone would be beaten and bruised after that kind of constant, relentless assault.

At the farthest corner, Nara saw the battlefield. It was hidden in the snowy mountains – a large, sprawling land – riddled with countless bodies. Vultures circled above, swooping down to peck on them. Barricades of barbed wires fenced the land in, so that no one could cross into each other's territory.

Nara had thought that he would never see all of this again … but here he was. He frowned, disappointed that so much time and energy was still going into the war. Over what? A nuclear weapon that would result in *more* wars.

This battle would end if there was no Pashupatastra to fight for.

Nara walked to the gates of the fort just as a loud bell began to ring. He saw archers lining up on the first floor of the fort and a dozen guards appear from the gates, beating the snow with their boots.

Nara raised his arms in surrender, though he found it mildly amusing that they were treating him like a high-level threat.

But that also spoke volumes about the security of the palace.

From behind the guards, a broad, heavy figure emerged. He was short, with matted hair and a tattoo of the trishul on his chest. A large leopard skin was thrown over his body to help him through the winter. His eyes were tired, and there were fine lines around them. An axe dangled from his waist.

'Identify yourself!' the man yelled.

Nara casually got off his horse.

'Hello, Bhairav,' he said, smiling.

Bhairav's expression changed. 'By the grace of Lord Mahadev, is it you, Nara?'

Nara nodded. Bhairav gestured for the soldiers to lower the weapons. He moved forward to envelope Nara in an embrace.

'I can't believe you agreed to return, my friend.' Bhairav patted Nara's back. 'Indra said he would try to convince you. And it worked!' Nara could swear that Bhairav's eyes were moist with tears.

Fifteen years ago, when Nara served Lord Rudra, Bhairav had been second-in-command. A middle-aged man back then, he had aged, and the change was visible. He looked like he'd been to hell and back.

'It was for you, so I had to,' Nara said, patting his friend's back, recalling how they had befriended each other after Nara had seen Bhairav crying one day. When Nara had asked him what was wrong, Bhairav had confided about his son, who had been kidnapped by Hiranyaksha during his rule. When Hiranyaksha died, Bhairav had tried to search for his son, but had failed to find him. He had then got to know that his son had been brutally killed by Hiranyaksha.

'You haven't changed a bit. Still a bad liar, eh?' Bhairav said now, a knowing smile on his face.

Nara chuckled. 'How is Parvati?' he enquired after Bhairav's wife.

'Oh, she's fine,' he said. 'Come in, old man, I shall have a feast prepared for you.'

'Old? Look who's talking!' Nara scoffed.

'I still have my glory days ahead of me,' Bhairav quipped, and Nara nodded, smiling, though he could see that his friend appeared quite grey, withered and beaten.

As Nara walked through the palace, the guards watched him in awe. He was the fabled hero, and now he had returned. Some might hate him for leaving the war; others were in awe of him. But he didn't care.

He was here. The prodigal son had returned.

Inside the fort, carts laden with meat, vegetables and fruits, the armouries and stables, the ground, everything was covered with a thin layer of snow. Men, women and children of different Tribes, including the Manavs, populated the place. Everyone seemed weak and exhausted, even the soldiers. Most of them were Nagas and Yakshasas, while some were Simhas – wearing their skin, the large tufts of mane around their head acting as a helmet, the gauntlets made of deceased lions.

The Simhas worshipped lions because lions represented strength and aggressiveness. They wore the skin of the deceased lion that they had once had as a companion. It was in their culture – every young Simha born in the Tribe would get a lion cub as a companion. The two would grow up together, and learn from each other. And when that lion died after completing its life cycle, its hide would be worn by the Simha. In this way, their spirits would merge and they would live on forever within each other. And to preserve this hide from rotting, a special mixture of soap, eggs and salt had to be rubbed over it every second day.

I stopped wearing mine a long time back.

Simhas used spears and swords, mostly handheld weapons that didn't require them to attack from afar. They were aggressive and at the forefront of every war. But most of all, their prime weapons were their hereditary and fatally sharp claws.

The females of the Tribe, the Simhis, were also warriors, used mainly for scouting and hunting.

Nara shook his head, dismissing the thoughts of his Tribe, and focused on the large bull statue made of silver standing in the middle of the fort. It was a statue of Nandi, the mount of Lord Nataraj, the first Shiva. Nandi was worshipped as a god of strength here.

'How is everything going?' Nara asked Bhairav.

'What do you think?' Bhairav sighed. 'We don't have enough food for the winter, and we rely on hunting for food, though Indra has promised that he will send us supplies. We have families to support, soldiers to feed. Every second day, Andhaka sends his forces down to the field and if we don't retaliate by fighting them, they come close to the fort,' he said, shaking his head.

Nara clenched his jaw and Bhairav noticed this.

'But look on the bright side!' he said, trying to lighten the mood for his guest. 'Even though these are dark days, by the looks of it, we are winning. We are surviving. And that's what's important,' he grinned and thumped Nara's back.

Winning? Surviving? Nara looked at the unhealthy, starved men and women around them.

'Andhaka has to stop sometime,' he said.

'That's what we thought,' Bhairav said. 'That's what we hoped would happen, but it didn't. Instead, he just kept at it. His forces are being supplied continuously by Hiranyakashyap.'

Nara arched his brows. 'Why can't we shift the Pashupatastra to a more discreet location?'

Bhairav shook his head. 'I wish we could, but Lord Rudra planned to keep it here. I cannot go against his words. As long as my breath remains, I shall be here, defending it from the forces that want to use it for evil.' His words were brave, heroic, and Nara wanted to interrupt his friend and tell him that, in this world, heroes often died.

'What about Indra using it for wrong too?' he asked instead.

Bhairav raised his brows. 'Still don't like him, do you?'

Nara scoffed. 'Who does? Do you?'

'He has helped us a lot. He's funding us, and for me, that's a blessing. As long as I am Shiva, I have to protect this land, which was passed down to me from Lord Rudra, before I pass it down to someone else.'

Nara nodded. He wanted to say more, but before he could, a tall, husky man with a beard and long, wavy hair, similar to Bhairav's, appeared. He whispered something in Bhairav's ear, whose eyes dimmed with worry as he turned to Nara. 'My dear friend, I'm afraid the feast must be delayed. I have some work to attend to.'

'Of course.'

'This is Veerbhadra,' Bhairav introduced the man to Nara. Nara noticed that Veerbhadra had a large scar across his eyebrows. 'He's my commander and soon to be a Shiva,' Bhairav added.

Veerbhadra smiled and nodded, bowing to Nara.

'Let's go,' Bhairav said to Veerbhadra, and taking Nara's leave, they turned and walked out through the main gate.

Nara walked on alone, his horse trotting beside him. Up ahead, he stopped next to a street seller with a cart full of ornaments. He saw a lion totem amongst the other items and smiled.

'Lookie who's here!' a voice called from behind him.

Nara turned to see a Simha with a black mane around his face and grey skin over his body. Around him stood other pale-skinned Simhas. Nara knew the voice, and even though it had been years, the face looking at him was oddly recognizable too.

'Mrig,' Nara breathed. 'You have grown.'

'We all had to, old man,' Mrig said, crossing his arms across his chest as the other Simhas chuckled with him, 'since you left us all alone.'

Nara sighed. 'I am sorry.'

'Save your sorry.' Mrig came forward, leaning close to Nara and Nara could see how big he had become. 'Tell me something, how was your vacation?' Mrig reeked of alcohol. In fact, all of them seemed drunk.

But the Simhas never drink.

'It was not a vacation,' Nara said, his voice grim.

'If it was retirement, old man, why did you return? This war doesn't need cowards like you on the battlefield. Simhas have one code of honour – to not leave their Pride behind,' Mrig said, his voice full of scorn.

Something I didn't respect.

'How do we …' Mrig walked around Nara, as he spoke, 'believe you won't leave us again during a battle? Tell me, please. I mean, for all we know you'll run away again when we need you.'

'I won't this time,' Nara said.

'Words are hollow, old man. Learn that.' Mrig stood next to his group. 'You are not even wearing your skin. You are a loser, a coward.'

Nara ignored him. The humiliation stung, but he decided that it'd be better to leave and find his quarters at the camp. Just as he was turning away, he heard it. All of them did – the bells and then the horns.

Someone shouted, 'Andhaka's army has returned to the battlefield!'

Mrig ran towards the gate, but just before he exited, he turned and called out to Nara, 'Let's see if you are a coward or if you can still be what you used to be!' And with that, he left with the other Simhas to join the battle.

Nara hesitated for a moment. He hadn't expected the battle to begin so quickly.

He grabbed the bag from his saddle on the horse. He walked to an isolated place, ignoring the men and women who were running around, the soldiers grabbing spears, swords and shields, the rams were being brought to the main gate.

I have to move fast.

Nara opened his bag, revealing the golden mane, the golden gauntlets and the overall skin that wrapped his back and front like armour. He saw his skin. He wore it, first fitting the mane around his head, then wrapping the skin around his tight, muscular body. It fit perfectly. He tied the whole thing with a leather belt.

And then he stood up, breathing hard. He could feel the spirit of the lion in him now. He could feel the power of the animal inside him. He was a Simha now.

And then he pulled off his gloves, revealing his large claws.

He had considered getting a weapon, but shook his head.

No.

I'll do it without one.

And then he ran towards the gate.

Here I come, Andhaka.

9

PRAHLAD

Hiranyakashyap left. Anuhrad left.

Prahlad was all alone. Not literally, though.

He got the king's office – with its walls and ceiling of solid gold, its stacks of papers, shelves lined with books and the hanging scrolls. On the walls were paintings of Pataal. Prahlad had never been to Pataal, not even on a vacation. Hiranya had told his sons that Illavarti was their new home and there was to be no looking back.

Prahlad walked to a painting that showed the holy river of Pataal – it flowed through a ravine, bluer than the water here in Illavarti. There were groves and beautiful maidens close to it, splendid jewels that grew from the colourful trees.

Devas characterized Pataal as hell – from where the demons came, but if they had the opportunity to see these paintings, they'd know how beautiful it really was.

He walked to the other painting, and saw how the ground represented in it was black, white, purple and blue. Prahlad realized that there were so many colours that played in the light of Pataal.

He recalled one of the conversations he had had with his father when he was small.

'Why don't we just leave for Pataal, father?' a young Prahlad asked.

Hiranya smiled, as he patted the boy's head. Prahlad was playing with a few wooden blocks and was building them into a castle. 'I wanted to do that, son. It was my brother's dream to conquer this land, Illavarti. I always thought we were happy, content in Pataal. But now, this is no longer the case. I would have left and stayed in my homeland if the truce had been honoured. Now, I stay here, not for my brother, not to conquer the land, but for your mother. I will not leave for Pataal, nor will you, until we have our revenge.'

Prahlad nodded glumly. 'Are all Asuras like my uncle? They want to conquer other lands too?'

'No. In fact, they are very happy there. That's the problem with us, my child,' he paused. 'We always strive for more when we should be content with what we have.' He sighed. 'My brother was never like that. He wanted to do what Lord Harigriva couldn't.' Harigriva was one of the Asuras during Lord Matsya's time, Prahlad recalled. 'And greed for greatness made him fall.'

'Are you worried that you will end up doing the same?'

The king smiled and Prahlad could sense great sadness behind that smile. 'I was like that before your mother's passing, my child. But I realized, one should wage wars for noble purposes, not for sinful ones.'

A beautiful painting drew Prahlad back from his memories of the past. The painting showed the entire island of Pataal.

It had strange, intricate carvings and there was no sun, only dark skies, but Prahlad remembered his father telling him that Pataal glowed with energy and light due to the amount of jewels it had. The Sun was never a privilege granted to Pataal, to the Asuras. But they lit up their streets from the jewels they mined from the land.

And they made sure that the light never left them.

Looking around his father's quarters, Prahlad could see that Hiranyakashyap was doing the same thing. Even at night, his father's room would shine and gleam because of the jewels he had used in its construction.

'Your father was always a lover of art and culture,' a voice said, breaking into his thoughts.

Prahlad turned and saw a bald, old man walk into the room with stacks of books and scrolls. White cloth was draped around his chest.

Narada, his guru and mentor, who had taught him everything since infancy.

Prahlad instantly went to help Narada with the books and kept them on the table. 'Guruji, you should have told me. I could have come and helped you.'

'Heh,' the old man chuckled as he walked to a chair, his posture upright and his demeanour energetic. 'You are a ruler now, Lord Prahlad. You should not worry about such small matters, my dear.'

'Yes, Guruji,' Prahlad said.

'What do you think about the paintings?' Narada asked.

'I find them nice.' Prahlad sank into his chair.

'Your mother was very vocal about them. Do you know she was the cultural minister before Amarka?'

'I was not aware of that.'

'She introduced your father to art. Very wise lady, indeed.'

'My father loved her a lot, didn't he?'

'He has made it his mission to right the wrong against her. Love is a small word for what he felt for your mother, your highness,' Narada smiled, pulling the scrolls on the table towards him. 'As a king though, you need to sign a few things,' he passed them on to Prahlad.

'What are these?' Prahlad read the scrolls and saw that they were supply lists for the vendors, bazaar finances and merchant inclusions. There were a lot of numbers and calculations, and he didn't understand most of it.

'Should I dull your mind with the details of what they mean?' Narada smiled as he asked.

Prahlad chuckled. 'Nah, I trust you.' And he began to sign the scrolls one by one. As he did so, he asked, 'Tell me something, Guruji, before Kashyapuri was formed, before the Dakshini became an Asura empire ... whom did the people worship?'

'Why do you ask, my lord?'

'I just ...' Prahlad sighed, recalling the feeling he had had before he had entered the battle. 'When I was in battle and could feel I was losing, I wished for someone to pray to. Asuras don't believe in idol worship. They don't believe in gods, but in attributes. I wish I had a god to worship. You are a guru, aren't you? Who did you worship?'

'That's very philosophical, my lord,' Narada said thoughtfully. 'We have only one god we worship – Lord Vishnu.'

Prahlad had heard about Varaha Avatar, the soldier of Lord Vishnu who killed his uncle. Apparently, Lord Vishnu sided with good, with Dharma.

'What about Brahma?'

'Brahma was worshipped for his inventions.'

'And Shiva?'

'That's a war title. You meant to say Lord Mahadev. Let me explain. During the creation of Illavarti, three gods formed out of nothing. Vishnu was the preserver. He was the chosen one to fight evil. Brahma was the first Prajapati, the first man before even Manu. He was behind many inventions that we see around us, thus he never had a temple ever dedicated to him because he always believed himself to be a man first. Then there was Lord Mahadev. He is worshipped by the Ganas of the north. The Gana have a leader called Lord Shiva, which is a war title, passed down, and supposedly a Shiva is chosen by Lord Mahadev.'

'And Lord Vishnu is a warrior like Shiva?'

'Depends on how you want to see it. For me, he was the heroic god, and he promised to return in every Yug to fight his enemy.'

'Enemy?' Prahlad arched his brows.

'Yes. The Adharm. In his Yug, when he was supposedly alive, the enemy was none other than evil Kaliyan. And he was an Asura.'

Prahlad got shivers down his spine. He knew about Kaliyan. His father had talked about him – he was the first Asura. 'Ah, that's why Asuras are hated.'

'Absolutely.'

Prahlad looked his guru straight in the eye. 'But you didn't answer. Who do you believe in?'

'Lord Vishnu for his goodness, Lord Brahma for his creativity and Lord Mahadev for his strength,' he said.

Prahlad envied Narada for the privilege of having a god to look up to. 'Faith is important, right?'

'Most important. Faith strengthens us and makes us believe,' Narada said.

'Believe what?'

'In being a better person.' Guruji smiled.

And then a voice boomed inside the room, 'But faith used to destroy the foundations of our government is terrorism.'

Prahlad turned to see Shand, the finance minister, and Amarka, the lanky culture minister, entering the room.

'My lord,' both ministers bowed in respect to Prahlad.

'Why do you say that?' Prahlad asked Shand.

'Haven't you heard?' Amarka said, his voice slick and thin as he narrowed his raven eyes at Narada. 'You should have told our king what's bothering this society.'

Prahlad glanced at Narada, who said, 'I thought I wouldn't burden him on the first day.'

'He's a king, my dear man!' Shand snapped at Narada. 'He has to be burdened.'

'What is it?' Prahlad stood up, his voice louder and more urgent.

'There's a terrorist organization operating in Kashyapuri, my lord,' Amarka explained, his nostrils flaring as he continued. 'They call themselves the Vishnusena, which literally means of an army of Vishnu bhakts. They want to tear down our Asura government and take back Kashyapuri from the Asuras and restore it to the dharmic way of life.'

Prahlad responded, 'Kashyapuri was never built on anything.'

'It was built on a Manav kingdom, my lord,' Shand said. 'A kingdom of men who were followers of Lord Vishnu. And now they are unhappy and want their land back.'

Prahlad arched his brows as he looked at Narada. 'What can we do about them?'

'They are unorganized, my lord,' Narada said. 'We don't know when and how they attack. Their last offence was when they tore down the black market by killing the merchants and displaying their heads alongside notes declaring that there won't be any other black market as it is against dharmic practices,' he said. 'Other times, they ended the moneylending racket and brothels and a lot of unethical practices.'

Shand grunted. 'Those *unethical* practices, Guru Narada, form fifty per cent of our treasury.'

Kashyapuri had a black market? Prahlad hadn't even known about it. 'Why do we have a black market?'

Shand, the finance minister, added, 'Lord Hiranyakashyap believes in multiple sources of income, my lord. In the black market, the merchants give good bribes and in return they want no interference from the government when they sell drugs, illegal weapons and women.'

'And my father *allowed* that?'

'These are commodities civilians want to consume and pay for. In return, the merchants give us a sixty per cent cut if we don't interfere and turn a blind eye to these illegal activities, and so we do. It has built up our treasury and merchants are also happy, for these activities, albeit questionable, are lucrative and taxes according to the laws can't be applied on them,' Shand explained.

'But women aren't commodities!' Prahlad exclaimed, hitting his fist on the table. 'That is wrong. I don't want blood money in my bank. We can raise taxes, but this is not how we should rule.'

'Taxes are burdensome to a middle-class or lower-class individual. Your father knew that to increase profitability in every part, make everyone happy, one must make some sacrifices of morality and ethics,' Amarka added.

'But is it fair?' Prahlad asked.

'The world is not fair, my lord,' Shand shrugged. 'It was your father's decision, my lord. You can take it up with him when he returns, if it is worrisome to you.'

Prahlad sighed, leaning back in his chair. Women were sold? Drugs were peddled? Weapons were given to *anyone*?

'Though ...' Narada began, chipping into the conversation, 'there won't be a black market any more, because the merchants are afraid of what the Vishnusena did. They aren't opening their stores for a while now.'

'That's true,' Shand smugly agreed.

Prahlad was unhappy about all of this. He sat there, in deep thought.

'My lord, as the acting king, you must condemn the Vishnusena and what they did, and offer protection,' Shand said. 'Otherwise the market will remain closed and we will run in losses.'

'So what?' Prahlad challenged the minister. He found that Shand's words were really irritating him.

'*So what*, my lord?' Shand chuckled. 'This is the same money that funds the army engaged in this war, the money that the soldiers are paid, the stipends that go to the Pishach and Rakshasas. This money will help us win the war. If we don't have it, we will lose the war against the Devas.'

So the money from the black market is to serve his revenge. But would my mother approve of it? Prahlad realized that he hadn't known his mother well enough to answer that question.

Prahlad knew what duty called for, but somewhere deep down, he knew what the Vishnusena had done was right. He tried to shake off the thought and said instead, 'What was my father's decision then?'

'He had told General Holika to hunt them down, one by one,' Amarka said.

Hunt them down?

'So my aunt is after them.' And with that he was assured that they would be hunted down all right, because his aunt was a genius in spy activities and was an indomitable warrior.

But do I want them to be hunted? Because of them, an illegal market had been stopped, its evil merchants scared.

'Great,' he said, but his voice was uncertain. He wanted to know more about the Vishnusena. 'Thank you, everyone,' he smiled at the gathering in his room. 'You are dismissed for today.'

They all nodded and left as Prahlad stood there for a few minutes. Then he walked up to the window from where he looked out at the lavish fountain, the pathways snaking across the field and cherry trees that beautifully lined the palace.

What will be the Vishnusena's next move? And are they right or wrong?

Prahlad felt torn between his father's need to defeat Indra and his own instinct to do everything in his power to serve the cause of *right*.

He didn't know why he felt this way; there was no reason or logic to it, but he knew that he had to find them.

And find them before Holika did.

Prahlad called out to his Royal Guard, the king's personal soldier. Captain Viparichit entered. Prahlad had known him since they had been children together. He was a little older than Prahlad, close to Anuhrad's age, and he was tough. They all used to play together, until Viparichit, who was a low-born in the Asura hierarchy, joined the army to serve the crown.

'My lord,' he bowed.

'Please,' Prahlad said. 'I've told you before. You are a friend. No formalities.'

'Not when you have the crown over your head,' Viparichit laughed. He was a cheeky boy, with dimples and darkish hair that stood on his head, spiky like thorns.

'Funny.'

'What can I help you with?'

'What do you know about the Vishnusena?'

'It's a terrorist group. Your father and your aunt detest them,' Viparichit said.

'But do you believe in their cause?'

'Governments are built for a purpose. They are destroying that purpose. Be it right or not, that's not for us to decide. We have to serve the government, no matter what. Even if it is wrong.'

Prahlad nodded. 'You are right.' And he *was* right. After all, no matter how much good they did, they were challenging an institution and disrespecting it. They were challenging his throne and his father's throne and that was wrong. 'We need to find them.'

'But your aunt is already on the lookout.'

'I know, but she won't be merciful. These people, they cannot be killed. They have to be imprisoned and tried; I don't mind that, but my aunt … I know her. She doesn't believe in prison. She will kill them and gut them and I can't let that happen under my watch. They are the believers of Lord Vishnu. If my aunt kills them, the other civilians who are followers of Lord Vishnu will revolt, and I can't let that happen. Not everything has to end in violence.'

Viparichit seemed impressed. 'What do you have in mind?'

Prahlad smiled. He had a plan.

10

NARASIMHA

Nara came forth on the battlefield.

And in front of him, he saw the enemy. They were in hundreds and they were standing with ballistas, holding long arrows. The cavalry was in the front and infantry at the back, with large shields. Most of them were Rakshasas and Nagas were on the other end, with a few Manavs among them. They weren't moving and Nara saw the central figure – a black stallion, bigger than any horse he had ever seen, on which sat a young man.

He was short and bald, with bleached skin, and he had a blindfold on his eyes.

Andhaka.

Bhairav was not on the battlefield, but in the purple tent close to it. They had a camp close to his army, outside which more than five thousand infantrymen waited in silent attention for Bhairav's command.

Nara saw Mrig talking to the Pride of Simhas close by. They were there in the hundreds, listening to him, as they huddled together.

All of this happened under the overcast skies of the north, the mountains around the arena lending a claustrophobic feeling to the scene.

Nara entered the camp just in time to hear Bhairav.

'I don't understand!' The Shiva thumped his hand on the table. He sat with Veerbhadra, planning the battle strategy. 'You are saying we don't have ballistas of our own?'

'We have onagers, my lord,' Veerbhadra said, gesturing to the giant contraption that worked like a catapult and could launch large rocks.

'And they have shields to stop them.'

There was a constant muttering going on as Nara's attention was directed to the nurses who were feeding the soldiers loaves and soup, to energize them. Others were tending to the wounds of the injured soldiers. There was so much tension and horror around that Nara felt like he'd never left the war.

He walked away from Bhairav, directing his attention to Mrig, since he was part of the Simha army, but when Mrig saw Nara, he shrugged. 'You are not allowed to fight with the Pride, old man.'

Nara wanted to protest, but he decided to stay silent. So he was alone in this war. But then, wars were fought by lonely souls.

A horn blew, followed by the beating of drums.

'He's starting it already!' Bhairav yelled from the tent. 'Gather your javelins, everyone! Archers, prepare your volley!

Shields high, to deflect their attacks. Are the battle rams ready?'

Nara breathed in deeply and flexed his muscles, readying them for battle.

'Nagas – cavalry! Simhas – in the front, leave no one, my boys. And Yakshas – archers!' Bhairav ordered, as everyone got ready to charge.

The Shiva came next to Nara. 'Are you ready?'

Nara sighed. He was … *hopefully.*

And then the drums beat faster. And he heard it, as loud as anyone can be:

'ATTACK!'

The command came from Andhaka, who lifted his spear, pointing it towards Bhairav's army. The basilisk-looking Rakshasas leapt from their place, rushing towards them. To tackle them, the Simhas stepped forward.

Nara followed them, followed by the Nagas who came charging on their horses.

And it began.

As the armies clashed against each other, shields were broken, limbs torn and men killed.

For a moment, Nara was blinded by the mist and snow, by the storm of swords and shields. He shook his mane, pulling himself back to the battle.

Suddenly a man appeared in front of him from nowhere, and Nara dodged, using his claws in the process to scratch at his back. The man dropped down on his head.

Another figure, daunting and dark-skinned, attacked Nara.

A Rakshas!

An axe was struck at Nara's shoulder, plunging into it. He screamed in agony as he used his claws to cut the wooden handle and then used the blade to strike the head of the Rakshas, jamming it in and throwing him in the snow.

Nara fell to the ground; his head was spinning as the deep gash of a wound on his shoulder bled profusely.

I have to get up.

Just then, an arrow struck him in his arm. He pulled it out and turned to see a woman standing with a black cloak over her. She was a Naga.

For some reason, Nara stood there, confused.

I can't kill her. She must have a family. She must have a child.

She shot another arrow at him, and this one plunged into his chest. He knelt on the ground, sighing, trying to let the pain subside while he thought.

Should I kill her or not?

Somehow, he felt like he'd been tied up, unable to move.

And then suddenly, a figure lurched at the Naga woman, pushing her to the ground as it tore the skin from her head and hair with long, deadly claws.

It was Mrig.

He got to his feet and put out his hand for Nara, who tried to grab it just as Mrig pulled it back. 'You have become too slow, old man.' With that, he turned and disappeared into the battle.

Nara felt defeated. He clenched his jaw, slammed his fist on the ground and roared in anger. He stood up and tried to act confident as he clawed a Manav who had appeared in front of him. The man fell back and said, as he fell to the ground, 'I had a daughter. You've made her fatherless.'

It felt like a dream. Was it really? Nara panted. The war was affecting him. Not physically. His wounds would heal.

But emotionally, he felt weak, torn.

He hadn't felt like this before, while defending the village, defending himself. But now, the horror that surrounded him was reminding him of the very reason he had left it all behind.

Two Rakshasas came towards him with their spears as Nara began to deflect their blows with his hands.

Just as he somersaulted back and decided to charge at them, the two Rakshasas stood still and said to him, 'We are innocent.'

Nara shook his head, and he realized that it was all in his head. The Rakshasas came forward and slammed their fists across Nara's face, and then using his blade, stabbed him in the stomach with the sword, twisting it inside his guts as Nara felt shivers of pain shoot through him.

'Are you really a Simha?' the Rakshas asked him, a malicious grin on his face. He had oily hair and a tough, leathery skin. 'Doesn't look like it.'

And then … Nara saw the truth.

He felt angry because he knew now – *they were not innocent.* None of them were, not in this battle. His mind was playing tricks.

This is it.

Nara grabbed the sword that had plunged into him, holding the hilt as the Rakshas continued to push it in deeper.

But he couldn't.

Nara pulled out the blade from his abdomen and tossed it to the side. The Rakshas looked bewildered, fear in his eyes.

This is enough.

Nara leapt from his place, roaring as he did, his mane golden in the winter sun as he quickly clawed the two Rakshasas in one go. A third Rakshas came towards them with a shield and a sword.

He used the shield as Nara continuously scratched the armour, and then the Simha punched his hands through the shield, grabbing the neck of the Rakshas and choking him.

He roared again, beating his chest.

A slithering pain went down his spine, spinning and swelling in him as he fell on the ground. He saw where the pain had come from. A spear had plunged into his back. A spear that belonged to Andhaka.

Andhaka pulled out the spear and walked around to face Nara, bringing the blade of the weapon close to Nara's neck.

Nara grabbed the spear, wounded and beaten but using the last of his strength to push Andhaka to the ground. And then he used the blind warrior's spear against him, but Andhaka, despite his blindness, dodged the blow. He rolled to the side as a smile danced on his lips. He pulled out two long daggers from his scabbards that were hidden under his coat and then gestured for Nara to come forward.

Nara charged at Andhaka and, using all his might and strength, climbed onto him, holding him by the throat.

Nara's claws plunged into the skin of the blind prince and Andhaka writhed in pain and horror, as he tried to pull away, but couldn't. Nara held him down, punishing him, torturing him.

Soon, Andhaka stopped struggling.

The blind prince is dead.

Nara smiled as he fell back to the ground, his wounds bleeding, exhaustion overpowering him and darkness clouding his vision.

11

PRAHLAD

Prahlad had a bad feeling about this.

But it's all right.

He reminded himself that he had to take certain daring steps to effect change. He knew the members of the Vishnusena were essentially good people, but he also knew that they had to be stopped and imprisoned.

Not killed.

Just a while back, he had heard of what his aunt Holika had done. She had weeded out supposed suspects from the village, forcing them to reveal the truth about the Vishnusena. When no one would tell her anything, she had cut their heads off. Holika was extreme and unstoppable, ever since she was made responsible for the welfare of the state by his father. And she acted independently. She was tall and black-haired, with golden irises and a thin mouth. She walked elegantly and wielded her signature weapon, the twin swords, ruthlessly and mercilessly.

And she was a force to be reckoned with.

As a king, Prahlad wanted to stop Holika, but she worked independently, and he had no control over her. She had her own paramilitary force of Asuras – women and men with whom she fought and killed the spies of Indra and other rebel forces.

Prahlad, wrapped up in a muffler and cloak, walked out into his courtyard, coming out of his palace from the back gate and exiting to reach the streets where Viparichit stood in a cloak himself, muttering while holding something shiny.

'What are you doing?' Prahlad asked, tapping his friend's shoulder.

'Oh,' instantly Viparichit smiled, hiding the object, 'nothing, my lord.'

Prahlad arched his brows, and grabbed the object in Viparichit's hand.

It was a ring.

'You plan to propose to someone?' Prahlad grinned.

Viparichit blushed. 'Erm, I was … uh … yes,'

'Why so bashful about it? Congratulations, brother,' Prahlad embraced the confused Viparichit, who hugged him back.

'Th-thank you,' Viparichit smiled. For the Royal Guard, he was often nervous. 'I would have told you after she gave me an answer. I was actually uh … right now, practicing what I'd say to her.'

Prahlad nodded. 'Of course. Who is the lucky girl?'

'She works in one of the brothels.'

Prahlad raised his brows.

'No, no.' Viparichit shook his head. 'She's not an escort. She helps there.'

'A Royal Guard of the Crown marrying a helper of a brothel?' Prahlad didn't like the concept of brothels in the first place, but Shand had told him that brothels paid good tribute as well as appeased the nobles who sponsored the wars that Hiranyakashyap fought.

Everything comes down to money. But then, it's an empire and every empire runs on dirty money.

'I plan to ask her to leave her job after we are married.'

'And go where?'

'Settle in a good house close to the palace, give her a good life. She's a low-born as well, and migrated from Pataal with her mother when she was small.' Viparichit lowered his eyes. 'She says she will not leave her job since she is emotionally drawn to that brothel. Her mother used to work there, you know.'

Prahlad smiled warmly. There was earnestness in his friend's face. Low-borns in Asura culture were given jobs of slaves, servants, cleaners, prostitutes and whatnot. Viparichit had been luckier than most, and grew up to work as a crown's guard, probably because of the good friendship he had with Prahlad and Anuhrad. He also lived inside the royal grounds.

And now, he was thinking of getting married. It warmed Prahlad's heart.

But back to business.

'Do I look like the king?' Prahlad asked.

Viparichit shook his head. 'We should go. It's time.'

'Where do you plan to take me first?'

'There's a merchant whom I've paid well to speak about the incident of the black market. Let's start there.'

Prahlad nodded and began to follow Viparichit through the crowded streets of his city. He hadn't been in the nooks and corners of the capital, since he was always in the protective environment of his chariot whenever travelling the streets.

He looked at the crowds, the bonfires to beat the cold of the afternoon, the people of every Tribe talking to each other, food carts and caravans, announcements for theatre shows and musicals. The smell of food, various dishes of meat, chicken and fish, floated in the air of Kashyapuri.

He also saw occasional members of Holika's army riding through the streets on their horses, stopping to talk to people and get information out of them. But he couldn't see his aunt.

And hopefully, we won't. If she caught them ...

Prahlad didn't even want to think of what his strict aunt would do to him if she saw through his plan.

'What is your exact plan, my lord?' Viparichit asked, as if reading Prahlad's mind.

Prahlad had little idea of that himself. 'Once I know their location, I'll send the guards to get the Vishnusena and have them imprisoned.'

'And how does that stop Lady Holika from killing them?'

'They'll be under my care then and I'll make sure there is a trial. She knows that she can't publicly kill someone without a trial if they are in prison. She can do it on the streets, but not once they've been officially jailed.'

'Let's hope you are right,' Viparichit said, adding, 'my lord, may I speak freely?'

'Of course, my friend.'

'Please do not take offence at what I say.'

Prahlad hissed. 'It's all right. Speak. What interim king am I, if I don't listen to my subjects, and let fear dictate their thoughts.'

'My lord, you don't speak like any other ruler out there,' Viparichit replied, impressed. 'But what I want to say is, I feel like your real reason for finding the Vishnusena is not so that you can imprison them, but because you are finding ways to meet them, to know about them, because they intrigue you.'

They had reached the dark lane in the midst of the arched buildings.

Prahlad sighed. He was conflicted. What Viparichit said made sense. There was a little part of him that agreed too, but he was too adamant to agree. 'I've always been a curious child, Viparichit. And I want to know what drives a group of people to fight against a government for a god they have never seen or heard.'

'Will you pardon them if you think they are right in their belief?'

Prahlad knew that if he did, he'd be caught by Holika and probably put on trial for treason himself. He couldn't let that happen. For now, he told himself that he just wanted to find out who these people were and what went through their heads. Were they heroes or villains?

As they reached the lanes, he saw the carts and the small shops that housed different goods and merchandise – clothes, jewellery, weapons, medicines that were not sold at the local shamans, and more.

'So this is a black market?' he asked Viparichit.

'A less obvious one, yes.' Viparichit guided him to a narrower street where there was a small shop.

He saw the merchant – a bald man with big tummy and a scrawny beard, speaking to one of his customers, 'Oh, what is the demand for the age? I have got one that's ten, another of twelve and even one that's eight.'

What is he talking about?

Viparichit looked over at Prahlad and just gestured.

By the gods, he's a child trafficker!

As the customer shook his head and left, Viparichit came forward. 'Mustafa,' he called out to the merchant, who saw Viparichit and bowed with a sly, slick grin. The shop had a shack-like upper and lower berth, a small table and a small room in the back.

'Oh, you come again, guardsman,' he turned to see Prahlad, whose face was covered with a muffler. 'Who's your friend?'

'He's just a passing traveller, leave him be. Do you have the information you said you would gather from other merchants? The information about that day?'

Prahlad clenched his fist. He hated just standing there, unable to do anything. Child trafficking? His father allowed *that* too?

Who is he really? Do I even know him?

'It's called the Black Day,' Mustafa said, as he brought something out from underneath his table, pulling a leaf and chewing on it, probably a drug of some kind. 'They rode on horses and they had chakras in their hands, with which they killed the merchants. I rushed and I hid, and by some miracle, was saved. They also all wore a symbol.'

'What kind of symbol?' asked Viparichit.

'A lotus. The symbol of Lord Vishnu.' The merchant shook his head, and trembled a little. 'Their faces were covered. That's all we saw. We tried to fight back, but most of the shops were burnt and many lost their lives.'

'And yet you are part of this black market now?' Prahlad asked, masking his voice.

'A man's gotta earn, right?' the merchant slyly grinned. 'We have kept lookouts though.' He gestured at the building tops where men stood, holding spyglasses. They seemed like mercenaries. 'And now, hopefully, we won't have an issue.'

Viparichit nodded. 'Any other information you can give us that can help us track them down?'

The merchant mulled over that idea. 'Well, there was a struggle, a fight between a merchant and a girl, one of the fanatics. The merchant pulled back the hood from her face and I caught a glimpse.'

'And?'

'Her hair was red. Bright red. Very distinct. Never seen something like that before.'

Red?

A chill went down Prahlad's spine. He knew who the merchant was talking about. Only *she* had such distinctive red hair in the entire capital city. It would catch anyone's eyes. It had caught Prahlad's too.

The merchant continued, 'If only I had caught her, I would have had her used by a dozen men. We would wine and dine over her.' And he laughed, the thought pleasing him. Prahlad took care to keep his face impassive, looking unaffected.

But he *was* affected.

'Let's go,' Viparichit said to Prahlad, as he handed the merchant a pouch of silver coins.

Just as they turned to leave, Mustafa said to Prahlad, 'You want a girl for yourself, lad? I have them of all ages. Have some fun, you'll lose your sternness then.'

Viparichit intervened, 'We don't want anything. Thank you for the offer, Mustafa.'

'The younger the girl, the higher the price!' the merchant called, slapping his hand on his thigh and making a lewd gesture.

Prahlad tried to ignore him, but something stirred within him. He felt himself awakening–felt like he suddenly had a purpose. It was a short-term purpose, but this purpose, it had meaning behind it. Earlier, when he was in the war, he was fighting but he hadn't really cared about it. But now …

He saw hope.

Not in this world. But in himself.

I have a purpose. But what is it?

He stopped, turned around, and walked to the merchant's shop. Standing before it, he pulled off his cloak and muffler, and revealed his royal features to the man, who instantly recognized him.

'Prince Prahlad!' he exclaimed, as he turned to Viparichit. 'How dare you bring his highness here? My lord, you don't have to pay anything. You can take anyone for free and make a harem for yourself.'

Prahlad gritted his teeth, clenched his fist and then …

This was his purpose.

Grabbing hold of the slick merchant by the neck, he pulled him out of the shop. Mustafa tried to stand and run away, but Prahlad grabbed him and threw him down again on the ground.

Crawling, Mustafa began to move, but Prahlad instantly kicked him in the back. Viparichit ran forward, grabbing Prahlad's arm, but Prahlad pushed him away, taking the dagger from his sheath and then pulling Mustafa's hair. 'Do you have any daughters? How dare you sell women!'

'My lord …' the merchant was groaning in absolute pain, 'I won't again … I won't … I promise.'

Prahlad gritted his teeth. He didn't know where his anger was coming from. Perhaps because of the fact that for the first time, he felt like he was fighting for something that was *right*. That was *fair*. And not for the sake of appeasing a king or appeasing his father or taking revenge. This battle was for himself.

'Good,' he nodded, 'because you won't be able to any more,'

And then he slit the merchant's throat, the blood spraying across his face as he saw the life ebb out of Mustafa's body. And then he left the dead merchant on the ground, wiped the blood from his face and turned to Viparichit.

'Bring the guards and have them dispose of him. No one should know of this,' Prahlad said to Viparichit, who meekly nodded, looking at Prahlad with new respect and fear in his eyes.

Prahlad saw the Royal Guard's face and there was fear – the very thing he didn't want his subjects to feel for him, but he knew he was fighting for the right thing. This fear was right.

It had been born out of his act of killing an evil man.

Am I proud of this?

He asked the same question he had asked himself on the battlefield.

Yes. I am. Oh yes, I am.

He knew what he had to do next.

He had to find the red-haired Dhriti.

12

HIRANYAKASHYAP

The desert was killing him.

He had been travelling with his men for a while in the outskirts of Yakshlok – the city of the Yakshas, which was plunged in heat and sand. Lizards roamed the dry land and the red earth swallowed them. Hiranya had never liked intense heat, always preferring to stay in the north-west or the south of the land, where there was moderate heat and tolerable coolness. Even the chill of the north haunted him and it was surprising that a young boy like Andhaka could rule there for such a substantial period of time.

Anuhrad, his tougher, stronger son, was sent to the north and Hiranya was not worried about him, but he was concerned for Prahlad.

I hope he will rule well.

Hiranya had chosen Prahlad to rule as an interim king because he was getting older and he had to learn how to control the city, understand it well enough to take important decisions. Anuhrad was a warrior, but Prahlad was the wise one. He *could* be Hiranya's successor.

Though I haven't decided whom I will crown. It's too early to think of that.

And Hiranya told himself that he didn't have to worry. After all, his ministers were there to support Prahlad if he faced any issues.

And I'll anyway be returning in few days.

Hiranya sighed. His horse neighed and stopped at the sight of the sand dunes, enveloping a structure that seemed like a large fort. It stood against mountains. The sun was setting on the landscape, and the vultures were circling, waiting for his men to fall dead so that they could pluck the carcasses.

The soldiers stationed on the fort saw his men approaching from the watchtowers and then directed everyone in the castle to ring the bell. As the sound erupted, the gates opened.

Hiranya's horse was brown and large for a steed. Hiranya didn't like the colour black, and so, he made sure everything around him was full of colour.

I have lived long enough in darkness for most of my life.

Even now, the clothes he wore were pale, almost white, wrapped around him like a stretched canvas, protecting him from the heat and the dryness of the sun.

As his horse trotted on, he swallowed, felt his parched throat and took a sip of water from the flask he was carrying with him.

Hiranya, followed by his men, entered the gates of the fort. At the sight of him, everyone bowed, calling him their king, their lord. He was never arrogant about that. Sure, he earned his right to claim his authority over them, but when he migrated from the land of darkness to the land of riches, he never forgot his humble origins or where he came from.

Hiranya stepped down from his horse and one of his men approached him to take it towards the stables. The fort was huge, and lit up by blazing torches. The guards were all covered in light uniforms to beat the heat. Soups and meat were being cooked in the large kitchen of the fort. Two other dome-like structures flanking the structure acted as indoor complexes.

'Where is Vigyasa?' Hiranya asked one of the guards.

'My lord, he's at the shore,' the guard responded, referring to the sea nearby.

Hiranya followed the guard, who took him through a passageway of the fort towards the outside grounds, which were lined with caravans and carts belonging to the nomadic tribes of Yakshlok, who operated these vehicles. And they were all handled by Yakshas and Yakshis – a diminutive, bulging-eyed race with pasty faces.

'The merchants here thought they could help us, so we allowed it,' the guard said. 'Though they are not from the real land of Yakshlok. They are outsiders and don't believe in the occupied Yakshlok.'

'They ought to be in the company of our soldiers,' Hiranya's voice boomed. 'After all, it gets lonely up here.'

The guard chuckled and nodded.

Hiranya, stepping on the hard sand, walked further and saw the shore: by the sea that stretched to the other part of the land where the dome-like buildings with large conical towers and fortresses stood, surrounded by red limestone huts. He was seeing it after a long time – it was after all, Yakshlok, stretching wide and large like a painting. Hiranya wanted to inherit the hands of an artist and paint the landscape by himself.

Yakshlok was now ruled by the Deva general – Agni. Indra had methodically usurped the throne of the chief of the Yakshas, and as Yakshas believed their kings to be gods, he made Agni a god of fire so they could fear him. Hiranya had heard stories of how Agni used to mix chemicals and conjure fires – magic tricks that anyone could do, but the Yakshas were illiterate, and saw them as proof of his god-like powers.

He walked down the shore, where more Yakshas and Yakshis could be seen by their huts, guarded by Hiranya's soldiers. Single masts ships or dhows, as they called them, were docked by the shore. A few of them had double masts. There were fishing boats, alongside a few battleships that could journey through the seas.

Hiranya came forward to see his lieutenant Vigyasa. He stood a few paces away, speaking in sign language to a boatman. Vigyasa had lost his tongue at a young age, for he had been one of the miners back in Pataal. And miners were never supposed to have tongues so they wouldn't reveal to any outsider the secret of where the jewels of Pataal came from. Vigyasa had quickly become one of Hiranya's favourite men. He was completely devoted towards Hiranya's cause, and had risen in the ranks from a foot soldier.

As Vigyasa saw Hiranya, he stopped signing to the boatman and rushed towards the king, bowing to him as he got closer.

Hiranya smiled at him. 'What is the status, Vigyasa?' he signed to the man. The king had learnt sign language long back, since his father had been a miner in Pataal too.

'Hiring local traders to get modifications for our ships. Agni's navy is growing fast, so we need to match up with him,' Vigyasa communicated, his fingers moving rapidly.

'Indeed,' Hiranya responded. This was a naval battle and the sea was used for travelling by Asuras, not battling.

Vigyasa added, 'You should not be here, my lord. If Agni's spies see you, he shall know.'

'Do I look like I care?' Hiranya asked, his brows arching.

Vigyasa shook his head.

'What is our strategy? Why did you call me here? How much are we losing?'

Vigyasa made an apologetic face. 'A lot. He surprises us with his naval tactics, my lord. I have added catapults to our battleships now. Let's hope we are prepared for him this time.'

'Don't worry, I'm here now and I have brought a thousand men to aid us. We are going to see the end of Agni's reign soon.'

There was a spark of confidence in Vigyasa's eyes. 'And also there's another thing,' he said.

'What is it?'

'As you know, King Hiranyaksha, your brother was stationed here for the longest time before his unfortunate demise. He had the king's quarters, which after his death, were never used by anyone. Out of respect to him, I made sure no one entered it except the cleaners, who would dust off the rot and dirt.' Vigyasa's expression changed as he continued signing. 'One of the cleaners saw a lizard, which crawled under the bed when she tried to get rid of it. She lifted the bed, only to find the lizard gone. Then she realized that there was a hole under the bed, covered with a trapdoor. She pulled it up and it led to a cellar through a small passageway.'

A cellar?

Hiranya had never heard of this from his brother.

Did he keep secrets from me?

Vigyasa continued. 'The cleaner didn't enter, of course. And I didn't either. I have put guards outside his room now, so no one can enter the cellar. I believe it could be of some importance as Lord Hiranyaksha took extra caution to hide this spot. I believe you would like to see it for yourself.'

'He was a reader. Could be just his books.'

'A strange place to have a library, my lord,' Vigyasa smiled at that.

Hiranya opened his mouth to respond, and then: an explosion.

Hiranya's ears went numb for a moment as he fell to the ground. He crawled around as his eyes searched for Vigyasa, but everything was a blur.

He could feel someone touch his back. He turned to find Vigyasa, who was bleeding from the head, gesturing for Hiranya to leave the ground.

Hiranya struggled up on his feet and took in the utter chaos raining down upon his men. People were running around in a frenzy as the red huts went up in flames. The scorching heat was eating away at the energy and strength of his men.

And in front of him, he saw the reason for it all. There was a small onager from which a group of white-armoured men had fired an explosive close to the shore, blasting the people around it.

Hiranya saw a man standing amidst the roaring commotion – he was clad in a maroon sherwani with an open collared tunic and a blood-red dhoti. Everything he wore was a different shade of red. He had blazing hair with red streaks in it, and a wide smile on his face. Hoops dangled from his ears as he walked forward, men with crossbows flanking him on either side.

Anyone would be able to identify him.

Agni.

'I had to come here,' the so-called Lord of Yakshlok said, laughing. 'I had to. I absolutely had to.' He was delighted. 'My men told me you had come here, foolish as you are, but I couldn't believe it. I thought Indra would be the one to kill you, but alas, it seems like he will lose that privilege to me.'

As smoke rose around him, a burning sensation coursed inside Hiranya too. He was shaking as he pulled out his sword, as he struggled to hold the hilt with his two hands while Vigyasa did the same. A few Asura guards stood behind them, ready to charge.

'Always had the fight in you, didn't you?' Agni smiled. There was something sinister about the man. 'Illavarti is ours, my dear Asura brother,' he said, referring to the common myth that a single father was the progenitor of both the Asuras and the Devas. 'You know,' he put his folded hands behind his back, 'Indra did the best thing when he killed your wife. I mean, starting that war? Ballsy. And now, we are all reaping the benefits of this beautiful chaos, aren't we?' And he gestured to his men, who launched another round of fireballs towards them.

As the explosives came hurtling towards them, Hiranya leapt from his place and rolled across the ground, hiding behind the hut. The balls hit the ground, exploding into more smoke and fire.

'You are killing innocent civilians! Stop!' Hiranya yelled as he saw the headless corpses of children and women of the Yaksha race around him.

'I'm their god, Hiranya. I am *allowed* to kill them,' Agni laughed.

Hiranya saw Vigyasa hiding behind the huts too and he signed to him, 'Run. We cannot win this.' There were not enough guards with them and as hard as it was to accept it, the truth was that he was losing this fight.

'Come on out! It's not a challenge if you hide like this.'

Hiranya gestured, '*One ... two ... three ...*'

He jumped out in the open and saw that a few paces away, Agni was standing with his hands behind his back.

Agni's attention was directed at Hiranya, who suddenly shouted, 'Go!'

Vigyasa instantly made a run for it, followed by other Asura guards, all of them moving towards their fort.

Agni saw what was happening and bellowed to his men, 'Shoot!'

Agni's archers began to shoot arrows from their crossbows at Vigyasa and other Asuras. While most of them escaped, some of them were hit, and Hiranya saw them fall to the ground, wounded.

It was time for him to make a move.

He ran too, but not away from Agni. Towards him.

Charging at the so-called god of fire, Hiranya pounced as he closed in, his blade drawn.

Agni dodged with a single swift move of his feet. Hiranya had heard about how the Deva was a brilliant dancer. As he pirouetted away from the attack, he gestured for his soldiers to lower the crossbows. He wanted to shoot Hiranya himself.

He pulled out a blade from inside his sleeve and slashed it across Hiranya's stomach, inflicting a deep wound.

Hiranya backed away and then, with a roaring sound, returned the attack. Agni deflected it with ease, and then, stabbed Hiranya twice in the back.

Hiranya fell to his knees.

'Your brother was a better fighter, at least.' Agni knelt close to Hiranya, looking straight into his eyes as he whispered, 'It's a tragedy Kayadhu died. I would have liked to have some fun with her.'

Hiranya's eyes blazed with anger as he stood up, roaring and grabbing Agni by the throat, lifting him up from the ground and choking him. Agni's face turned a bright red as he struggled, blood pooling into the whites of eyes. Hiranya's anger was blinding him, and he was about to end the fire god's life when—

Multiple arrows pierced his chest.

The pain was excruciating as he fell back. Agni dropped to the ground, spluttering and trying to regain his breath.

Hiranya staggered as five more arrows knocked him out. A horse galloped towards him and on it was …

Vigyasa!

The Asura lieutenant dodged the arrows and grabbed Hiranya's hand, pulling him up on his horse.

Hiranya slumped on the horse as Agni's Manav soldiers prepared to launch another attack with their crossbows. Agni coughed and got to his feet.

Vigyasa raced the horse towards the fort, where they would be protected. Hiranya was losing consciousness and a lot of blood, and his vision was blurring fast.

I don't feel good.

'Run!' Hiranya heard Agni shout after them, 'Run, you scavenger. Our story has just begun!'

And then the king of the Asuras closed his eyes in defeat.

13

NARASIMHA

I have killed Andhaka.

Nara was muttering in his sleep. Then suddenly, his eyes opened and he found himself in a dark room.

A lone fire was lit in the corner, burning the logs in it. There was a strong chill in the air that sent a shiver down his legs, right to his toes. He was lying on a flat, hard surface. He turned his head towards the fire and shooting pain brought him back to reality. His eyes finally focused on a woman treating his wounds.

She was wearing a long gown. Her eyes were majestic, and she had a small, well-defined mouth. Her hair, dark brown and lustrous, was pulled up in a bun. But most of all, Nara noticed a tiny mole on her cheek that lent her a certain uniqueness, setting her apart from the women he had met before.

And she looked familiar. Strangely familiar.

She was applying an ayurvedic cream upon his wounds, massaging it in and then bandaging the wound with a damp cloth. She noticed Nara had awakened and was looking at her.

'How was your sleep?'

'Who are you?'

'I'm a nurse,' she said.

'No. You are not.' Nara focused on her face. She seemed so familiar. 'I have seen you somewhere.' He could feel the effort of speaking. Exhaustion threatened to take over his body again.

'I *am* a nurse,' she stressed, avoiding his question. 'And you are a strange man, to speak like this to me after I've spent my day tending to your wounds.'

Nara realized he was being rude and sighed. Instead of being apologetic about it, he asked her another question: 'Where's my skin?'

'Safe in the corner. Don't worry, I washed it and kept it for you,' she said. 'But I wonder, why do you think you know me?'

Nara didn't know why, but he recalled the village he had attacked at the orders of Indra only to learn that it was a Manav Gurukul. Several Manav families lived there. Hiranya had tricked them into attacking innocents and since then, Nara had begun to question the very idea of war. And in that village, there had been a girl – a young girl, with a mole on her cheek.

'Because...' he said, and stopped. 'Which village are you from?' He knew this question would corner her.

She stopped tending to him and looked at him with an impassive face. 'I see,' she said, softly.

Nara waited. When she didn't say anything, he asked, 'What?'

'I see that you remember.' She shook her head. 'I was in a village, a long time back, a village you and your Pride attacked.'

Guilt washed over Nara's soul. 'I'm … uh …' He couldn't believe that the same girl whose village he'd destroyed was now supporting the army responsible for killing her family; was tending to the wounds of the leader of that army.

'We were Nishads,' she said, still bandaging Nara. 'Forest dwellers, who never hurt anyone. And then out of nowhere, we see Simhas surround our village, believing it to be an Asura hideout. You attacked us and wreaked havoc, until you finally noticed our eyes and realized that none of us were Asuras.'

Nara clenched his jaw. He remembered that day like it had been yesterday. 'I'm sorry. I didn't know … I … I have been trying to redeem myself since that day.'

The woman nodded. 'I understand.'

'Do you, really?'

'I do. Why do you think I'm here? Because I understood how Hiranya tricked Indra and his army,' she said. 'He planned it all, and you were his executioner. You didn't know any better. And that's why I'm here, to ensure that it doesn't happen again.'

'And how do you do that as a nurse?'

'The north forces us to do multiple jobs for a single purpose,' she said. 'I am a nurse, but I also scout the villages with other nurses to see whether there is something or if it's another hoax to kill innocents.'

'We all learn from tragedies.' Nara got up from the slab and struggled to walk towards the fire. Waist down, he was clad in a loose rag, and the flames cast a glow over his hairy chest.

'But that doesn't mean we are supposed to face them in the first place. No one deserves to be unhappy,' the woman said, washing her hands in a bowl of water. 'No one deserves sadness. I let my tragedy motivate me into leading a positive life and helping others. Not everyone does that. Sometimes, evil is borne of tragedy. And that's the worst kind of evil,' she finished.

Nara could feel that her words held some special meaning. 'What makes you say that?'

'Andhaka,' she breathed, and drew close to the fire, warming her hands. They stood close together, watching the flames dance. 'He was abused as a child.'

'Abused?' Nara narrowed his eyes, thinking about the man he had killed. 'How do you know that?'

'As I told you, I scout a lot of villages to help the families there and prevent casualties of war,' she said. 'And in one of those villages, I met a physician. He had taken care of Andhaka after the blind prince was wounded in one of the battles. The physician told me that Andhaka used to tell stories of how his father – to teach him strength–used to beat him, lash him and cage him.'

Nara could feel his heart racing. He could almost imagine the horrible scenes. 'What kind of a monster would do that to his own son?' he wondered out loud.

'Hiranyaksha was mad.' The woman sighed. 'Andhaka was a product of his madness. But this childhood of abuse made him into the warrior he is today, and now no one knows how to defeat him.'

Nara quizzically raised his brows. 'But I killed him in the battle.'

'No, you didn't. He's still out there.'

A chill ran down his spine.

'What are you talking about? Just before I lost consciousness, I choked him to death. I remember it.'

The woman shrugged. 'If that was the case, how come Andhaka was seen again in an attack he launched at the fort earlier today?'

How is that possible?

'But ...' Nara didn't complete his sentence. He grabbed the nearest shawl and raced out of the medical quarters. Outside, he saw that his room was a part of a small complex like a hospital, where nurses were tending to other wounded soldiers.

Nara stepped out. He was barefoot and the snow numbed his feet as he walked towards Bhairav's camp. Inside, the Shiva was discussing something with a Naga chief and Veerbhadra, as well as Mrig. On seeing Nara, Bhairav looked up, worried. 'Are you okay now?' he asked.

'I killed Andhaka,' Nara announced. The others looked back at him, perplexed. Everyone, except Mrig, who grinned.

'Okay,' Mrig's eye shone with delight, 'and then you made love to fairies. We believe you.'

'No, no.' Nara shook his head. 'I *killed* him, with my bare hands. I remember it clearly.'

Bhairav clenched his jaw. 'I believe you, Nara. But how is it possible then that he was here at the morning attack?'

'There's something there.' Nara was panting now, wrapping the shawl tightly. 'I don't know what it is, but there is something about him. Something only he can do. It's impossible that man I just killed in the last battle was reborn today.'

'Stop talking nonsense, old man!' Mrig scolded. 'You killed Andhaka in your dreams, that's all.'

The Naga chief coughed to draw attention. 'I didn't think this would come up, but one of my soldiers had also shot a spear into his spine once. He also believed that he'd killed Andhaka. I was about to tell you, Lord Bhairav, but um … another attack happened and he was there and I thought my soldier was lying, showing off. I thought he just wanted to get promoted so I refrained from saying anything.'

'Hmph!' Nara grinned. Here was some proof that he wasn't deluded. That was consolation at least.

'This is absurd. Could he be using Vidhyadharas?' asked Lord Bhairav, his long locks dancing around his head.

Veerbhadra intervened with his gruff voice. 'No, my lord. Vidhyadharas can manipulate energies of nature but do not bring back men from the dead. Also, what they do is purely an illusion.'

Bhairav nodded. 'We will figure this out.'

'Stop believing this nonsense, Lord Bhairav,' Mrig said loudly. 'Nara is lying to your face. He doesn't have the guts or the brawn to kill Andhaka. He's old. He's weak and now he's delusional. I would request you to relieve him and send him back to where he came from.'

The utter and absolute insolence …

'You need to address me with respect, Mrigsimha,' Nara spoke through gritted teeth.

Mrig smiled mockingly as he came forward, standing next to Nara, nose to nose. 'And what will you do if I don't?'

Nara returned his gaze, dead-eyed, the predator's urges pumping within him. He bared his teeth, his muscles tensing.

'Gentlemen!' Lord Bhairav stepped between them. 'This is of no importance. We cannot fight amongst ourselves. Our enemy is out there and he's using magic to fight us. We need to find ways to defeat him rather than quarrelling amongst us.'

'I have an idea,' Mrig said, looking at Lord Bhairav. 'Why don't we just use the weapon Andhaka is trying to take? Blow him up with the Pashupatastra. I mean, we are losing so much of our resources protecting a weapon that we can just use to our advantage.'

Nara interjected: 'And let innocent villagers die in the crossfire? Sonitpur is an usurped city and there are Manavs and Tribals who live there too.'

'And what kind of lives are they living, caught in this war?' Mrig said. 'Believe me, Lord Bhairav. Let's use the weapon.'

Lord Bhairav looked at both Simhas, raising his brows. 'I cannot. Lord Rudra told me one thing – to not use the Pashupatastra if there was even one innocent's life at stake. And already, we failed in doing that when we used the weapon and … well, I cannot let that happen again.'

Nara didn't know what Bhairav was referring to, but he was curious. But before he could ask more, Mrig stood up, glared at Nara and left the table to join his Pride. Bhairav resumed his discussions with the Naga chief and Veerbhadra.

Nara walked away too. He wanted to rest and clear his mind. As he left the camp, he saw the nurse coming towards him. 'What did they say?' she asked.

Nara told her what the Naga chief had said.

'It's true then.' She sighed and Nara was happy that there was another person who believed in him.

'What's your name?' he asked her.

'Chenchen,' she said. 'You need rest. Let me take you to the quarters.'

Nara nodded as he gave his hand to her and she guided him to the medical quarters. As they walked, he heard the familiar, irritating voice call out behind him. 'Need a woman to guide you? Old man, I'm telling you for your own safety, you are not needed here. I mean it, leave. Otherwise, you'll be killed.'

Nara flared his nostrils as he turned and saw Mrig and the Pride laughing. Chenchen ignored them.

'He's not the right leader for them,' Nara whispered to her.

'Do you think you are?'

He pursed his lips. 'I used to be. I don't fit the bill any more. But looking at him now, I feel like I might still be better than him, at least.'

She nodded. 'Then why don't you do something about it?'

Her words hit him like a brick.

Why don't I do something about it?

'Old man! Why don't you give your wench to us? She seems like a fine piece, and we would all love a taste,' Mrig's voice boomed again.

Chenchen raised her brows and shot an angry look at Mrig in return.

'Ooooh, terrifying!' Mrig chuckled, and so did the other Simhas.

Nara shook his head. 'I have to stop him.'

'Ignore him,' Chenchen whispered.

Nara thought that Bhairav was the one who should have been doing something about all of this, but he was busy planning the battle strategy with his men. He wasn't here to see what was going on.

'Hey whore, why don't you put your granddaddy to sleep and then come here for some fun?' Mrig laughed.

'Why are you doing this?' Nara turned, his eyes flashing in anger. He was getting really annoyed by Mrig now, especially since he was directing the nastiness towards Chenchen.

'I don't want you here,' Mrig's face turned impassive. 'Leave.'

'Why?'

'Because I believed in you, old man. When I was young, I followed your footsteps, heard about the great Narasimha – the arrogant warrior who fought everyone. And now look at you, broken and withered, a sad nutcase who needs a woman to carry him to bed and shit and piss.' Mrig spat on the ground. 'I really looked up to you, man, and you betrayed my trust.'

'But I am here now,' Nara said. His abdomen had begun to hurt him, but he still managed to walk up to Mrig, Chenchen by his side. 'I am helping. Don't you see?'

'Simhas worship strength, and I don't see any left in you.'

'You are …'

Before he could complete his sentence, Mrig suddenly punched him. Nara was taken by surprise and fell to the ground, the snow hitting his face. He could feel his teeth – broken and bloody – on the ground. Chenchen grabbed his hand and tried to pull him up.

'See! That's what I am talking about. You lack basic instincts. I mean, you are not ready for this war. Why don't you piss off and leave this fine woman with us so that we can have some fun?' Mrig grinned.

Nara wanted to say so many things, but he controlled his anger. They were part of the same team, not the enemies. He flared his nostrils and turned to leave with Chenchen.

'I don't like how they talk about you,' he said to Chenchen.

'Leave it. It's fine. He's harassing me to anger you.'

'Well, it's working.' Nara shook his head.

'I have always believed that there are two kinds of people. The ones who do things and the ones who boast about it.'

'What are you saying?'

'He keeps calling you old, weak. Why don't you show him that you are neither?'

Nara arched his brows. He considered Chenchen's words, and then loosening his grip on her hands, he turned back and walked up to Mrig, who was still laughing with his team.

'Mrigsimha!' Nara cried, holding on to his bandaged torso.

Mrig looked up, bored. 'What is it, old man?'

Nara didn't want to do this, but he looked around him and saw that everyone was staring at them – the soldiers and villagers – agog with curiosity. Bhairav though, was still in his camp, unaware of what was going on outside. Hopefully, he'd remain there. He had other bigger things to worry about. This was Nara's problem, and his problem only.

'I challenge you to a fight,' Nara announced. 'You wanted to know if I'm still strong. Well, let's find out. If I win, I will lead the Pride from here on. If you win, I will leave this place.'

Mrig's smile wavered, as if he was trying to frame an ideal response to this.

After a few moments, the younger Simha nodded.

'All right,' he said. 'But there's one thing I want to change in your clause. If *I* win, I get to kill you in front of everyone.'

There was a split second's pause, and then Nara nodded. 'All right. I accept your condition.'

14

ANUHRAD

Anuhrad hated his father now.

There weren't a lot of times when he hated him. In fact, most of the time, he was quite proud of him. But not any more.

Prahlad was supposed to be sent here for this bloody solitary confinement. Not me.

He was always the better one. He was always the better fighter, a better strategist. And he was the ideal son.

And yet he had been sent here – to this dungeon.

He was with the Pishach, who were stationed at the main city of Sonitpur. He walked alone with his guards inside the palace that belonged to his cousin, Andhaka. As he did, he saw the dead trees around him, a long, lonely path that stretched to the towers around the mansion. It was a fort, but partly broken, as if it had been damaged recently.

Sonitpur was a dead city. Sure, there were people around, but he could see their dull expressions, their hopelessness. It looked like Andhaka had sucked the life out of them.

As a child, Anuhrad hadn't met Andhaka often. When they had met, Andhaka had been ... strange. Quite often, he would mutter syllables in a voice that was so much like a girl's. He was an albino, with light skin and reddish irises, which were hidden under the blindfold he almost always had on. He had been born blind ... or at least, that was what Anuhrad believed.

Lost in his thoughts, Anuhrad looked at the city of Sonitpur again. The entire place was covered in snow.

He noticed fanged creatures lurking in the trees – wolves.

Anuhrad was wearing thick armour that covered his chest and lower abdomen. The armour would protect him if he was attacked. He had a fur cloak and a hood that was pulled back so that the guards could recognize him. A bronze breastplate covered his chest and a blade was sheathed along his left thigh.

The wolves left the tower and came running towards him. Up close, they sniffed him as he remained still. He had heard somewhere that wolves could smell fear, and if they did, they'd attack.

I don't fear them.

They were of white and grey, with long ears and blood on their teeth.

They sniffed him for a while before retreating behind the trees again.

Anuhrad, taking a deep breath, continued on. Up ahead, he saw a corpse that had been torn apart by the wolves. Blood pooled on the white snow and for some reason, it looked more like art than gore.

He saw the guards in front, close to the gate outside the fort. At the sight of Anuhrad, they pulled out their spears.

They were of Rakshas origin and they knew who Anuhrad was. They bowed to him, opening the door.

Anuhrad entered the castle, welcomed by arched doors and a long winding staircase. There was no ceiling and flakes fell from the sky. The wooden floor creaked and Anuhrad smelled something strange … the distinct smell of death and decay.

He felt isolated from the world. He could hear owls hooting in the background.

'Is anyone here?' Anuhrad called out, but there was no response.

He was considering asking the guards stationed outside about where to go, when he stepped on something and it cracked. He looked down and saw that it was a skull.

A human skull.

What is this place?

'Is it you, Prince Anuhrad?' a voice called out.

He turned to see a short, hunched man standing a little distance away.

'Who are you?' Anuhrad asked.

'Your humble servant,' the man said, his fingers locked together in front of him. His voice was stuffy, like he had a cold. 'I am Kalanemi. Master will see you in the dining hall.'

Anuhrad nodded. He was famished, but at the same time, uneasy. 'Might I ask when you plan to clean this damned place?' He walked towards the man and up close, he saw that Kalanemi's face was covered with boils. His skin was red and streaked with dirt. His thin hair flapped at his shoulders like paper.

'What happened to you?' Anuhrad asked.

'I have a disease,' the man said. 'Please come in, prince.'

Anuhrad sighed when he saw the room he'd followed Kalanemi into. There was a small library in one corner, and hanging torches from where the warmth and light emanated. In this room, the ceiling was well etched and there was a long table with multiple chairs. There were guards, standing close to the windows and the entrances, and they remained impassive.

Anuhrad went to the table and rested his blade, taking a seat. He saw the food on the table – roasted chicken and loaves. He was so hungry that he wished he could begin eating without his cousin.

'Where is the *master*?' Anuhrad asked, chuckling. 'Why do you call him that?'

Kalanemi looked at Anuhrad as if he was from another planet. And before Kalanemi could speak –

'Because I asked him to,' a girl's voice said.

Anuhrad turned to see a relatively short man with skin white as snow. He wore a dark red blindfold and seemed absolutely hairless. He had on strange clothes – a black tunic and black pants over which he wore a coat, buttoned up to his throat.

He walked slowly to the table and sat next to Anuhrad, quite as if he could see, as if his blindness was just a hoax.

'Andhaka,' Anuhrad would be lying to himself if he said he was happy to see his cousin. 'It's nice to see you.'

'Hmmm ...' Andhaka sighed.

'Shall we start eating?' Anuhrad asked.

Andhaka was leaning back, his pale fingers moving restlessly. He did not answer.

'What's wrong?' Anuhrad said, eager to begin the meal.

'You didn't ask me about the progress,' Andhaka said softly.

'Progress with what? The war?'

Andhaka nodded.

'Well, during my journey, I heard that you'd died in battle. I didn't believe them. I knew they were just rumours.'

Andhaka turned his face to his cousin. 'I did die.'

For a moment, Anuhrad thought Andhaka was joking.

But is this creep even capable of making a joke?

'Then how am I lucky enough to see your ugly face today?' Anuhrad laughed.

'That's not very nice,' Andhaka said. 'I was … I am … I am ill.'

'I know you have that skin disease, but my dear, you look awful. If your plan is to scare your enemies to death, I am sure it will work,' Anuhrad joked.

'I don't intend to scare them with my face,' Andhaka said, touching his cheek as if extracting the warmth of his body.

'How did you come back from the dead, cousin?' Anuhrad asked, as he finally gave up and began eating, stuffing pieces of the loaves and the chicken into his mouth.

'Everyone has secrets. I have come back from the dead many times. And every time I do, I multiply,' Andhaka said, his voice so unwavering and daunting that Anuhrad felt a chill go up his spine. 'Initially I had considered not multiplying, but I now feel glad that there are many of me.'

'Do you always speak like this?'

'Does it bother you?' Andhaka asked. And then, when Anuhrad didn't answer, he added, 'I can smell that it does.'

'You can smell ...?'

'I can smell expressions and feelings, since I cannot see them,' Andhaka said. 'I hear heartbeats and know when someone is lying or hiding something.'

Great, no privacy with this man.

'Father said,' Anuhrad swallowed a lump, as he directed the topic elsewhere, 'you are doing a good job. Frankly, what help do you need from me? You look like you have it covered here.'

Andhaka ignored that and turned to Kalanemi, who stood in one corner of the room, half hidden in the darkness. 'Please bring me my feast.'

'Yes, master,' Kalanemi said and left the room .

'You are not eating this food?' Anuhrad asked.

'I don't like ... *normal food*,' Andhaka said just as Kalanemi re-entered the room with a head in his hands ... a human head, the top half of which was severed, revealing the brain.

Disgusting.

Andhaka pushed his hand inside the skull and tore at the brain. He began to eat it, blood dripping on his clothes and his skin.

Anuhrad pushed back his chair and took his plate to the other end of the table. If he kept sitting close to Andhaka, he'd lose his appetite. 'Why the hell are you having that?' he asked his cousin.

'Hmmm?'

'Why the ... oh, never mind,' Anuhrad massaged his head. 'I'll be taking an inn in the city.'

'But I have a room prepared here.'

Yeah, as if I'm going to live in this crazy place.

'No, I don't want to be any trouble. I'll take the inn,' he said, his nose wrinkling at the sight of his cousin eating a human brain.

Andhaka nodded. He put the skull on the side and used a hand towel to wipe the blood from his fingers. 'You are upset about my diet.'

'You smelled wrong, cousin. Upset is not the right feeling. Plain disgust is what I feel.'

'Hmmm, all right. It's just that as a child, I never ate anything other than the men I killed.' He shook his head, as if trying to recollect a sad, petrifying memory.

'Uncle allowed that?' Anuhrad asked, shocked.

'Father endorsed it,' Andhaka responded. 'He always believed in eating one's kill.'

'That's for hunting, cousin. You hunt animals so you can cook and eat them.'

'I never had the privilege of hunting animals. For some reason, they never seemed interesting to me. Pure souls, they were. Did you meet the pack of wolves I groom outside?' He smiled like a child. 'I always had animals, but Father didn't allow me to keep pets, so I kept them in secret. Once, he was about to enter my room and my dog kept barking. My father heard it and I was afraid. I knew that if he found out, he'd do awful things to it. So I killed it. It was sad. Very sad.' He lowered his head, his lips pursed.

Anuhrad didn't recall his uncle behaving like that. He had always been ... jolly and funny and warm. This account of his from Andhaka seemed far-fetched, almost unreal.

'Do you still play the flute?' Andhaka asked.

Anuhrad shrugged. 'I haven't got the time.'

'Perhaps you can do it later, once you settle in.'

Anuhrad nodded. 'Sure. But you didn't answer my question. Why did you need me? What can I do? You have two Kalakeyas at your disposal too, so what can a young guy like me do for you?' he said, referring to the Danavs, who were nowhere to be seen, but he knew that the towers outside belonged to them.

'I don't like to use them. They eat a lot and are moody about when they want to go to the battlefield,' Andhaka said.

'Well, they are Danavs. What do you expect?' Anuhrad thought about the relationship his father Hiranya had with the Kalakeyas and the Poulamos. By nature, the Danavs were lazy. They needed to be forced to work and given a lot of food in return. His father didn't use them unless it was absolutely necessary, thus, most of them were stationed at Hiranyapur, where they got fat and snored and drank. Most of the Danavs didn't want to come to Illavarti because they thought it meant too much work.

'I wanted company. I was alone here,' Andhaka said, answering the question Anuhrad had asked earlier. 'I fear loneliness. What do you fear?'

'My dear weird cousin, I am not a wench here to satiate your loneliness. If you don't need me, I'm leaving now,' he said and hit his fist on the table, pushing his chair back and making a move to stand up.

'No,' Andhaka tapped on the table himself and the wood creaked. 'Don't, please. I do need you …'

'That's easy to say, difficult to do.'

'You don't understand, no, hmmm ... you don't.' Andhaka kept shaking his head. 'I don't care about Pashupatastra. If I get it, I shall hand it over to my uncle. But I don't fight this war because of that. No. I volunteered to come here because I have a secret.'

Anuhrad clenched his jaw. He looked at his cousin. He felt sorry for him, but then he also felt that Andhaka was wasting his time. 'You call me here to tell me you don't care about this war? What if my father finds out? He will send you away from here.'

'But I won't let him know. He funds the army here. It's helpful, but ... but you need to understand me,' Andhaka whispered. 'Please, understand me and sit down. We were always different. But I know we can work things out. Please sit down.'

Anuhrad did so.

'You are a good man, Anuhrad.' Andhaka nodded to himself. 'Thus I will reveal one of my secrets to you. I am not fighting this battle because of my uncle. I fight this battle for myself, for a purpose, and I want you to help me achieve that purpose, because I'm unable to do it alone. You will be the key to my victory. You are a great strategist and a good listener too. So please, please do this.'

Anuhrad exhaled, finally realizing that there might be a reason for his presence after all.

I didn't waste my time coming here.

'What is that goal if not the Pashupatastra? You do realize we need that weapon to disarm the Devas ...'

'I don't care. I told you, if you help me with this goal, you will get the astra. But you need to help me. I sincerely beg you to do it. Will you?'

'Will I really get the astra by the end of it?'

'I won't have it any other way,' Andhaka said.

Anuhrad agreed. 'All right, I will help you reach your goal. What is it? What do you want me to do?'

'Assist me in killing Bhairav. In killing the Shiva. Hmmm ... before we get the weapon.'

'Why? Why do you hate him so much?'

Anuhrad saw Andhaka hesitate, his fingers trembling. Then he said, 'Because he's my biological father.' He turned his face up to the ceiling, a grim smile on his face. 'And I shall never forgive him for what he did to me.'

15

PRAHLAD

Prahlad saw her from afar.

He stood there, close to the royal gardens where Dhriti was watering the plants. He looked at her – such a sweet, childlike girl that it seemed impossible to think of her as a member of Vishnusena.

Perhaps it was some other red-haired girl …

But Prahlad's instincts told him otherwise. He watched as Dhriti stopped watering the plant and looked around. She plucked a flower and tucked it behind her ear.

Prahlad couldn't help but laugh at her innocence.

It was so … *nice.*

I might be wrong about her.

And then suddenly, she spotted him and instantly straightened up, threw the flower to the ground and grinned nervously at him. Prahlad walked to her, but before he could say anything, she spoke.

'I'm so sorry, my lord. I am very sorry,' she said, her voice anxious. 'I didn't mean to …'

'No, it's fine. You like flowers?'

'Oh …' She nodded. 'I like them all. I like lavender, roses, tulips … see, my hair is like a rose.'

Prahlad looked at her, using the opportunity to search for a scar or a wound, something that would give away the fact that she belonged to a terrorist group, but there was nothing there.

Perhaps, I'm mistaken …

'Tell me more about yourself, Dhriti,' he said.

She swallowed and fidgeted, silent.

'What's wrong?' he asked.

'No, it's just, you are the prince of Kashyapuri and you are asking about me. It's just … well … overwhelming,' she laughed at herself.

Prahlad smiled. 'It's all right. I am trying to strike up a friendship with you.'

'But I am a low-born!' She pursed her lips. 'We can't be friends.'

'I don't believe in caste dictating our relationships. Do you want to be friends with me?'

'Of course!' she exclaimed, but then realized that she might have sounded too excited. 'I mean, no, I mean yes, I mean, oh, my dear …' she slapped her forehead.

Prahlad had an idea that would help him find out whether she was just acting innocent or if she was actually a part of Vishnusena. 'Do you believe in gods?'

She shook her head.

'Are you saying that just because I'm here?' he asked.

'No, my lord. The palace made sure I was an atheist before I started working here.'

Prahlad had heard about his father's strict policy of not letting believers work in close proximity to him, his sons and his ministers. Guru Narada had been an exception, because he was very good at what he did and King Hiranya hadn't wanted to lose out on a meticulous education for his children.

Or was there another reason?

'But why do you ask, my lord?' she looked at him with earnest eyes.

'Because I want to believe in one,' he replied, surprising himself with his honesty to her.

She looked at him, nodding. 'I know. Faith is important. Though it has never sided with me.'

'Why is that?'

She clenched her jaw and Prahlad could see that this was a question she found difficult to answer.

'That's a story for another time, perhaps,' she finally responded.

Prahlad smiled, trying to keep things light.

'I should leave, my lord. Lots of work to do around the palace,' she said, bowing and taking her leave.

'Of course,' he said. 'Please go ahead.'

And then he tried his plan. As she turned to go, he casually put his foot in front of her. Without noticing, the girl stepped on it and instantly tripped. Prahlad didn't let her fall, but grabbed her. She muttered, 'By the graces of Lord Vishnu! I was about to fall …'

Prahlad held her, one arm around her waist as he watched her intently. For a moment, he forgot why he'd done what he'd done. There was something about her, and the way she looked back at him, it was evident that she felt something for him too.

Concentrate on the plan ...

'I thought you were an atheist,' Prahlad said to her, smiling.

'I ... um ...' she straightened, pulling away from his grasp. 'It was instinct. I didn't mean to ... I mean, I don't. Did you do that on purpose, my lord?'

Prahlad raised his brows. 'Do you mean to imply that your prince purposely trips girls?'

'Oh! No, no,' she giggled, realizing what she had just implied. 'I mean to say... I am not a ...'

Prahlad blushed too, and averted his face. He could feel his cheeks burning. 'Look, it's all right if you believe in Lord Vishnu. You don't need to hide it. I won't hang you for it. I am not my father,' he said.

She nodded, smiling.

'And please, help me if you can in learning more about Lord Vishnu. I want to find my faith, for I have none. My culture doesn't allow it. But I am of a different mind.'

She didn't say anything, but her expression spoke of a certain scepticism. Prahlad could see her trying to make up her mind about speaking, contemplating whether or not to tell him something.

'I need to leave,' she finally said. 'But I will let you know soon if I can help you.'

'Thank you.'

She nodded, flustered, as she began to walk away. Prahlad's chest tightened as he watched her go. He had loved holding her.

I don't know what is happening.

As he watched, she stopped and looked back at him, stray red strands of hair playing with her face.

She smiled.

And he smiled back.

By the graces of Lord Vishnu, her smile is disarming.

'Is your romance over, my lord?' a laughing voice came from behind him and Prahlad swung around to look at Viparichit.

When he turned again, Dhriti was already entering the cook's cabin.

'What were you doing talking to her, my lord?' Viparichit asked.

Prahlad didn't say much. 'Just keep an eye on her. And alert me when she does something suspicious,' he instructed.

Viparichit nodded. 'All right, my lord.'

It was night when he heard a knock on his door.

'Come in,' he called out, rubbing his eyes.

Viparichit stepped into the room. 'My lord?'

'Viparichit? What time is it?'

'Time to follow Dhriti, my lord.'

Prahlad sat up, instantly alert. 'What do you mean?'

'I had been keeping an eye on her like you'd asked me to, and even though it's after curfew, I just saw her leave from her quarters for the administration wing, so I thought I would update you.'

Prahlad jumped out of the bed and grabbed his cloak. 'Let's go.'

'What do you plan to do with her?' Viparichit asked they walked out.

Prahlad didn't answer and increased his pace, heading for the door.

'Shouldn't we just arrest her, my lord?' Viparichit said, quickening his pace to keep up with Prahlad.

'We cannot arrest her if we don't know for certain that she's guilty.'

'It doesn't matter. We can arrest her first, and then torture her until she opens her mouth.'

Prahlad narrowed his gaze and looked at Viparichit. 'I don't even know what to say to that.' He shook his head. 'I do believe she's a nice person.'

'If she's part of Vishnusena, I'm not so sure about the niceness, my lord.'

They made their way down a flight of stairs, towards the administration wing.

'Are you sure she's here?' Prahlad asked.

'No, she might have left, but I have a feeling that she is meeting someone here. Someone she works for.'

They got to the bottom of the staircase, to the intersection that led to two corridors on opposite sides.

'You take the one on the left and if you find her, don't attack. Just see if she's doing something suspicious and, if not, leave her be,' Prahlad instructed.

'Do you think her getting out at this time has something to do with the Vishnusena?' Viparichit asked.

'I don't know. She's leaving her quarters when she's not supposed to, to go somewhere she's not supposed to,' Prahlad smiled to himself. 'Whatever the reason, we need to find out the truth, and I believe we will.'

After all, why would she go to the wing with the ministers' offices?

'All right, my lord. I'll go check and brief you.' And he took off.

Prahlad slowly walked into the other corridor. Since this was an old wing, there were not too many guards stationed here. As he passed the empty offices, he crossed Amarka's office, and reached Shand's. The door was open. Was this where Dhriti was?

Is Shand part of Vishnusena?

But he had sounded completely opposed to it. Was that one of his tricks?

Prahlad stood against the wall and listened to the voices coming from within the room.

'Chief, he's on to us.' It was Dhriti's voice, but she no longer sounded like a nervous young girl.

'Are you sure?' a voice responded – a distinctly familiar voice.

Shand?

'He was asking me about my religion today. I *am* sure. He's investigating us and he hinted that he wants to join us.'

'We don't know if we can trust him,' the voice whispered back. 'For now, let us continue what we are doing.'

'Yes, chief. Why are we meeting here, though?' she asked.

'My office was out of the question for today's meeting. Holika's guards have been crowding my office corridors.'

'I see. Whose office is this?' Dhriti asked.

It's not Shand.

A chill ran down Prahlad's spine. He leaned a little more, and looked into the room.

Inside, he saw the hunched, bald, figure of an old man, standing across from Dhriti, whose back faced the door.

Of course. Prahlad swallowed, his throat dry.

Narada.

16

HOLIKA

Holika poked the suspect with a cattle prod.

Strictly speaking, she should have been using something else for the torture, but there was nothing else around. A dagger or a sword would have killed the man.

She stared at him, hanging upside down from a hook in the wall, his skin fiery red, his naked body like a fat infant's, with red bruises and piercings from the prod peppering the flab. And he was weeping like a child too.

Holika was enjoying herself, especially because all of this was happening in a humid, dense room where the only shimmering light came from the grills that were five feet above them.

'Tell us about them,' she put the prod aside and flexed her arms before landing another blow on his stomach.

He cried out in agony and looked at her with pleading eyes. Holika's armour was tightly fitted and her hair was tied back. While age had brought wrinkles, she was still an exceptionally beautiful woman.

'I don't …' the man cried, 'I don't know them. I don't. I will swear on whoever you want me to.'

Holika sighed. She turned to see her Asura guards watching her with worry. Not worry for her, but for the man she was interrogating.

But Holika didn't care.

'When we came to the black market to investigate,' Holika began, as she knelt close to the man, blinking her golden eyes, 'you saw us and you ran. Why did you run if you have nothing to hide?'

'I am just a thief who stole some food and I was worried you might catch me.'

Holika shook her head and grabbed the cattle prod again, smacked his stomach with the blunt end and plunged the sharp end into his naval. 'You are quite fat for a man who wanted to steal food. Tell the truth and you will live. I give you my word. Your loyalty to the Vishnusena will not save you. But loyalty to me can go a long way.'

The man, sweating profusely, watched her intently, as if contemplating the proposal. 'I …'

'Yes, tell me.'

'I am not part of them.'

'All right,'

'I swear I'm not.'

'Okay.'

'I just did some business with them.'

'For what?'

'Weapons. I supplied them with weapons.'

'So basically,' Holika chuckled under her breath, 'to destroy the black market that supplies illegal weapons, they bought illegal weapons from the same market?'

'The weapons I brought were not illegal. They came from outside Kashyapuri. I purchased them at subsidized rates because they were made in local towns. The Vishnusena paid for them, but I gave them a discount.'

'All right, and?' Holika asked, irritated at the apparent sincerity with which the Vishnusena operated.

'That's it.'

'There's nothing else you know? Any facial description?'

He blinked. 'One time, I saw the man who dealt with me … here … in Kashyapuri.'

'Where?'

'After the deal, he left for your palace.'

Holika arched her brows. A spy amongst the ministers, or the people of the palace?

'What did he look like?'

'He was old.'

'There are many old people employed in the palace. Anything else?'

'He was just old and had white hair, you know. And he seemed quite intelligent, knowing what kind of swords and bows they needed. Could have been an acharya, or perhaps a guru.'

That was not enough information, but it did help her rule out a few people. 'Why were you hiding this?'

'I was … I am loyal to my clients. But I won't put my life at stake for them.'

'Good,' she slapped him playfully on the cheek as she leaned back and stretched her arms.

'Will you let me go now?' the man asked, and Holika ignored him, walking away. As she passed the guards, she whispered to them, 'Take him out of the city and kill him.'

'My lady,' one of them said, 'didn't he just reveal important information?'

'And that is the reason I want him killed,' she said, her wide, kohl-smeared eyes blazing as she stared at the insolent soldier who had dared to question her orders. 'If by chance he opens his mouth, he can jeopardize this mission.'

'All right, my lady,' the guard began to move when Holika grabbed him by the neck.

'Don't question my judgment again.'

He nodded meekly.

Holika left him, sighing, as she walked out of the prison. More of her guards were stationed outside.

'My lady,' one of them came forward, 'a guest is waiting for you, outside the prison gates.'

'Who?'

'Simhika.'

'Uh, okay, thanks.'

By the heavens, I'd forgotten about it completely.

Holika walked outside the gates. She saw the glittering city lights in front of her and stood staring at them, enamoured. She turned to see a young girl with round eyes, a simple smile and bangles up to her elbows standing next to her.

Simhika.

'Uh,' Holika awkwardly opened her arms, offering an embrace. Simhika shrugged and stepped back.

'I had to search for ages before I could find where you were, Mother.'

'I'm sorry. I um … I was busy.'

'Even today?'

Simhika wasn't really Holika's daughter, but both of them had spent enough time together to think of each other as family. A long time ago, Holika had seen Simhika working for the maidens in the brothel. Feeling bad for the girl, she'd offered to help her with her reading, after which both of them had become close. Simhika still worked at the brothel, but not as a prostitute – she was a cleaner.

Holika didn't approve of the job. She wanted Simhika to work in the palace as a warden or something else, but Simhika refused, saying the brothel was where her biological mother had worked till her violent demise. And Simhika wanted to stay and work where her mother had worked. It was, of course, an offensive place to live in according to the civilians, but brothels were where women had the freedom to earn, especially low-borns who could find no other work.

Holika hated the idea of Simhika working in a place where women were the followers of men, but she respected Simhika for her choices, and let her continue.

'I know today is your birth date, and I so apologize. I did bring your gift.' Holika came forward, holding her daughter's arm and lovingly looking at her.

Simhika smiled. 'Really?'

'Yes. It's back in my room. Let's go and get it, all right?'

'Sure.'

Holika snapped her fingers and her guards stepped close, ready to follow them.

'Do they have to come with us?' Simhika asked.

Holika thought for a moment. She was not really loved by anyone in the city except for Simhika, and she needed protection.

But then, today was a special day.

'Are you bothered by them?'

'Kind of, yeah. I want to spend some quality time with you … *alone.*'

Holika smiled. She signalled for her guards to leave and they promptly dispersed. They began to walk as Holika put an arm around Simhika. But she couldn't stop thinking about the old man from the palace that the black market merchant had mentioned. Who could it be? There were many old ministers in the palace. Narada had white hair too, didn't he?

I should talk to Narada, ask him a few questions.

Simhika coughed to get Holika's attention back.

It can wait. I should concentrate on Simhika today.

'I have something to tell you,' Simhika said.

'Sure.'

'I think I am in love.'

'Really?' Holika chuckled, though she was afraid of who the man was. She didn't want her daughter with just another chauvinist degenerate. 'Who is it?'

She smiled, almost blushing. 'He works in the palace. His name is Viparichit and he's the Prince's … er … I mean King Prahlad's Royal Guard.'

Holika grimaced. She didn't want Simhika marrying a low-born. But she didn't show her distaste either. Instead, she said, 'I look forward to meeting this gentleman.'

17

NARASIMHA

'You of all people should know that this is wrong.' Bhairav stood in front of Nara, who was putting on his skin over his dhoti.

'My lord,' Nara sighed. His ribs hurt. His entire body was paining from the last battle. 'It is the right thing to do. I have to win back the respect of my Pride.'

Bhairav shook his head. 'For what?'

'So that I can lead them. I know I can do it better than Mrig. I fear how he handles the group, the wine they consume, the amount of Somas they take and by the graces of Lord Vishnu, Mrig has some seriously dark thoughts,' Nara explained. 'He's no leader.'

'Are you?'

Nara didn't know how to answer that. 'I don't know. But I know I'm better than him.'

'What if Andhaka attacks again and what if you are not alive to help us during that time?'

Nara chuckled. 'Are you so sure then that I'll lose?'

'Just look at yourself, Nara.' Bhairav placed his hand on Nara's shoulder. 'Don't do this. I won't be able to stop it. This is suicide. By the graces of Lord Vishnu, I hope he protects you.'

Nara smiled. 'Doesn't he protect the good?'

'What makes you think you are not a good man?'

Nara contemplated that. He didn't know. He had done some horrible things in this life. Killing Chenchen's village folk. Hurting Virata. Hurting Shantanu. Hurting so many innocents – all in the name of war. But he had fought on the side of goodness, hadn't he? 'I won't lose,' he said to Bhairav.

Bhairav clenched his jaw with disappointment. Then he lowered his head and walked out of the hut.

'He's right, you know,' Chenchen said as she entered the room. 'I heard what he said, and it *is* suicide.'

'You should be happy that the person who attacked your village is about to be killed,' he sighed.

She looked at him, her eyes unreadable.

'How did you save yourself that day?' he asked her.

'I hid in the well with the rest of the girls. It's the elders who were the biggest victims, unfortunately.'

'You didn't have parents?'

She shook her head. 'My father left my mom quite early and then she died from an illness a few years before the attack. Not enough medical care was given to her. And that is one of the many reasons I am a nurse today.'

'Do you hate me?' he asked.

She looked up. She was so close that Nara could smell her scent. She smelled of fresh lavender.

'No.'

'Why not?'

'Why should I?' she paused, her fingers on his chest. 'Your ribcage is broken.'

'I'm a Simha. I heal.' Their Tribe healed rapidly. 'You didn't answer my question,' he pressed her.

Chenchen pulled back and leaned against the wall, folding her arms. 'I don't hate you because …' she said, exasperated, 'I don't know! Back then, I did. But now, I see you not as an enemy but as someone who is good. Your past doesn't define you. Your present does. What you do now will define the person you are going to be.'

'Do you think I will win?' he asked her.

'Do you believe in yourself?'

Nara thought for a moment, and then nodded. 'I do.'

'Good. Then I believe that you will win.'

Nara smiled and she did too. 'Can you do something for me?' he asked.

'Yes,' she said without hesitating.

'Can you touch your forehead to mine?'

'Why?'

'It's an expression of prayer in our Simha culture – of support.'

She blinked and then she came forward. She leaned in and Nara did too. Their foreheads touched and, for a moment, Nara could feel her warmth, her skin, her soul and her life. He pulled back, smiling. 'Thank you.'

She nodded and he walked out of the hut, stretching his muscles but not to the point of hurting his body.

Outside, he saw people of all kinds were gathered in wait. Mrig was standing in a small pit. He was in his skin too.

Nara and Mrig stared at each other, and then Nara looked at Bhairav, who was shaking his head in disapproval.

And then he saw his Pride, who had lost faith in him. They were standing around, grinning. All of them clearly supported Mrig.

Nara saw Mrig pulling out a vial of blue liquid. It was the Soma. And it was wrong to overuse it. While it strengthened your core, too much of it could be harmful, and drive you mad.

'I thought you would have scampered away, old man,' Mrig grinned, and the Pride roared in support. 'Don't worry. I'll make your death swift,' Mrig added. 'After all, you were our king once. I have to give you some sort of respect, at least.'

Nara nodded. 'You know, I'm not that old and it really upsets me that you keep calling me old, son.' He glanced at Chenchen, who smiled at his comment. 'And you look quite old for your age too.'

Mrig sniffed in anger. 'You shall meet your death today, old man.'

'Enough banter, lad. Show me what you are capable of.'

Mrig didn't hold back. He sprinted towards Nara, who put his hands in front. Mrig punched him twice, but Nara kept blocking his blows, waiting for the right moment to return the attack …

The moment he saw it, he threw his punch and hit Mrig's face. Mrig fell on the snow, spitting out blood, and then stood up again.

His eyes fell on Nara's heavily bandaged ribcage and he grinned. He sprinted and used his head to smack Nara in the chest.

Nara fell back as Mrig came on to him and rather than hitting him on the face, he began to pound his claws over Nara's ribs.

Slivers of pain began to shoot through him. Nara was almost teary-eyed. He glanced at Chenchen, who was looked petrified with worry.

Nara exhaled and used most of his strength to grab Mrig by the throat and push him back. Nara got to his feet, his one hand against his ribcage.

'You are weak, Nara. You are a Simha no more,' Mrig mocked.

'You don't get it.' Nara walked forward, his claws drawn. 'This isn't just a challenge. This is me taking back what's rightfully mine.' He paused. 'To you, I am the god of death and my claws are my scythe.'

And then Nara pounced on Mrig and clawed his face. For a moment, Mrig seemed bewildered, and then he lunged forward, hoping to use his claws, when Nara swiftly turned, stressing the muscles around his ribs as he grabbed Mrig's forearm and twisted it. He flung Mrig across the ring, but Mrig stood up and laughed.

'What was that about?'

Nara grinned. 'I just twisted your brachioradialis muscle.'

'What's that?'

'You won't be moving your hand, for a while,' Nara said, his education as a physician in his other life coming into play.

Just as Mrig realized what Nara had done, Nara sprinted towards him, this time knocking Mrig in the rib. The force made Mrig fall back. The next moment, Nara had tossed him in the air, through the crowd and to the hut, where a torch hung low.

'I am not old, Mrigsimha,' Nara gritted his teeth. 'I am *experienced*.'

He walked up to Mrig and held out his hand.

'Let me lead the Pride now,' he said.

Mrig watched Nara in absolute horror. Nobody would have believed that Nara could have the upper hand. But he quickly gathered his wits and shook his head.

'Never!' he roared, and then he clawed the hanging torch and threw it at Nara.

Nara dodged it, the embers bursting and trailing smoke before mixing with the snow.

An arrow flew through air and plunged into Mrig's head.

Nara turned to see where the arrow had come from and saw Bhairav … but the Shiva looked like he'd had nothing to do with it. His eyes then found Chenchen, who was holding a crossbow after snatching it from a surprised Naga guard standing beside her. Nara grinned and Chenchen shrugged.

'He broke the rules. No external weapon was allowed,' she called out.

Nara saw Mrig's lifeless body lying there. He wished that one of his own Tribe had not lost his life, but in the end, Mrig's stubbornness had killed him.

He wanted to thank Chenchen and he would, in his own time. Now, he walked to his Pride, who stood in hundreds, wearing their skins. Nara was in pain, his skin hairy and greasy. And his mane wasn't the royal golden colour it used to. But he still had the spirit of Simha in him.

'I apologize to my kind that I abandoned the battle. But I accept my mistakes. I came here to prove to you and myself that I am strong. I still have the spark. And now, I need your loyalty. You need a better leader to guide you through this. Lord Bhairav …' He pointed at the Shiva, 'He wants our help and we need to give it to him, with as much loyalty and discipline as we can muster.'

A deep silence ensued.

Nara looked at Chenchen, who with her crossbow, seemed uncertain too. But then he heard it … a thump.

It was the sound of a chest thump.

And slowly, each member of his Pride began to thump his chest. The noise grew and buzzed, accompanied by roars and whoops.

Nara knew what this meant. It was the sign of approval. He thumped his chest too, and roared back. He saw Bhairav, who stood with a smile on his face.

After the roars and the thumps died down, he stepped away and walked towards Chenchen.

'Thank you,' he said to her.

Chenchen didn't say anything. She leaned her head forward. Nara knew what she was doing, and so he leaned forward too. He could feel her soul again and this time, he hoped that she could feel his. Perhaps she did, because her hands wrapped around his as they stood close together.

And for the first time in a long time …

Nara felt like a hero.

18

HIRANYAKASHYAP

He saw Kayadhu.

She stood there, holding their child.

Hiranya came forward with a smile dancing on his lips. It was in a garden, and he recalled the garden was part of his palace. Kayadhu had curls that bounced on her shoulders and as she looked up, she returned her husband's smile.

'What happened?' she asked.

Hiranya didn't want to say anything. The silence spoke volumes about the beautiful scene he was witnessing in front of him. 'Your labour was arduous, my dear. You must rest instead of roaming the palace,' he said. Prahlad had been born just a few days ago.

'My dear Banjan,' she referred to Hiranya's childhood name, 'you need to stop worrying about me. Don't you forget, I'm as tough as you.'

Hiranya smiled as he leaned forward, kissing his wife's lips softly. 'I know you are. I still remember the first time I saw you.'

'I was a high-born and you were a low-born and we saw each other when I came with my father to the bazaar,' Kayadhu said. 'I remember it very well. And I saw you with your exhausted face, selling us fruits. You seemed near dead.'

'Thank goodness that in our culture, a man's deed can lift him out of the caste he's born in, and make him a noble or a slave,' he said, referring to the Asura way of life back in Pataal. 'Otherwise I would have remained a miner's son, a fruit seller.'

'And look at everything you've achieved. You are special,' she said.

Hiranya smiled. 'You are quite the flatterer.'

'What did you like about me?' Kayadhu asked. 'I've never asked you this.'

'I ... um ...' A soft smile played on Hiranya's mouth. 'I remember how you beat a bunch of goons who tried to rob you once.'

'So you liked the fact that I was fighting like a man?'

Hiranya shook his head. 'It's not just men who have the right to fight. Women have every right to do whatever they want to do. And you showed me that day that you cannot be forced to back down.'

Kayadhu nodded, as she lowered her head to look at infant Prahlad. 'I want him to grow up in a good household, where he respects women, where he respects culture and where he sides with righteousness.'

'All the qualities that I have,' Hiranya grinned and Kayadhu nudged him with her elbow.

And then suddenly, a knife came out of nowhere and slit her throat. Blood began to spray over Hiranya as he grabbed his lifeless wife and the infant who was splashed with his mother's blood.

Hiranya gave a cry of rage and looked around, spotting the assailant.

It was Indra, with a bloody knife in his hand.

Hiranya's eyes flew open and he jolted up, sweating as he clenched his fist and punched the wall in anger.

A thin crack appeared on it.

Fury boiled in him, and he jumped out of his bed, trying to calm himself down.

I gave him a chance, and instead, he betrayed me, broke the truce, and killed her.

With his teeth gritted, Hiranya walked to the window, and saw the wondrous desert fort that lay beyond. Vigyasa was in one of the towers, stationed at his quarters. The fort was large and had its own holdings and was packed with guards, several Apsaras to make the guards happy, and Gandharvs, who served drinks and food.

And then he saw the Danavs. He had specifically told Vigyasa to wake the two Danavs up and to guard the two main gates of the fort. They were fifteen feet high, holding customized maces in their hands. They had a small force of Rakshasas deployed with them.

The very look of the Danavs was daunting – shaggy-haired, with bulbous noses and droopy eyes; they were exceptionally obese but one impact from their clubs and the enemy's face would be smashed to pulp.

There was a knock on the door.

'Come in,' Hiranya said. He was bare-chested, with his muscles protruding from the thick mass of hair. His moustache was drenched in sweat, along with his wavy hair.

A familiar face looked in.

'My men heard something,' Vigyasa signed and shut the door behind him. 'Thought it was a quake. I was pretty sure it was you. Having bad dreams?'

Hiranya had spoken about his nightmares to Vigyasa a long time ago.

'I always do. What is it?' he said to the lieutenant.

'Everything is well fortified after the last attack. I'm sure they won't think of attacking for a while,' Vigyasa signed.

'You were sure they wouldn't attack earlier too. But they did. We are in a losing battle. Agni has weapons, and we cannot compete with him. We had the Danavs, but now because of food and drinks, they are incapable of fighting a war.'

Hiranya shook his head, and looked at Vigyasa. 'Now that you are here, show me my brother's room. I want to see the cellar,' he said, recalling what Vigyasa had told him.

Vigyasa nodded. He pursed his lips and signed for Hiranya to follow him. Hiranya did, walking the lonely corridors of the tower, passing rooms and guards who stood with their spears. Finally, Hiranya reached a door where two guards stood. At the sight of Hiranya, they bowed and turned away from the door.

Vigyasa motioned for Hiranya to enter the room.

'I'll be outside,' he signed.

Hiranya nodded and unlocked the door, entering a large room with a bed, a mat over which a chillum was placed, and large stacks of books on big racks. The entire room was filled with books and manuscripts, for while

Hiranyakashyap was always interested in art, Hiranyaksha had been interested in books.

Hiranya turned his attention to the bed and lifted it up with one hand. His eyes fell on a carpet. He put the bed on the side and then lifted the carpet. There was the hole Vigyasa had talked about. Lifting the lid on it, he saw a ladder leading down.

Hiranya grabbed the nearest torch and descended down the stairs. It was pitch black, apart from the glow from the torch. Granite walls surrounded him. Hiranya didn't particularly like this kind of darkness, but he had to brave it and, swallowing a lump in his throat, he walked on, his heart racing.

Why would my brother have a hidden room under his bed?

This question was killing him, but he was about to find out. He felt a thrill of excitement as he saw what lay before him once he reached the bottom of the stairs. He was in a room with just a small table on which stacks of paper were kept. There were even papers stuck on the wall.

What was my brother researching?

Hiranya kept the lamp on the table and began to read the papers.

Brahmashastra … He was researching the invincible Kavach that belonged to Lord Brahma …

Hiranya looked at one of the papers on which an armour was drawn. It was his brother's drawing for sure – haphazard and not at all pretty to look at, but the details all there. There was a gem studded in the armour's centre. Under the sketch, a line read, '*This is the Kaustabha Mani that energises Lord Brahma's armour*'.

Hiranya saw another paper which read, '*It has similar structural powers like the Mani which was used for Pashupatastra*'.

Mohini's myth, Hiranya thought.

The story was from the days of Lord Bhasmasura, a few years back before the Hiranya brothers came and wreaked havoc. It was said that the Asuras wanted Soma – the celestial drink. The Devas gave it up after being defeated innumerable times by them. They put Mohini, an Apsara and an Avatar of Lord Vishnu just like the scum Varaha who killed his brother, to be the bridge between the Devas and the Asuras. They said that Mohini would do the Churning that would result in the Asuras being the first to drink the Somas. Unfortunately, it was a ploy. The Churning was fake and there was nothing of consequence that emerged. And it was a way to bring all the Asuras to one place, so they could all be burnt alive.

Unfortunately, Mohini was stuck with the Asuras in the fire and she died too. Out of her ashes, Lord Rudra, lover and friend of Mohini – created five gemstones, Manis of absolute power. Since they came from the ashes of an Avatar, the manis had the power to fuel energy into ordinary weapons. One such weapon was the Pashupatastra.

As Hiranya read, he felt his eyes moisten with tears. It felt like his brother was speaking to him.

'*The Brahmshastra is protected by a valiant spirit who guards the temple. The spirit is there to make sure that only the right person could gain this armour.*

I lost because to get this magical armour and his sword that is of utmost power, one must go through the Trials set up by this spirit. The Trials challenge your mental, physical and emotional state. If you pass through them, you will get the armour and if not, you will be sent home.

I have tried multiple times, but it is tough. It is a challenge. I don't know when I'll try next but to defeat Emusha (Varaha, that boar!) I have to find this Kavach which will make me invincible to any attack.

Unfortunately, it only belongs to the worthy. And I have proved myself unworthy every time.

And that is wrong because this armour, this sword was left by Brahma for the Danavs and the Asuras.

Hiranya arched his brows.

What does he mean? Why was the Kavach left for Asuras?

Hiranya began to look through the pages and saw another folder with papers covered in writing – the description of Brahma – a faint character sketch of the First Man of Illavarti who led an utopian tribe from which every tribe grew and became what they are today. There was a genealogy chart –

'BRAHMA

Succeeded by Mariachi (Saptarishi at Pataal, one of the original progenitors of the Dharm/Adharm prophecy)

Succeeded by: KASHYAP …

A chill ran down Hiranya's spine.

Succeeded by …

HIRANYAKSHA and HIRANYAKASHYAP.'

Hiranya threw the papers on the desk. The truth hit him like a ton of bricks.

So Brahma is my ancestor.

Hiranya picked up the papers and resumed reading, steeling himself.

'Brahma left the armour and the sword for us, his favorite Tribe – the Asuras, originally called Daityas. Everything changed once the Devas, the other Tribe of Brahma, left for Swarg, an island north of Illavarti, and the Asuras left for Pataal. They migrated with the respective Saptarishis and their race was born in abundance.

But originally at Brahma's death, he had promised to leave his armour for us, and now because of that mysterious spirit, we are unable to have what is rightfully ours.

I seek to try the Trials again but every time I do, the riddles change, and the games turn my head.

I know whatever I learnt from the malicious spirit. The spirit is ancient, and we don't know where it has come from, but it holds some powerful significance. I seek to know its identity soon.

But for now, I shall go and give it another try. But if I don't, and if I'm unable to or if something happens to me before I do, I want my brother Hiranyakashyap to try it because he's a good man, a good father, a good husband. I hope he does. I hope to tell him about my discovery of the armour soon.'

And the diary ended there.

Hiranya grabbed the lamp and moved away from the desk. He took the important papers with him, which included the map to the Temple of Brahma, and walked towards the staircase, thoughts swirling in his mind. He was losing a war. And he had no choice but to do the impossible – what his brother had failed to do.

If my brother couldn't get to the armour, how will I be able to?

But then, he couldn't give up without trying.

After all, his ultimate goal was to kill Indra. And now he knew how to do it. He was going to find the Kavach.

And he was going to make sure he passed the Trials of Brahma!

19

PRAHLAD

He felt betrayed.

I'm going to do something about it.

Prahlad was frantically pacing around in his room. He didn't know what to feel about the fact that the very guru who had taught him and nurtured him was part of a terrorist organization.

But are they really terrorists?

They were more like vigilantes – doing good for the public and punishing the greedy and the elite. But that meant that he would be one of their targets too, since he was the king's son and currently the acting king.

What could he do about his discovery? He felt conflicted. He believed in the cause of the Vishnusena. He knew that now. And one of the reasons for understanding the moral side of their work came from his father's teachings.

He recalled an incident from when he had been old enough to understand the inner workings of the court.

Father and Prahlad were in the hall, the one where the throne of gold and sapphire stood. Hiranya's hands were around Prahlad's shoulders. 'You are going to be a king soon.'

'I know. After Anuhrad, of course,' Prahlad responded.

'Anuhrad is brash, my child. He's older, but he's brash. I might give him a try, but not now.'

'But I thought we would leave for Pataal.'

'We will.' Hiranya knelt, looking at his son, while in the background, the throne stood, dominating the room. 'I have no reason to stay here since your mother is no longer with us. But this country needs an able ruler. If the Devas get their hands on it, they will destroy it.'

'But we are Asuras. They call us demons.'

'My child, a demon is not called one because of where he comes from, but what he does, what his deeds and his choices make him. One might say that by killing your mother, Indra is also a demon now.' He smiled. 'Remember, a good man will always know when there is evil around him. Now, whether he does something about it or not is up to him.'

'Are you a good man?'

Hiranya arched his brows. 'Perhaps you can call me noble, my child. Your mother's death has brought out the worst in me. I have to do things for this empire, for this throne, that I'm not proud of. But you don't. You have no reason to. I am an uneducated, brash man from the streets of Pataal, but you … you have a different upbringing.'

'Do I have to bend rules for the empire? Hurt the good for survival?'

'That's a hard question. I believe being right is subjective. I am sure a day will come when you will face a conflict – to

choose the empire or to choose what's right. And I cannot tell you what to choose. I have seen my share of battles. You will too and you will have to deal with him.'

'What would you have chosen?'

'My empire, any day. It took us years to get where we are. But you will be a different ruler.'

'But father,' Prahlad breathed, 'how will I know I am good?'

'You won't. Others will determine that for you. But goodness, my child, is not something you learn or are born with, but something you choose.'

Prahlad returned to reality. He had no idea where this strong surge that made him want to hurt evildoers came from. He had killed that merchant, but then that merchant may have had a family.

I made a child fatherless.

And now, after having committed a crime, he was hurt by Narada's treachery.

And he was hurt by Dhriti.

But they are doing the right thing … and my people, my men … they are wrong.

The Asura Empire was important. The throne was important. But was it more important than being right, than being good and kind? Prahlad didn't know. He didn't have the answers.

There was a knock on his door and he looked at it. Massaging his forehead, he asked for the person to enter.

It was Narada. Prahlad had called for him, and he'd finally come.

'My lord, yes, what is it?'

Gritting his teeth, Prahlad directed Narada to the chair with a gesture. Narada came forward and sat down, meek as ever, looking at Prahlad with an innocent expression. Prahlad didn't know whether this old, hunched physique was really a deception from the mastermind behind Vishnusena's activities.

'I have been meaning to ask you.'

'What, my lord?'

Prahlad pursed his lips. 'Why?'

'What do you mean, why?'

'Why are you conspiring against the government with your men?'

Narada's face remained impassive. 'I don't know what you are talking about, my lord.'

'I know my father is not perfect. I know this empire isn't perfect. But please, we can discuss it, we can work together to undo what my father did. By causing mayhem, you are disrespecting what my father built and what I want to continue to build.'

Narada was baffled. 'But my lord! I don't know what you are talking about.'

'I saw you and Dhriti. I know about you two. And I called you here to propose a truce with Vishnusena. I didn't want Holika to catch you, since she will kill you and your followers. Initially, I considered putting you all in jail, but Holika will get you there too, and I don't want you … regardless of your treachery, I don't want you to get hurt. Or Dhriti to get hurt.' He fell silent.

Narada arched his white brows. 'What do you have in mind, young king?' he asked, an unspoken admission of his guilt in his words.

For a moment, Prahlad was taken aback by how easily Narada had changed his demeanour from a fumbling old man to a determined, focused one.

'Why? Why do this?' Prahlad asked again.

'I have my reasons. I am not going to tell you why I do this, and what I have done before. But it is personal and there is definitely a major reason for me to be involved. If you know about me, about us, why have you not executed us yet?'

'Because I'm not like other rulers. I want to work with you, but without disrespecting the empire.'

'The empire will have to be disrespected. Do you know what it stands on? On the innocent bodies of Manavs who have been killed and tortured to create this petty, structureless empire of yours, helmed by a disabled ruler who has emotional issues about his wife,' Narada said, clenching his fist. 'We live in oppressed times and Vishnusena will bring the revolution of the liberation.'

And then he came forward to Prahlad, standing upright in front of him. 'I am not saying you are not a good king, lad. You are. I promise you that. I see goodness in you, but you must understand that there is no middle ground here. You can have plans and strategies and truces to solve it out, but the empire will end, your father's sacrifices and hard work will end. People need to be free to worship Lord Vishnu, Lord Brahma. We need a world where women can walk freely without being sold like pigs, where men can earn through hard work rather than gambling or being pimps or selling guns.'

Prahlad pursed his lips. 'You plan to create a utopia. I get it. The perfect world is a perfect lie, Guruji. You will end up burning a hundred more innocents in the process of achieving what you want.'

'BAH! Your men hurt more innocents than we ever could.'

'But you are in the process of doing exactly what you are trying to prevent. You will end up doing more damage than you think you can. I plead with you … work with me and we can solve it together.'

'And I plead with you, my boy, to work with us. Leave this throne and join us.' He held Prahlad by his shoulders. 'There's greatness in you. Embrace that. Use your influence as the interim king to aid us in our cause and finish the tyranny of your race. I believe Lord Vishnu will give you a second chance, to be reborn as one of us.'

And before Prahlad could even think or ask how, the door opened, revealing a tall, onyx-haired woman with ink on her arms that swirled into a beautiful design. She had multi-coloured strands of hair and her clothes flashed vibrant colours. Prahlad gasped.

Holika.

Prahlad stood in the corner, behind his desk, as he tried to remain composed. Narada did the same.

'I was looking for you,' she said.

'I was here.' Prahlad smiled. 'Aunty.'

'Not you.' Holika gazed at Narada. 'Him.'

'What is it?'

'I want to take him for questioning,' she said, bringing her guards in.

'For what?' Narada cried out loud. 'I have done nothing.'

'Yeah, well, we will see that.' She shook her head. 'I hope you have no issues, your highness, about the fact your guru is being taken.'

By that time, the Asura guards had grabbed on to Narada's arm, as he was trying to pull away, but he wasn't strong enough.

'I want to know why,' Prahlad asked his aunt, respectfully.

'We have received information that there is a mole working inside this palace and we believe it is Narada, and that he is playing a pivotal role in the Vishnusena.'

Prahlad looked at Narada, whose eyes pleaded with Prahlad to do something.

But what could he do …

Narada had made it clear that he was going to destroy his father's empire. And as much as Prahlad had begun to dislike his father, he knew that he couldn't betray him.

'Do you have any reason to believe that Narada is not part of the Vishnusena, and that our intelligence is wrong?' Holika asked. 'Since you know Guruji better than anyone else in this palace. Your testimony could be beneficial in proving his innocence.'

Prahlad remained quiet. He didn't know what was right – to side with Holika or to help Narada.

Finally, he shook his head. Holika nodded. 'Take the man away,' she said to her guards.

Prahlad saw Narada being dragged from the room. Holika went with him, closing the door behind her, leaving her nephew standing in his room, alone.

I did what my father would have done – save the empire.

But he hadn't done what he really wanted to.

Perhaps, I am not a good man after all.

20

ANUHRAD

He found Andhaka under the blood red tree.

Anuhrad had been summoned by Andhaka a few days after the big reveal – that Bhairav was his father. Anuhrad had been left speechless, for this was something he hadn't anticipated, not in a million years. In fact, he always believed Andhaka to be his blood cousin, but he wasn't. He was a Manav, the son of the Shiva.

The army didn't go to battle any more, but the spies brought regular news of how the enemy was building defences. One of the spies close to Bhairav's camp even told them that there was a new leader of the Simhas, called Nara, who had returned from a small village to challenge Andhaka.

Close to the tree, Anuhrad saw Andhaka sitting like a child, arms folded and legs crossed, as the blood red leaves fell around him.

There were no guards around and Andhaka looked weak and fragile in his jet black clothes. For a person who couldn't be killed, he certainly didn't look invincible.

'You are here,' Andhaka sighed.

'What is it? Why did you call me?'

'You never played that flute for me.'

'I don't play it any more.'

'Why?'

'Because well … it was something someone liked me to do for her, and since she left, I don't feel like playing it for someone else. I only played it for her,' Anuhrad said.

'I understand,' Andhaka said. 'Hmmm, one of my fathers is dead and the other is alive. You never told me how you feel about it.'

'That's your personal business, man. I am just helping my father get the nuclear weapon.'

'Indeed, hmmm.'

Anuhrad moved restlessly, wanting to leave, but he felt obliged to ask what he hadn't before. 'How do you feel about it, being Bhairav's son?'

Andhaka played calmly with a leaf like a child. 'I don't feel anything. I remember the day I was told the truth by my adopted father,' he said. 'I just want to kill him.'

'Why?'

Andhaka lifted his head to Anuhrad. His face was placid. 'Because he put me in the demon's hand.'

'What do you mean?'

'Your uncle, hmmm, wasn't a very nice man, Anuhrad.'

Anuhrad clenched his jaw. 'I don't know if I should trust your words, freak. I mean, you with your strange habits, you could be lying and truth be told, I really don't give a shit about what you went through with my uncle. While you sit here and mull, we need to go ahead and get that weapon.'

'I called you here for a reason. And it wasn't to get that weapon.'

'I know. You want my help in killing Bhairav.'

'Hmmm, there are yet more secrets to be revealed, Anuhrad. Only a few have been spoken of till now.'

Anuhrad couldn't guess what Andhaka was hiding or whether he was really hiding anything at all. 'I don't trust you, blind boy. Let's just do our work.'

'You are different, hmmm. You try, but you are different.'

'From whom?'

'From other demons.'

And by demons, he meant Asuras, as the Devas and the Manavs called them.

'You have a heart. Prahlad is too young to help me. You ... you have a heart unlike others.'

'Is that why you called me?'

Andhaka shook his head. 'Impatience is a virtue. Without impatience, we might never reach where we want to. Now ... hmmm ... I didn't tell you about Hiranyaksha.'

'I don't want to know.' And frankly, Andhaka was afraid of finding out something that would tarnish his image of his uncle further.

'All right, I won't bother. You can leave.' Andhaka turned his face to the tree, dismissing Anuhrad.

Anuhrad gritted his teeth. He was not angry at Andhaka. He was angry at himself for what he was going to do next, but his curiosity was piqued now. 'All right tell me.'

'There's nothing to know, Anuhrad. It's very simple. He damaged me so much ... that I want to kill the man who let him take me.'

'But my uncle never showed any ...'

'Hmmm, he was good at hiding it. At social outings, he would be perfect, but not indoors. You see, I was not always blind,' he said.

'What ... but ... how?' Anuhrad asked, shocked into a reaction.

'Hmmm,' Andhaka sighed. 'Hot, burning coals.'

Anuhrad squirmed, the image of Andhaka as a child being tortured like that too gruesome to imagine. 'Why would my uncle do that?' he asked.

'To make me aware of my other senses. He said no one cares about smell or hearing. They care only about what they see and seeing is deceiving, hmmm,' he said, and then paused before adding, 'It was not just that ... he ... put me to these tasks, pitting me against lions until I got mauled by them and then ... one day he burnt me, said I should be immune to fire.' And Andhaka pulled his sleeve up to reveal his skin – the puckered, burnt patch of skin still there. 'Do you know what it means to be that young, and face pain and death every day?

'He told the truth about what had really happened. How he had kidnapped me as a child from Bhairav and Bhairav hadn't done anything to stop him, since he was busy following Rudra's instructions on defeating the Asura army. He didn't care about saving me. Hiranyaksha told me everything because he said he wanted me to be strong,' he nodded to himself. 'You know what I believe?'

'What?'

'It was not about teaching me grand lessons, hmmm. It was just about the torture. Always. Every time. He loved it. He loved hurting me.'

Anuhrad stepped closer to Andhaka. A pang of guilt went through him. 'I am sorry,' he said, putting his hand on Andhaka's shoulder. He could feel Andhaka trembling, as if recalling those memories was physically hurting him.

'Your father was good,' Andhaka said. 'But your mother made him evil.'

'What do you mean?'

'Pointless wars,' he breathed.

Anuhrad pulled his hand away. 'My mother died because of that degenerate. The war is not pointless, freak.'

'Hmmm,' Andhaka nodded, bobbing his head back and forth. 'I do not mean to disrespect Aunt Kayadhu's life. She was a beautiful and strong woman. But do you think fighting the Devas will bring you anything?'

'It'll bring us revenge and triumph.'

'Then what?'

'Then …' Anuhrad went silent. 'Then we shall conquer and rule and …' he was confused for a moment. 'All right, I get your point, but it's for Mother.'

'It must be.' Andhaka rose to his feet.

'I am sorry for what happened to you. You didn't deserve it,' Anuhrad said, feeling like he had been too brash with his cousin, who had suffered enough.

Andhaka didn't respond, and instead changed the topic. 'Come with me.'

Anuhrad followed Andhaka, who walked towards the pathway that led to the two towers where the Danavs slept. Andhaka was flaring his nostrils and Anuhrad noticed that he was letting the smell of the place guide him to it.

'He caged me,' he said, his voice shrill and high. 'He caged me and poked me with fire prods. His Danavs used to crush my back and I would sit with the shaman every day. He hurt me every day by smashing me on the skull. Everything apparently in an effort to make me tough!' His feet kicked the snow. 'I was just fifteen! I was small! I didn't know what to do!'

Anuhrad wanted to calm him down, but he couldn't since he didn't know how to pacify this situation. And then Andhaka stopped, looking at the guards who came out of nowhere and stood around the towers where the Danavs were. They had strange blue plants.

'What are these, Andhaka?' Anuhrad asked, horror on his face.

'Hmmm, I did something … one of my spies, he stole a crate of Somalata plants from the camp and gave it to me.'

The guards began to sow the plants around the towers.

'Why didn't you tell me?' Anuhrad asked. 'Father told us to give the Somas to our guards for strength.'

'We don't need chemicals hurting us, hmmm,' he flared his nostrils. 'We are not Devas. We are not Asuras. We are men guided by the light.'

And then the guards lit fire from the torch lamps to the vines, growing a swirling flame around the towers – letting the Somalata plants explode.

The Danavs were inside!

'Why are you hurting the giants?'

'Because that *demon*,' he snarled, 'was proud of them. And now I want to show him what I can do. And now, I have you to do it.'

The tower gates were closed and Anuhrad could hear the Danavs trying to escape the tower but failing. The towers exploded and fire and smoke rose in the air with the wind. Anuhrad wanted to stop the madness, but he didn't know how. He knew his father would kill him for letting the Danavs die.

He turned to find Andhaka, who came forward, and grabbed Anuhrad by the face, pulling him close. 'Remember, this is not the war of Danavs and Asuras or Devas. It's our war. We are greater than them. We are good, important people made out of tragedy and pain, and pain shall be the reason we rule.'

'Why? What will it bring you?'

'I want to prove them wrong. To prove that we are not weak, that our tragedies don't make us weak. To prove to them that we are stronger than anyone else. But most of all, it'll be good to live once again where we have monopoly. He told me I was weak. I was, yes. I am not any more.'

Anuhrad looked at the guards who stood around them, watching the towers burn.

'Why aren't your Asura guards stopping you?'

'Because they are afraid of me, my dear brother.' His palms pressed tighter on Anuhrad's cheeks. 'They are afraid of the fact that they can't kill me. No one can. And also, because they believe in my cause.'

'Your cause?' The fire before them grew, and Anuhrad felt the heat from it burn his skin. He could feel *fear* in the air as the Danavs fell.

'After I kill Bhairav and take the Pashupatastra for us, I'm coming for the throne.' And then for the first time ever, he smiled a genuinely bright smile. 'And I am going to end the Asura Empire, for what they did to me … and for what they did to you as well.'

Anuhrad was shocked. 'What did they do to me?'

'Oh. You don't know,' he smirked. 'Well, I know. Oh, I have known for a while.'

21
NARASIMHA

Everything was all right … for *now*.

The Pride followed Nara, listened to him as he guided them. Nara knew that he would eventually have to leave them again after defeating Andhaka, since his reason for coming to Mandara Hills had been to prevent the Pashupatastra from being used by the blind prince. But he was loathe to leave. He had begun to like the place – and like Chenchen. She was … warm. That was the right word. And she was supportive of him; she understood him. He wanted to be around her.

She saw who he was, even when he didn't know it himself.

Bhairav was mostly fortifying his defences and asking for help from the villages that could spare more people. He was also sending ravens across to Indra for more soldiers and supplies in preparation for an attack.

One day, when Nara was teaching his Pride how to use the Somas responsibly – the trick was to not mix them with alcohol or any tobacco product – they saw a large cloud of smoke in the sky above Sonitpur. The city was ablaze.

Bhairav stood beside Nara. 'What is he up to now?' he asked.

'It's coming from the towers,' Nara replied.

'Why is he burning them?' Bhairav wondered. 'He's always been unpredictable. Once, he raided the nearby villages and picked up young boys and men.'

'Why?'

Bhairav shrugged. 'We can only guess.' He clapped his hands to catch everyone's attention and gestured for them to get on with their work. 'Listen, Nara. Since Mrig is not here, I want you to aid Chenchen's team today. They are visiting the villages.'

Nara was pleased, but maintained an impassive expression on his face.

'We need donations from the villages. In return, we provide them with medical aid and tend to their sick. Chenchen's team collects the donations – food, supplies and other necessities – that aid us in battle. I want you to go with her as protection. The enemy has been known to target nurses.'

Nara nodded. 'It'll be done, Bhairav. But we need to figure out our own strategy, otherwise we will keep defending ourselves. We need to find a way to launch an offensive on Sonitpur and kill Andhaka.'

'We shall,' Bhairav said grimly. 'I want to end this battle too, much more than you do. And we will.'

Nara smiled. As he began to move away, Bhairav whispered under his breath, 'I have been considering using the Pashupatastra.'

Nara froze. He looked at Bhairav's face, which was twisted with worry and guilt. 'Are you serious?'

'I just … we have to do something before all of us die. We can draw Andhaka to an isolated place and then use the weapon. Maybe this time, innocents won't have to die,' Bhairav said, looking at the leader of the Simhas with pleading eyes. 'We are losing, Nara.'

Nara clenched his jaw.

This is bad.

But he didn't say that, shrugging instead. 'We will talk more when I return from the villages,' he said, and walked towards the nurses.

He saw from afar that Chenchen and the other nurses had packed their things and mounted the horses. Nara grabbed his horse too and asked two Simhas to follow him. He was no longer in his dirty, grimy skin. It had been polished and cleaned, and now shone golden. He looked like a proper lion-man, a true Simha leader.

Nara turned his horse towards Chenchen and began following her team.

'Are you always going to follow me?' she asked, a small smile playing on her lips.

Nara sighed. He couldn't return her smile; Bhairav's words about the threat in the village had worried him, and his reason for accompanying her was a grim one. 'I'm supposed to guard you and your team.'

'Really? *I* need protecting?' she raised her brow. He knew she was referring to the time she had saved him from Mrig.

Nara smiled. They climbed uphill, the nurses and the two Simhas behind them.

'Oh, so he does smile?' Chenchen laughed, and Nara felt his heart glow.

Chenchen guided them through the snowy landscapes, the hooves of the horses digging into the snow. The angry skies thundered as they at last reached a small village – parts of it barricaded. There were carts and caravans parked here and there, and a few huts lined the roads, bearskin spread on them for warmth. There were pots on burnt logs, being used to cook food, and small fires around which the natives huddled in an effort to keep warm.

While Chenchen and her team began their work, Nara and his Simhas took different positions and stood guard. Chenchen began to talk to the villagers, giving them bags of ayurvedic ointments and creams. And Nara saw how charming she was, without even trying.

As the nurses scattered to gather supplies, Nara watched the villagers. Most of them had their faces covered against the snow, and a couple of them had protruding eyes and twisted mouths.

Chenchen saw him staring and asked, 'How does it make you feel, looking at them?'

'Why do they look like that?' Nara wondered, frowning.

Chenchen was passing around a bag to people who were dropping apples, raw meat and other food supplies in it. 'Their deformities are a result of the nuclear weapon. A few years ago, Indra wanted to try the Pashupatastra and he did, blasting a particular area, isolated though it was. However, just a few miles away, there was a village. The radiation from Pashupatastra …' she took a few apples from a woman who, Nara noticed, had no nose. Next to her, another woman with white spots on completely dark skin waited in line.

'That weapon caused these innocent people to go through mutations,' Chenchen said.

Hatred for Indra boiled inside Nara. He now knew what Bhairav meant when he referred to that *one time* the Pashupatastra had been used.

'After that, Indra and Bhairav tried to lock the weapon down, believing it was of no use to either the Devas or the Asuras, except as a last resort in an extreme situation,' Chenchen said.

Nara knew that Bhairav felt immense guilt for actually trying the Pashupatastra and harming civilians unknowingly. Perhaps the Shiva wouldn't have agreed to use it if he had known its consequences.

Nara felt himself stiffen as he looked at a child who came forward and dropped a single loaf of bread into Chenchen's bag. The boy was completely bald and hairless, down to his eyebrows, and his eyes were a fierce red.

'I believe,' Chenchen said, smiling at the boy as she accepted his donation, 'I believe that we don't need this weapon at all, not even in a dire situation. I believe, no matter how much they try to prevent it, it will end up hurting innocents.'

Nara knew that she was right. Hadn't he hurt innocent civilians despite trying his best not to? Wasn't that why he had left the war … at least that was one of the reasons, other than the secret that haunted him. He shook his head and tried to forget about it. He didn't want to remember, didn't want his past to catch up with him. If he did, the cycle of prophecy would begin.

As if to make sure, Nara looked at his chest. He was free of the symbol of Vishnu. It was all right.

'Are they not angry?' he asked Chenchen. 'For what Indra did to them? It is surprising that they are still offering donations.'

'You won't like the answer.'

Nara understood what she meant. 'They don't know it was us who used the weapon,' he said.

Chenchen shook her head. 'No, they don't. Indra told them that it was the Asuras who did it, especially Andhaka, and they believed him. Indra said that in order to kill Andhaka and take revenge, they needed the villagers' help. Hence the donations.'

'How did Bhairav go along with this?' Nara knew Bhairav to be just and fair, and believed that he would never knowingly deceive the villagers.

'He had to, since he and his people need Indra more than Indra needs them. Also, Indra convinced him that the truth would bring about a rebellion, and that sometimes, lies are nobler than the truth. Bhairav had no choice but to try to lighten his conscience by sending medical aid to the villagers. We ...' She looked at the nurses, 'We are like his puppets, working for his redemption.'

Before Nara could reply, a shriek rang through the air. He closed his eyes, trying to track down the direction the sound had come from. It was from the east. And before he could move, a volley of arrows came flying towards them.

Instantly Nara stepped in front of Chenchen and the people, letting the arrows plunge into the skin. He roared and pulled them out, hurtling them back at the black-armoured archers, who rode towards them on horses.

An arrow hit one of the riders, and he fell, but the rest of them dodged the attack and continued drawing closer to the villagers, shooting arrows as they approached.

Nara walked forward, using his hands to deflect the arrows. He lunged at a rider who had come closer, tearing and clawing at him. As the archer fell, the horse neighed and fled.

Where are my Simhas?

He turned and saw that they were fighting the other archers. One of them was injured while the other one was using his blade to fight back. Nara rushed to their aid and clawed the Asuras, tearing them apart.

Once they had taken care of all the attackers, he looked around to see the villagers cowering in fear.

He walked to Chenchen, his breath strained. 'We need to leave. One of my Simhas is losing too much blood and won't be able to fight back if they return.'

A boy Chenchen was holding protectively said, 'They will return.'

Nara arched his brows, his blood growing cold. 'What do you mean?' he knelt before the boy.

'They are stationed close by and wait for the nurses to come,' the boy said. 'They find out when you'll be here for the donations and they strike at that moment and attack you all.'

Nara nodded. 'Why?'

'They look for the weapon, sir,' The boy was shivering. 'I heard them once. I snuck up to their hideout. They were speaking of a weapon you have. They have been told to find the weapon and they won't give up until they do.'

Nara touched the boy's head and smiled. 'Thank you for letting me know, kid.' The boy gave a watery smile in return and left for his hut.

'Let's leave,' he told Chenchen.

'Are you going to find that hideout?' she asked.

'No use. They know that's what we'll do, since we've deflected their attack. They'll find a different way of attacking us now.'

Chenchen nodded, grabbing the supplies and making her way to their horses. Nara helped her mount her horse while the villagers watched them. He saw women holding their children, men covered in turbans and cloth to hide their deformities, orphans who were pale like snow and the decrepit huts dotting the landscape.

Nara was quiet as they rode back. Chenchen rode by his side. 'Are you all right?' she asked.

'I am not fine with how Indra is treating the people around him. I am not sure whether we are serving on the side of good any more.'

Chenchen spoke, 'We serve the lesser evil, Nara.'

Nara nodded, but a thousand thoughts ran through his head. Most of all, he was angry with Indra.

He hurt them and then blamed it on someone else. That coward can't even own up to his mistakes.

They will not stop until they get the weapon.

'What are you thinking?' Chenchen's voice broke into his thoughts.

'The weapon is the root cause. I believed it could be used for the greater good at the time of crisis, but after seeing these villagers, and the way it has destroyed their lives, I no longer believe that. It's pure poison. And even without being used, it is harming us. I have to do something about it. Andhaka will not stop looking for it if I don't.'

And Bhairav is growing desperate enough to consider using it again.

Chenchen arched her brows. 'What do you think you can do?'

'What do you think I should do?' Nara asked her.

'You seem conflicted,' she said.

'I am. What choice do I have?' Nara shook his head. 'I follow a leader – *we* follow a leader – we can't even trust. How are we so sure that he won't end up using the Pashupatastra against us one day?'

Chenchen sighed. 'All I can say is that one always has a choice.'

'I know. That's why I left. My choice was to not be part of it.'

'And be a coward?' she chuckled. 'You aren't a coward, Nara. You are so much more than that. That was not the choice you had.'

'What then?'

'To be better,' she said, 'than Bhairav, than Indra, than anyone else.'

Nara was quiet, mulling over her words. She was right.

We all have to make choices that define us.

'I know what to do,' he said, finally breaking the silence, letting a smile wash over his face.

'What?' she asked, looking at him.

Nara looked up at Bhairav's fort; at the big golden bull Nanda towering over it.

'I have to destroy the Pashupatastra. The Asuras don't deserve it ...' he looked at Chenchen. 'And neither do the Devas.'

22

HIRANYAKASHYAP

He rode under the scorching sun.

The map was leading him nowhere, but Hiranya was determined to find the temple – the so-called Temple of Brahma that stood in the regions of Yakshlok. The region was dusty and barren, the sun's orange rays bleeding over the landscape.

Hiranya was exhausted. He was parched, he needed to save the water he carried for as long as he could. His joints ached and his feet hurt. He rode through the day and would rest with his stallion close to the caves at night, when the weather was cooler.

Today, as he walked he saw in front of him the darkness of his nightmares – his wife. She was standing a few yards away. He could see her. She seemed so real, and he jumped off his horse, running towards her. As he drew closer, she disappeared in a puff of smoke and he realized that she had been just an illusion.

Anger boiled within him, and he dropped down to the burning sand, punching it with his fist. He wanted to die. His lips were dry and he felt like giving up.

I shouldn't have come alone.

But his brother had written in the diary entries that no one else could know of this place. So Hiranya had come alone, and was now in the middle of a desert that was slowly sucking the life out of him.

He finally got up, and as he did, he looked around and saw something that stunned him – some distance away, there was a large cave over which stood a huge statue, broken and dilapidated, its bearded head as large as a battle tower.

He quickly opened the map and realized that somehow, he'd reached his destination.

Is this the place?

He mustered his strength and climbed back on his horse, riding towards the statue.

He reached it and dismounted from his horse. Walking under the shadow of the statue, he saw that inside the cave, there were blazing torches lining the wall. Vultures perched over what looked like skulls and bones, pecking at them.

Men have come here and died horrible deaths.

He saw bats and lizards in the cave as he moved forward. Finally, he reached what looked like a door, and opening it, entered a room with blue walls, in the middle of which stood a strong suit of armour and a sword resting against it, both things lit up by a ray of light. And studded in the middle of the armour was a gem – the Mani.

This is it.

Hiranya saw that three slabs of stone surrounded the armour, and they were covered in strange symbols. He ignored them and came forward, reaching out for the armour. The beam of light hit his hand and he pulled it back, crying in pain,

It had burnt his hand!

Tears of pain pooled in his eyes and he looked up to see a smoky figure materialize before him. A ghost-like figure in a hood, suspended in the air.

'It isn't that easy,' the figure said, the sound like that of a hissing snake.

Hiranya saw that the apparition's face was yellow, with no nose and red eyes. His mouth had a strange, viper-like tongue.

'Who are you?' Hiranya asked.

'We are the spirit that your brother must have told you about.'

Of course. So he's literally a spirit. Great.

Hiranya massaged his burnt hand. 'How did you know I would be here?'

'We know. We know everything.'

'Who's "we"?'

'We is me,' the spirit gestured with his thin, papery hands. 'You are a volunteer sent to retrieve the weapon? Isn't it a beauty?' He floated around the armour, grinning a horrible grin. 'We protect it with the utmost care and love. But most of all, we know it deserves to be given to the worthy.'

'How do you judge worthiness?'

The spirit looked at Hiranya, hissing. 'Do not play dumb with us. We know you know about the Trials. The question is, are you ready to embark on them?'

Hiranya felt a tendril of fear within his heart, but instead of answering, he asked a question. 'Who are you?'

'We are the guardian of the armour, appointed by Lord Brahma himself.'

'I see. And why has Lord Brahma left his armour here?'

'It is to be given to the worthy. For years, no one has been worthy enough. Not even your brother.'

Hiranya remained impassive. He knew this was it. He had come to the place to achieve greatness, to prove himself worthy so that he could wear the armour, fight Indra and win the war. 'If I do this, if I get the armour, no one can kill me?'

'No one except …' the voice faltered and rose again, as the blue light formed a figure of a lion-man. It was just a figure, but the roar – Hiranya could feel the roar in his heart. 'Except the Avatar of Lord Vishnu.'

'A Simha?' Hiranya knew about the previous Avatar – a mere Manav who sported the symbol of a boar and had killed his father.

'The prophecy by the Saptarishis stated that the bearer of the Brahmshastra can be only defeated and killed by the Avatar – whether the Avatar rises in this Yug or not, that depends on the Avatar himself.'

Hiranya had to take that chance. 'But can I kill him before he kills me?'

'There are many ways in which you can twist the prophecy. The prophecy doesn't guarantee that the Avatar will kill the bearer of Brahmshastras. It is only *capable* of killing him,' the spirit laughed. 'So are you ready, son of Kashyap?'

Hiranya clenched his fists and gritted his teeth. He knew he had to do this. And he knew that if the Avatar ever did rise, he, Hiranya, was capable of killing him. He had to take that chance and he knew that the risk would be worth the reward.

'What do I have to do?' he asked.

'Choose your first Trial.'

And suddenly, the slabs began to rise, turning into pedestals, and the symbols on them began to gleam brightly.

The first symbol was of a man fighting a bigger man. 'The Trial of strength, of physicality,' the spirit said.

The second pedestal showed a man sitting in the lotus posture, meditating. 'The Trial of mental awareness, of how you use your brain in times of conflict.'

The third pedestal had a strange design Hiranya couldn't interpret.

'What is this one?' he asked.

'Only when you pass the first two Trials will you know the third one's meaning, for it is the toughest of all. So which one is it to be, son of Kashyap?'

Hiranya thought.

'It's your choice,' the spirit hissed. 'And whichever pedestal you choose, you have to step on it to begin the Trial.'

Hiranya knew what he was best at, and so he stepped on to the first pedestal.

Let's see who I'm going to have to fight to prove my strength.

'Good choice,' the spirit said. 'And now to begin, you must have this.' He brought forth a strange blue liquid out of nowhere in a small vial.

'What is this?'

'Every challenger who participates in the Trials must have it. It's the Soma. It gives one great strength.'

'I don't believe in it. I already have strength.'

'Not as much as you will if you take this. Believe us, it's good. Otherwise you won't be able to get through even the first part of the Trials.'

Hiranya clenched his jaw and took the vial. He swallowed the warm liquid in a single gulp.

'Good, good. Are you ready?' the spirit asked.

Hiranya felt his stomach grumble, liquid kicking in. He could feel a surge of strength shoot through him, energizing his muscles.

A slow smile lit up his face.

'Yes.'

23

PRAHLAD

Prahlad knew there was someone in his room.

He had woken up from deep sleep when he heard his window open. The hairs at the back of his neck stood up. His arms were tightly crossed over his chest and he was breathing softly.

He didn't have his sword close by, so he had to remain still, with his eyes closed, and pounce from the bed when he had the chance.

He could hear the figure was approaching him and before he knew it, it stood right at his bedside, breathing. He heard the sound of a blade sliding from its sheath.

Who would want to kill me?

Many people ... many.

Prahlad opened his eyes slightly, hoping to catch a glimpse of the figure. He saw that it was wrapped in black clothes and there were large eyes staring down at him.

Prahlad swallowed a nervous lump as the figure held the blade against his throat.

'You don't have to do this,' he said softly. 'Please.'

The figure froze, its eyes watching him with hate.

'We can settle this some other way,' he said, repeating, 'you don't have to do this.'

The figure pushed the blade closer.

Prahlad suddenly caught a glimpse of red strands that had escaped the hood.

'Dhriti,' he said, 'I know it's you.'

Dhriti stood still, the blade still held against Prahlad's throat. She remained silent.

'I am sorry for not doing anything for Narada,' Prahlad said.

She didn't move. 'I wanted you to be part of us, part of this cause,' she said at last, her voice choked with tears. 'I was wrong.'

Prahlad wanted to say so many things, but he chose to remain silent. He felt too confused to know the words to say.

Dhriti broke the awkward silence between them. 'You don't realize the value of this cause. You have sent our leader to prison. Our leader!'

'It was not my fault. Aunt was on to him,' Prahlad explained.

'She's a maniac and you know that. You are intelligent. You aren't like others, Prahlad.' Her blade was touching his skin, almost cutting him. 'When you told me you wanted to believe in something, you thought you were lying to me … but you were lying to yourself. You *do* want to believe in something.'

'And destroy the empire my father built in the process?'

'This very empire is suffocating us,' she said, her voice rising. 'You haven't seen the world like I have. I have been an orphan for the longest time and I have seen things you won't believe. I have seen women being abducted, men being beaten, farmers being forced to pay heavy taxes. I have seen so much, and that is why I joined this cause. I was not blind to it, like you have been. Your father is not a good ruler. The Asuras have to die and you can help us. You know they are evil,' she explained, lowering her voice.

Prahlad listened, still silent.

She asked, 'Do you know why Narada started the Vishnusena?'

Prahlad shook his head.

'Because after Kashyapuri was ransacked and Hiranya began rebuilding the empire, Narada set up his Gurukul in the village close to Kashyapuri. Hiranya had become paranoid and was doing everything to increase security, to see if there were spies within his empire. He believed a rumour that there were a few spies hiding in Narada's Gurukul, and so he burnt down the entire Gurukul … even the children inside.'

Prahlad was horrified. 'Father would never—'

'He's been blinded by his thirst for revenge,' she said. 'When he learnt that the Gurukul belonged to the very guru he had appointed for his sons, he instantly realized his mistake and gave Narada an important role in the office to make amends. Hiranya was guilty. But Narada … oh … he was angry. He slowly began building his team, realizing the murders weren't the only acts of evil the king allowed, or ordered. There were other things – attacking the poor, feeding the elite so his war could be funded by the rich nobles that run this city.'

Prahlad listened with growing horror as she continued. 'And the very man who inspired and rallied people to defend themselves against their violent oppressors is now in prison because of your sadistic aunt, who will end up killing him while we sit here helplessly.'

'I'm sorry.'

Prahlad felt the blade press closer, the rusty smell of it filling his nostrils. 'I am shocked by what Narada went through. I am … I am sorry. I don't know what else I can do.'

'You have already done what you shouldn't have done.'

'You are right.' Prahlad sighed. 'I do want to seek faith. The void left behind by my mother, it has left me in shambles. Anuhrad is like my father, but me … I am different. I do believe in the Vishnusena and their cause.' He felt the pressure of the blade ease and reached out to hold her hand, looking straight into her eyes. He felt his fear subside. 'Thank you for coming tonight.'

She stared back at him and he could feel her gaze searing his soul.

He continued, 'I'll right my wrong. I want to be part of you all. I want to help you.'

'What do you mean?'

'We are going to save Guru Narada from the prison, Dhriti.'

24

ANUHRAD

SIX YEARS AGO

He was nineteen.

But he did not receive any special gifts on his birth date. Instead, he had to follow the same strict routine he adhered to every other day.

He woke up in the morning and went for a long run. Then, after a breakfast of something healthy, be it fruits or meat, he had to attend javelin practice. Then, archery, followed by a healthy lunch. By dusk, he was subject to lessons on warfare from Narada, after which he had to go on a run again.

The day would end with a sword fighting lesson and a wrestling match against his father.

His father, who didn't mind breaking his bones. In fact, he relished it.

Sometimes Father can be quite demented.

His birth date was just like any other day, and ended in a bruised back and a feeling of crushing exhaustion.

While he rested on the grass after the wrestling match, his father, clad in his trademark golden dhoti, walked up to him. 'You must be strong enough to lead this empire, son. I am teaching you everything I can so that you toughen up and lead us to victory against the likes of Devas. I don't want Indra's son Jayant to end up stronger than you.'

Anuhrad nodded glumly.

He goes and on about how the Devas have the Somas. So even with enough training, will I be able to defeat those with Somas running in their veins?

'The Asuras have a hard exoskeleton, something the Devas lack,' Hiranya said, as if reading his son's mind. 'Learn to make good use of it.' Hiranya wiped his sweat. 'Remember' – he knelt down – 'this is all for your mother. Alright?'

Anuhrad wanted to ask him about many other things; most of his questions were about why his younger brother Prahlad received a milder treatment while he was always pushed into a warrior's lifestyle. But whenever he asked the reason for his training, all he would receive was a lecture on how this was vengeance for his mother, and he would grow quiet.

Anuhrad wanted to be a musician; he wanted to join theatre and learn different art forms, travel with the troupe. But here he was, doing his duty, practicing and learning about his responsibilities until the duties of the throne overpowered him.

There's nothing like free will for me.

'You were born nineteen years ago on this date,' – Hiranya thumped Anuhrad's sore back –'and I have a gift for you.'

'Thank you, father. What is it?' Anuhrad asked, afraid that the gift wouldn't be something of his liking.

'You are joining a royal hunt right now.'

'But it's night!' exclaimed Anuhrad and as he leaned forward with indignation, a searing pain shot down his back.

'How does that matter? It's good for your senses. Assassination attempts happen mostly at night. You must be prepared to act in the dark. You have to ally with darkness, make it your friend,' Hiranya explained.

Anuhrad clenched his teeth. 'All right, Father. Who am I going with?'

'Andhaka,' he said and Anuhrad's chest tightened at his cousin's name. 'After all, who knows darkness better than him?' Hiranya added.

Andhaka was the quiet sort. He was bald and white and had slimy lips. He wore tight-fitting clothes and wrapped his limbs around his body as if he were hiding scars. Anuhrad didn't meet his cousin often, for he didn't like him, but when he did, it was mostly for work or at family reunions.

And today, it was work.

They were in a secluded part of the forest behind the castle. They walked alongside, with a dozen guards behind them. They kept their distance, but were there to ensure that the princes were not assaulted by an outside threat. Andhaka wore a black blindfold. He didn't speak much. He was using a stick to walk through the overgrowth.

'I point. You shoot,' Andhaka commanded.

Anuhrad had his bow and arrow prepared. He hadn't gone hunting in the night before, and it felt odd. Most of the deer would be fast asleep.

'To master the night, hmmm,' Andhaka said, his voice wheezy and high-pitched, 'one must concentrate on other senses ... shoot!' he pointed to his left.

Instantly, Anuhrad, without doubting his cousin's intention, pulled back his arm and released an arrow in the direction Andhaka asked him to.

There was a loud yelp and Anuhrad narrowed his gaze in recognition.

It was a dog. A puppy.

'It's a pup,' said Anuhrad, his heart sinking as he rushed towards the dog and knelt down next to it. 'You made me kill an innocent beast!'

'Doesn't matter. We must eat it,' Andhaka squirmed in anticipation.

'Are you crazy? There's enough food in the castle,' Anuhrad was horrified.

'Father doesn't let me.'

'What do you mean?'

Andhaka didn't respond. 'Please, I am starving.'

'No, get lost! Creep!' shouted Anuhrad, to which Andhaka just lowered his head and felt his way out of Anuhrad's sight.

Anuhrad looked at the dog for a while. It lay lifeless under the moon. He pulled the arrow from it.

'You shouldn't have done that.' The voice came from the trees nearby.

Anuhrad looked around, but he couldn't find the origin of the voice.

'Up here.'

Anuhrad searched the trees and saw a shaggy-looking girl sitting on one of the branches, eating a mango. She looked strange and wild, with her hair all over the place and her skin dark. She was absolutely gorgeous. She jumped from the branch with surprising agility and landed on the ground.

'Be careful. My soldiers might attack you for coming too close to me,' Anuhrad warned, but she scoffed as she began to dig a small hole in the ground.

'You are a prince, aren't you?'

'Yes, I am.'

'You sound and behave like one for sure.'

'Do I?' Anuhrad shrugged.

As she dug, Anuhrad caught sight of the image of a hand-drawn tree on her bag.

'Y-you are a Nishad?' he asked.

She nodded. 'Name's Jyoti.' She picked up the dog gently with her hands and put it inside the freshly dug hole, covering it with mud. 'What are you looking at? Help me,' she said.

'Uh, sorry.' Anuhrad shook his head, and began to help her bury the dog he had just killed. 'Father once told me about you people. How you wouldn't join his campaign.'

'Let's focus on burying the life you just took.'

'I-I shouldn't have done this. It's just my cousin … he's a weird person.'

She stopped piling the mud and looked at him.

'We are not blind to the pursuits of the king. We just don't believe in him. By the way, I saw how you called that boy a creep. He's blind, you know.'

'How do I care?' Anuhrad grimaced. 'He made me kill this innocent beast.'

'Not really.' She rose and said a brief prayer. 'You were the one who did the deed, but now, you are blaming him. If you would have considered for a moment before shooting your arrow and really seen what he was pointing at, you could have saved an innocent. But you didn't. Thus, you behave like a prince. Just like your father.'

She dusted off her hands before continuing, 'Don't come to this place any more, *prince*. I won't let you hurt the residents of this forest.'

Anuhrad was fascinated by the girl, but her words stung, and he shot back at her, 'You can't tell me where I can or cannot go, woman. You are an illiterate and a forest dweller! And the likes of you have no ...'

She chuckled. 'Resorting to your princely behaviour, eh?'

Anuhrad instantly realized that she was playing him. He was not an arrogant person but he couldn't control his ego, even though he was not egoistical like his father.

'I am sorry,' he bowed his head.

She laughed out loud as she said, 'Well, good day, prince. I hope we never meet again.'

And she walked away, towards the lanterns that glowed like fireflies along a river in the misty woods. Anuhrad watched her go and he could feel his stomach twist. His bones felt hollow and his ears were hot.

Well, I hope we do.

It had been a few days since Anuhrad's first encounter with Jyoti. Every day after training, he would sneak out and send a written message attached to his arrow. He hoped she received them.

When he was not training, he would sneak off into the forest in the hopes of seeing her.

He was standing in the forest, looking around him forlornly, when he suddenly heard a voice.

'Have you forgotten that forest dwellers can't read?' she called from above.

He saw her descending from the tree, holding what appeared to be written notes from him.

He shrugged. 'A prince is too busy to consider small matters like that. But as long as the message is clear, words are meaningless, aren't they?' he asked.

She laughed again, making his heart skip a beat.

They talked about nature, about animals and flowers. Anuhrad learnt that Jyoti was from a lower-caste family, but she could scavenge the mountains well and was an excellent cook.

His gaze soon fell upon a wooden instrument that she carried.

'Is that a flute?' He looked at the instrument sticking out of her bag.

'Yes! Can you play it?' she asked.

'Barely,' he said.

Anuhrad always wanted to show off his musical talent, and one day he had brought his instrument to play to his father. He had been crushed when Hiranya had said, 'You are not good at this, son. You better be good with swords.' His words had pierced Anuhrad like nothing else.

'Play it,' she encouraged him, passing him the flute. He raised it to his lips.

The sullen atmosphere of the forest lightened as Anuhrad played a melody unheard of in the lands of Kashyapuri. Jyoti looked at him for a moment, and then began kindling a fire, and took out a pan for the broth to boil.

The tune rang through the forest, and the flames danced as if to the notes of the song. Jyoti watched him closely as he played, and then glanced at the bag lying next to him, full of flowers.

Had he brought the flowers for her?

Her smile grew brighter, and she blushed.

'Who taught you to play?' she asked him once he'd put the flute down, pausing to regain his breath.

'My mother. I couldn't spend much time with her since she died young. But when my father used to leave for his campaigns, she had only me for company. And my brother, but he was an infant.'

Watching the pain on his face, Jyoti's own heart twisted, and she reached out and held his hand.

'It's beautiful. Come tomorrow evening to our village. Our headman lets our people perform – be it acting, mimicry, music or dance. Needless to say, he will be more than happy to host a prince,' she said.

Anuhrad grinned and promised to be there.

Anuhrad was at the Nishad camp. They had welcomed him with enthusiasm. Anuhrad knew that they were not a part of any caste; rather, they were outside of it. But Anuhrad could see they didn't care. For them, it was all about living in the moment. He could see them enjoying themselves, sitting around the bonfire with music filling the silent night. They all wore multicoloured clothes and a stall to sell jewellery made of inexpensive clay had been set up in one corner.

Once it was his turn to perform, Anuhrad was called to the centre. Hesitating, he came forward. He lifted the flute to his lips with trepidation, but once he began playing – the same tune he had played for Jyoti in the forest – his apprehension died down. People around him were swaying to the music, clearly enjoying themselves. He could feel himself being cheered on, supported. He felt like he had been a part of them all along.

He felt free.

Once he finished his piece, he received a huge round of applause and smiled. As he looked around, his eyes darted towards a shadow close to the camp.

He knew that shadow …

Anuhrad left the camp and instantly made a run for it. He could see Jyoti watching him. And after a moment's pause, she followed after him.

Anuhrad charged and pounced at the fleeing spy, grabbing his neck. 'Who sent you?'

'Your father!' the man exclaimed and Anuhrad slapped him hard.

He was furious. 'How does he know?'

'He has been observing your nightly activities, my lord. And people have been talking behind your back. A high-born Asura, our prince, getting close to the likes of forest dwellers? What a shame!' He escaped the grip of a stunned Anuhrad.

'Leave,' Anuhrad said, disappointed. His heart was pounding.

He saw Jyoti approaching them. Seeing Anuhrad's livid face, she enquired, 'What is the matter?'

Anuhrad struggled. 'My people are talking about my involvement with you. That is the last thing my father wants – rumours distracting him in the middle of his campaign. Rumours about us.'

'Talk to him,' she said, putting a palm on his cheek.

'About what?'

'About me,' she smiled.

Anuhrad wanted to, but he was afraid of his father. 'He wants me to join in his campaign, and if I tell him about you, he will think of you as a distraction.'

'You are above this bloodshed, Anu. You are greater than this. Why don't you come with us? We will be leaving soon and you can leave with us and start a new life. The life you live here in these castles, that's not a life you want. I know that about you,' she said.

'Can't *you* come be with me? To the castle?' he asked.

'Do you really want me to be there?' she said, cocking her head towards the castle. 'Do *you* want to be there yourself?'

Anuhrad knew in his heart that the castle was no place for her. Was it a place for him?

He knew what he had to do.

He had to choose between her ... and his father.

'I want to withdraw from your campaign, Father,' he announced as he walked into Hiranya's room. His father was working at his desk, documents and papers arranged neatly in front of him.

'Why?' Hiranya asked.

'I am tired of this life. I want to live the way I want to live.'

'Aren't you living the life you want to?'

'I am living your life, Father.' Anuhrad gritted his teeth. 'You want me to be the ideal warrior, the ideal son. But I'm not. This is not my place … I don't think I can be a prince.'

'It's the girl, isn't it?' Hiranya flared his nostrils, leaning back in his chair as he twirled his moustache. 'I was afraid your weak mind would be polluted by the woman. They are quite tempting when they suck you in between their legs.'

Anuhrad was angry but composed himself. 'It's not that. It's not her. It's more. I feel free there, with her people.'

Hiranya pushed his chair back and walked around his table, coming to stand in front of his nineteen-year-old son. 'All right, you may leave. You have disappointed me, Anuhrad,' he said.

'I know.'

And I don't feel bad about it.

'Just remember, once you leave … I cannot accept you back, no matter what. Because it will be a stain on my reputation that my own son chose a life without any caste. The moment you leave this room, you are an outcast for me, a nobody.'

Anuhrad nodded.

'She's not right for you, Anuhrad. You are a king while she's an outcaste. She comes from the people who lack a spine. Return to your destiny. Embrace it,' Hiranya tried to convince him.

'But Father, I love her and I will stay with her,' Anuhrad said for the first time and he believed these words.

Did I just say love?

But it was the truth. He could feel it in his heart. He knew that he wouldn't return.

I don't want to.

'All right, Father. Thank you for allowing me this freedom.'

He bowed and walked out of the room, on his way to a new life.

They were supposed to meet at the riverside.

With his bags and rolled-up clothes, he waited for her, but she was nowhere to be seen. Hours passed and the midday sun shone on his face when he walked towards the Nishad camp. He trudged along and finally reached the camp, only to see that ...

The camp lay before him, ruined and destroyed.

There were charred bodies on the ground. The last of the fire blew everywhere. The ground and floors were splattered with blood.

Anuhrad wept as he walked around. He could feel his soul being torn apart.

Jyoti...

He looked around for her, scanning the faces of the bodies before him.

No, no. Please no ...

Tears brimmed and flowed over his hot cheeks as he moved around frantically, turning the bodies and looking at each face until he found her.

She was close to a mango tree; her body had been propped against the tree. He ran and knelt next to her, his eyes meeting hers. She wasn't dead, but her eyes were full of pain, regret, and a long knife protruded from her stomach. She had been stabbed fatally.

'Anu ...' she held on to his hands. 'Help me ...'

Anuhrad tried to remove the knife, but she cried out.

'No, don't ... it's worse.'

'But you will ...' He knew she had lost a lot of blood and was moments from death.

'We only wished for a new beginning. Was it too soon?' she cried in anguish, holding his face. 'There was so much I wanted to share with you.'

'You are not going anywhere, all right. You are going to be fine. I just have to call the doctors.'

'Could we have avoided all of this if I hadn't met you?'

'Don't. Please don't talk like this,' he said, crying. 'Who was it?'

'The Mlecchas. They robbed us, attacked us.' She swallowed a hard lump and Anuhrad saw her eyes ... they had sunk in. 'Attacked my parents ...' she sobbed, 'Anu, it was wrong. It was so wrong. It's too early for me. For us.'

Anuhrad embraced her and kissed her on the cheek. And then he kissed her mouth and their tears met each other and he pulled back to see her smiling.

'Get that mango,' she said, asking for the fruit that lay a few paces away.

Anuhrad went to fetch it, but by the time he got back to her, the life had seeped out of her, and her eyes were blank.

Whom do I turn to now, Jyoti?

Anuhrad was shivering under heaps of blankets. He was back in his room at the castle. Prahlad sat beside him, patting his back. His young brother didn't say anything but his father did, emerging from the entrance of the room.

'I am sorry, son. It shouldn't have happened.'

Anuhrad clenched his jaw.

'The Mlecchas … I have sent a task force out there to find them.'

'I will join them.' Anuhrad's bloodshot eyes looked at his father in pain. 'I'll join them and kill every last one of those bastards.'

'You shall and we will help you.'

'Why?' he questioned his father. 'Because of me, your reputation was at stake. You didn't want to have anything to do with the outcastes.'

Hiranya knelt down next to his son. 'It doesn't matter, my dear son. I may have been angry then, but I can understand a broken heart. I love you and I don't care about my reputation. I promise to do right by you. But will you promise to do right by me?'

Anuhrad gazed at his father's golden eyes. He never thought that his father – a strict man with rules and norms – would have accepted him back so easily, despite everything that he'd done, despite him choosing another life. He realized that even though he had left his father to fight the battle alone, Hiranya would always be there for him.

'Yes Father,' Anuhrad said, a new determination in his voice. 'From now on, you have my complete loyalty, King of Kashyapuri.'

25

HIRANYAKASHYAP

He knew he was in trouble.

As soon as Hiranya stepped on the slab, the world around him whirled and spun, and he was sucked into a wormhole which spat him out on barren ground.

His eyes surveyed the surroundings and he realized that he'd been teleported somewhere by that pedestal. The world around him looked grey and dead.

Smoke filled the air, and the plants and the trees were either cut or dead. There was a pungent smell of corpses that infiltrated the place and as Hiranya walked forward, he saw a large dam – as high as fifty feet, in front of him. And wrapped around the metal dam was something harsh, something strong – a serpentine tail the colour of melted copper. The head of the beast lifted and Hiranya saw that its eyes were bright like the midday sun. Sharp incisors glinted in the harsh sunlight and the nostrils blew air in gusts. It was a serpent, but looked like a dragon.

Hiranya recognized the beast in this makeshift illusion created by the spirit. He had seen an image in a temple in Pataal where this dragon was worshipped as – *Lord Vritra.* He was a Danav and had a disfigured face, and was always portrayed as a Dragon who held the water dam from Indra. Vritra ruled Illavarti by controlling the water from this dam. He used to ask for high prices from the mortals, before Indra came and used his thunderbolt Vajra to kill Vritra.

Vritra hadn't seen Hiranya yet. He was busy scratching his ears with his claws.

The spirit appeared next to Hiranya. It hissed and said, 'Do you see your opponent?'

'I can't kill my own kind,' Hiranya said.

'It's just a projection of the past,' the spirit said. 'It's not Lord Vritra himself.'

'Why is he my opponent?'

'You shall know soon. For you must remember, your enemy is Indra and you need to know how Indra killed his greatest enemy. Your task is to identify your enemy's weaknesses.'

These Trials … he's training me against Indra's own deceptive powers.

'Was this the Trial for every other challenger?'

'No. The forms in which the Trials of Brahma manifest depend on the challenger himself.'

Hiranya walked forward, leaving the spirit behind. He had no weapons on him, and was clad in just his golden dhoti. His hair was oily and pulled back and his moustache was drenched in sweat. He knew this was just an illusion. Illavarti couldn't have actually looked like this during Vritra's time, but who knew?

The spirit caught up with Hiranya, 'Remember, you must think like Indra. You must think about how he killed Vritra.'

'It was with a Vajra.'

'The Vajra was just an instrument used to launch the attack. Indra knew *where* he had to attack. Find Vritra's weakness and you will get your Vajra to kill him.'

'I thought this Trial was about strength ...' Hiranya said. He was afraid, he could feel the fear inside him bubbling, making him feel nauseous. 'And I won't have any weapons?'

The spirit laughed. 'If it were that easy, they wouldn't be called the Trials of Brahma.' And with that, he dissolved into smoke.

Hiranya was as small as a mouse in front of Vritra, who was on the top of the dam from where water dripped. Hiranya also saw humans building the dam, working on it, worshipping it. He hadn't seen them from afar, and he noticed many, even thousands of them, working at the dam and around it. He saw other Asuras, and they were all copper-skinned, lashing at the humans and forcing them to work even harder.

Hiranya couldn't believe he was here – that he had been transported back in time to when Vritra had been alive.

As he drew closer, he saw the guards that worshipped Vritra approaching on their horses. The Dragon looked down at him from the top of the dam – its crimson-gold eyes blinking.

The guards came up to Hiranya, their spears pointed at him. One of them asked him who he was, and in response, Hiranya pounced from his position and onto the guard, pushing him down and then smashing his fist across his face.

The other guard fell back, his expression confused, clearly wondering who Hiranya was.

But Hiranya didn't stop. He took the spear from the unconscious guard and swung it at the other one, plunging the blade into his chest.

This will grab Vritra's attention.

The desert heat was making him feel uneasy, but he remained still, waiting.

I have to do this for Kayadhu. I have to pass this Trial.

The Dragon hissed, glaring at Hiranya, and then, hooking his talons on the wall of the dam, he leapt from it and landed on the ground, across from Hiranya.

The rest of the people around the dam – the soldiers and the guards – had gathered around, forming a semi-circle and watching the entertainment unfold.

Vritra's claws dug into the earth as the rays of the sun beat over both of them. Hiranya stood there, naked from the waist up, unarmed and unarmoured. He was ready. From this close, he could see that Vritra's skin was thorny, and looked rock solid, like it would be difficult to penetrate.

'Who are you?' Vritra asked, his booming voice making the earth below them tremble. 'And what do you want?'

Hiranya didn't answer.

Instead, he *ran*.

Hiranya ran towards Vritra, as fast as he could, his heart pounding as only one thought rushed through his mind – *Kayadhu*. And as he drew close to Vritra, he sprang from his position and close to Vritra, smacking him on the head.

The impact was not much, but it surprised Vritra, who instantly pulled his long head back.

Hiranya landed back on the ground, kneeling on one of his legs, his fist clenched on the ground as the sand swirled around him. The strength from the Soma felt good – he felt invincible under its influence, like he could control everything around him.

And then he felt a blow strike him. Vritra's tail had swung at him, catching him on his side. It swung again, and instead of leaping over it, Hiranya grabbed it, holding it off. The impact of the tail was so strong that he was pushed back, but he did not let go.

But then the tail rose and Hiranya realized he was suspended in the air, dangling from it … but he used it to his advantage, pushing himself forward and landing on Vritra's neck.

He dug his nails into Vritra's scales and the Dragon roared in anger. Hiranya began to climb the thorny skin.

I need to know where his weakness is. He must have a weakness.

Jumping from one part of Vritra to another, Hiranya reached the top, close to the Dragon's mouth. He tried to see if there was a way to kill him by attacking him there, but it looked difficult. Vritra's teeth were sharp and strong, and as Hiranya got closer, he noticed that the fangs were like mini blades. He grabbed on to them and instead of going inside the mouth, Hiranya slid onto the shoulder of the thorny dragon, grabbing hold of his hard scales. As he made his way to the top, he realized Vritra was swiping at him with his talon … trying to shake him off.

But Hiranya somersaulted in the air, missing the talons by an inch.

When he reached the top of Vritra's head, he saw that hiding on it was an old man who had sparks shooting from his fingers as he moved them, the way a puppeteer would to control the strings of his doll. It looked like he was controlling the dragon the same way.

What is going on?

Suddenly, Hiranya realized the truth. But he didn't say anything. Instead, he pounced on the man and the sparks from his fingers instantly died down, the dragon disappearing with them, as if it had been nothing but smoke and mirrors – an illusion.

Hiranya was holding the man as they fell on the ground, rolling in the dust. Without meaning to, Hiranya's fingers let go of the man. He could feel exhaustion getting the better of him. He opened his eyes and got to his feet, his body feeling weak when …

A blade came at him out of nowhere!

Hiranya stopped it with his arm, letting it cut his skin. He fell back. In front of him stood the old man.

Hiranya saw him clearly now. He was clad in a robe, and his beard was thick around his face. He was not an Asura. He was a Manav.

'Who are you?' Hiranya asked.

The old man didn't answer. Instead, he swung the blade at Hiranya again, who instantly rolled over and grabbed the old man from behind. 'Who are you? Identify yourself!'

As Hiranya held him, he could feel how fragile the Manav was. 'I'm … I'm Tvastr,' the old man answered.

'Tvastr?' Hiranya had heard about him. He was a Vidhyadhara, which explained the dragon illusion. 'Hold on, weren't you one of the young rishis, a powerful magician … and an illusionist,' Hiranya said, a smile on his face.

'Yes,' the old man replied. 'Why are you here?' he asked, as if he knew Hiranya.

'Why did you do it?' Hiranya recalled the legend of Tvastr. 'You are a Manav, aren't you? An architect … a builder who was sent by Indra to recreate Illavarti to suit the needs of the Devas.'

Tvastr nodded. 'Yes, I am. And I am here because this is my finest creation.'

'No, it can't be. Vritra was real. He was not a product of your trickery.'

'No, he wasn't. He was a disfigured king who migrated from Pataal, whom I met and befriended. I tutored him and he became like my son. And he was ill. So when he died, I created this illusion for him, so he would be proud of me … proud of his father.' He knelt down, crying. 'I was always a father to him. I wanted his legacy to live on, so he could be remembered as a Dragon and not as a weakling.'

Hiranya saw how a Deva had acted like a father to an Asura. It was unbelievable.

'I ruled in his stead,' he continued, 'so everyone could know how tough he was, so everyone would worship him and be afraid of him. He told me his plan before his death; he wanted the people to worship him and think that he controlled the waters, and so that's what we did.'

'Why did you betray your kind?'

'Because it doesn't matter where you come from, but where you end up. Both of us forgot about who we were and focused on what we meant to each other.' The old man sighed. 'I was doing what he loved, I was doing it for him and now … everyone will know because of you. He will be just another weak Asura lord and I'll just be an illusionist.'

Hiranya thought about how well the illusion had worked. Vidhyadharas were good at creating images that could also be so real that you could interact with them. But if you found the source, they would disappear, and the trickery behind them would be exposed.

Before Hiranya could say anything, he saw that a long spear was materializing in his hand. And the blade on the spear had a thunderbolt-like symbol.

A Vajra.

Vajras were weapons that carried the symbol of Indra – the thunderbolt. Their speciality was that they were made of obsidian.

The spirit had told Hiranya that when he found out where to attack the dragon, he would receive the weapon with which Indra had killed Vritra.

But Hiranya felt uneasy about killing Tvastr. He knew the deep pain of losing a loved one. And he didn't want to hurt Tvastr.

'Do what Indra did.' The spirit appeared by his side, whispering in his ear. 'Murder him and you will have passed this Trial.'

'But this trial is not about strength …' Hiranya tightened his fist. 'Why … I can't kill a father.'

Tvastr was crying softly before him.

'Exactly.' The spirit smiled. 'And isn't Indra a father?'

Hiranya blinked. And then a chill ran down his spine.

I was ready to kill a father.

'What are these Trials?'

'They are most unpredictable in nature, Asura king, and they will test you. Do the needful or else … you can return home,' the spirit explained. 'The point of the Trials is to bring you to the worst of situations and test whether you can overcome them.'

Hiranya came forward, flaring his nostrils as he grabbed the old man's head and pulled it back, the spear close to his throat.

'Please don't,' the sage begged, 'I will leave all this. Please. I will leave this. Please …'

Hiranya was panting. He could feel the blood rushing to his ears, his heart beating hard.

I have *to do this.*

'Please don't,' Tvastr joined his hands and begged.

The spirit on the side kept urging him on. 'Do it!' his voice hissed. 'Do what Indra did and win this Trial!'

But when Hiranya looked at Tvastr, he saw himself; he saw Prahlad and Anuhrad.

Hiranya let go of the old man and tossed the spear to the side, turning to face the spirit who was looming in the back. 'I can't,' he announced. 'I can't stoop to the level of Indra.'

The spirit didn't say anything, but hissed in anger.

Hiranya blinked and instantly he found himself back in the cave. The beam that was around the pedestal over which he stood, dimmed. The spirit was in the corner, muttering to itself.

'What happened?' Hiranya asked, as he touched his armour. He was standing on the pedestal, as if he'd never left; as if the whole episode with Vritra had never happened.

'This was not how it was supposed to be! You were supposed to kill him. You were supposed to do what your enemy Indra did. But the fact that you didn't, you … you …' The spirit was screaming with pain.

'I lost, didn't I? I have to leave …' Hiranya was disappointed.

But the spirit shook its head. 'I am bound to tell you the truth,' he said, his face twisting. 'Lord Brahma always believed that strength is not defined by taking a life, but by sparing one. It's easy to kill someone, but it's difficult to save a life.'

Of course. The test was never about killing Vritra. It was about doing what Indra didn't – saving Vritra.

Hiranya smirked. He felt relieved. 'What does this mean?'

The spirit shot him a dirty look. 'This means that you … you *passed* the first Trial.'

Hiranya grinned with relief. He had won a lot of contests in his young days, lots of battles and duels, but winning this one – it felt *really* good.

'What next?' he asked, broadening his shoulders.

'We underestimated you. You are unlike your brother. He was strong … but you … you are smart.' The spirit snarled. 'The rules must be changed now.'

'That's not fair!' Hiranya flared his nostrils.

'The Trials of Brahma aren't fair.' The spirit chuckled as it began to flutter around in the room. 'They are just and they keep changing.'

Hiranya clenched his jaw. 'What have they changed into?'

'Your second trial won't be so easy,' the spirit responded. 'Unlike last time, if you win, you will go to the third trial. But if you lose …'

Hiranya waited in anticipation.

'You will *die*.'

And then the spirit laughed.

26
NARASIMHA

'Tonight, we must end this war,' Nara began his speech.

The other Simhas looked up at him. They were all huddled in a small room, which was tough, since all of them were large and wide in their muscular frames. But they were all diligent enough to listen and agree with what their leader was saying. Chenchen was in the corner, arms folded, gazing at Nara as well.

'The war is not between Devas and Asuras. It's between egos. And the root of that ego lies under that bull.' He was referring to the golden bull Nanda, who stood in the middle of the fort of Shiva and signified strength and valour.

He had learnt from Chenchen that the Pashupatastra was underneath that bull which was guarded by the Nagas and the Manavs, the true worshippers of Shiva, ready to attack anyone who got too close, even the ones who were a part of this camp.

'We need to burn the astra down so Andhaka leaves us. And there's no greater weapon out there that could hurt us. The

Pashupatastra doesn't belong here. It never did in this world, and I swear on Lord Vishnu, I hope to him that there will be a time when they won't exist again. But for today, we – as protectors and guardians of this realm, at the side of Dharma, the residents of New Vaikuntha … ' he said, referring to the Simha homeland, which was mythically called the Abode of Vishnu, 'We have the responsibility of ending the reign of this nuclear weapon. Are you all ready?'

All of them nodded and then slammed their chests with their fists.

'Remember, no one has to be killed, only subdued.' He turned to the left flank of his group, that was standing close to the lamps. 'Take the eastern front.' Then he turned to the right. 'You all take the western one. I'll take the middle and go underground to search for the weapon.'

The response was a thunderous roar.

'Let's do it!' Nara returned the roar with his own, his golden skin glimmering in the shades of the fire.

As they dispersed and went out in the dead of the night, Nara walked up to Chenchen, who smiled when she saw him coming. 'You are doing well.'

Nara smiled in return. 'It's a choice, right? To be better.'

'You do realize Bhairav won't be happy about it?'

'I know. I'll take the Pride and leave for Vaikuntha then.'

At that, Chenchen moved uncomfortably. 'I see.'

Nara realized the reason behind her expression changing from concern to annoyance. He had begun understanding her. 'You are welcome to join us.'

'Only if you return alive,' she chuckled. 'What about Indra? Will he take this lightly?'

'Do you think so? Because I doubt it!'

Nara and Chenchen went out and stood under the moon's silver gaze. The guards were standing around Nandi as if nothing was happening.

'Wish me luck,' Nara said to Chenchen.

'You don't need luck. You need a miracle,' she said. 'And may Lord Vishnu give you as many as you need.'

Nara smiled as he gestured his Pride to move forward as planned. They all wore gloves, since they didn't want to hurt their peers, even by accident. Chenchen stayed behind while Nara rushed towards the front.

Nara moved in the middle, his gloved hands tightening as he saw his men had begun roaring and taking the people down – some were lassoed and some were tied to the ground. Nara had to do nothing but walk straight through. As one of the Nagas came out of nowhere, Nara instantly dodged and tossed the armed Naga to one of his men.

He saw people exiting their homes, taking in the rebellion that was happening. And he was okay with it.

This had to be done.

The light in Bhairav's tower was out, and so he had some time before Bhairav could realize what was happening.

Nara walked up to the large twenty-feet-tall bull. It had a glistening sheen all over it. The bull's four legs stood on a large wooden door.

I have to move them.

Nara began to push the bull and as he did, his muscles flexed, his Rudraksh beads broke apart and he gritted his teeth. Slowly, the bull began moving in the other direction …

'Don't do it,' a fragile voice called from the back.

Nara turned to see a matted-haired, bearded, bluish-skinned man standing behind him. His body was covered in scars, and he wore a leopard skin. It was Bhairav. At a distance, Veerbhadra fought against Nara's army.

Nara and Bhairav stood looking at each other.

'I have to,' Nara declared. 'You know that.'

'You are wrong. By destroying the Pashupatastra, you would have ensured that Andhaka wins.'

'But he won't get the weapon. For me, that's a win.'

'But imagine the lives we can save with the weapon!'

'And destroy many in the process too,' Nara clenched his jaw. 'Have you seen what these Astras do? The mutations they cause through radiations when dropped from above?'

Bhairav had no defence. 'I shouldn't have sent you to that village.'

'Well, you did,' Nara shrugged. 'But even if you hadn't, I would have found out the truth eventually. The weapon is bad for all of us, and none of us deserve it. Not you, a Shiva, not Indra, the so-called king, and not the Asuras.'

Bhairav pulled out his trident from his back. 'All right then, I have no choice but to stop you.'

'Why?' Nara felt betrayed when he saw that his friend was ready to kill him for a weapon.

'Because Lord Rudra wanted it to be safe and I follow his instructions. That's what I have always done. Even when I lost my son, I did what he wanted me to do – go back to where my post was instead of finding my son.'

Nara shook his head. 'And what has it yielded you? We are in a losing war. And Andhaka is using sorcery to keep himself alive. Imagine what he must have planned for the weapon. But if we take it away from him, it's over. We are safe.'

'But I cannot disobey Lord Rudra!' And with that, Bhairav came forward with the trident, ready to attack Nara.

Nara rolled to the other side, grabbing Bhairav from the back, taking care to not seriously hurt his friend.

'We don't have to do this. Please, understand!' he cried.

Bhairav elbowed him hard in the abdomen and Nara fell back.

'You don't understand!' Bhairav screamed, amidst the roaring violence in the background. 'You don't understand,' he repeated as he began to plunge and jab his trident in the snow close to Nara's legs, 'the only reason I'm a Shiva is because of my undying loyalty to Lord Rudra. The title of Shiva is an earned title and I earned it by showing what others didn't have …'

'Vision!' Nara yelled and as the trident came close, he grabbed the weapon with his two hands. 'You don't have vision, Bhairav. You are not surviving. You are dying and you need to see that.

'Being a Shiva is not about loyalty.' Nara pushed back the weapon with force and sprang up to his feet. 'It's about doing the right thing. You are not blind like Andhaka, but you are blinded by the power that the Pashupatastra holds.'

The Shiva lunged forward and roared in Nara's face, summoning his fearsome persona. Nara instantly dodged the weapon and punched Bhairav in the gut, pulling the trident away.

'Being a Shiva is about protecting your people.' Nara tossed the weapon to the side. 'Not destroying them in this fruitless war. Indra has got to you. He's not a good man. I don't even know what makes a man good. But whatever it is, he doesn't have it. There will be a day he will be tired of the Asuras and he will use this weapon to destroy countless people for the sake of his image.'

And that was when Bhairav's face changed. Suddenly, he stood still.

Nara faced him and nodded. 'I don't want that day to come, Lord Shiva,' he said, calling Bhairav by his title. 'I don't want to give him that luxury of choice of using the Pashupatastra one day. I want to take that choice away from him.'

'I'm sure he didn't send you to do this,' Bhairav seemed calmer now.

'No, he didn't. He told me I had an opportunity to save innocents this time by defeating Andhaka. I thought Andhaka was our enemy. No. He isn't. He's just a pawn in the big game – the big game of ego. The enemy was always out there and that is this weapon,' Nara said, pointing to the statue of Nandi.

Bhairav didn't say anything, but just panted and gestured for his men to stop fighting. Nara did the same.

'Thank you,' Nara smiled.

Bhairav walked to the bull and pushed it a little to reveal the small trapdoor in the floor. And then he opened it and began to climb down the hole.

Nara followed, entering the cave which was lit by torches. He walked behind Bhairav, who led him to a large clearing where the Pashupatastra was kept. It was a long, vertical weapon which had a gem studded in one end of it. It looked a little like a crossbow, but much more complicated. But instead of arrows, it had boulder-sized projectiles, which were perhaps the actual villains.

'This is a launcher to shoot them,' Bhairav gestured to the device. He pointed to the gem next. 'This is the lever which helps to launch the explosives, which only burst on heavy impact. They are made of Lady Mohini's ashes, comprising of minute Manis, that lead to the deadly explosions. The entire thing is called the Pashupatastra, but one can say that these rocks are the actual weapon. The launcher is just an instrument to release them.'

Bhairav began to pull the rocks out and started displaying them on the ground. 'I sure as hell hope,' Bhairav began as he took the torch in his hand and put it close to the rocks, 'you are right about this.'

'Do it,' Nara said.

Bhairav nodded and then he lowered the torch. The fire engulfed the rocks as soon as it touched them.

Nara, with his crossed arms, watched the fire of the weapon, finally taking the real villain of this war to its end. And he was happy, for by destroying this, he knew … he knew he had saved so many innocents. His purpose for finally coming here, for being pulled back into the war, was complete. The beams of the light that came from the fire reflected on their faces as Bhairav said glumly, 'What do we do now?'

'We set up a meeting,' Nara said, 'with Andhaka.'

'And do what?' his voice was grave.

Nara looked from the flames to the Shiva. 'We call a truce.'

27

HOLIKA

They were in the prison again.

Holika kept her twin swords on the table in front of her and then sat opposite Narada. At first glance, Holika noticed that Narada seemed like an ordinary old man, but there was something sinister under the surface, especially when she entered the room and saw Prahlad and Narada arguing.

Let's hope my nephew is not involved.

Her guards stood outside the cell. Inside, the lamps cast pale shadows on the wall. The smell in the cell was tough to tolerate, and there was no wind at all. It was a suffocating space.

'You've got the wrong man,' Narada said, his arms bound tightly with ropes.

'Could be, but I never liked you anyway,' she shrugged. She wasn't sure whether Narada was guilty, but her instincts told her that he was. She had to provoke him, make him talk so she could get to his nest and then burn every one of those spiders that threatened the empire.

He sighed. 'I don't know what I should say. So I will remain silent.'

'Do you know why I chose to free myself from the rule of my brother?' she asked, and Narada shook his hand. 'It's because I was tired of his rule. He was not Hiranyaksha, and you know that. Hiranyaksha was strong, unlike Banjan, who is … meek, fragile; especially after Kayadhu, and it hurts me to see him that way. And that's why I have my autonomy, so I can do what I want with my paramilitary force. So please, I ask you again … tell me what I want to know, otherwise I can do whatever I want to you and no law or trial will be able to help you.'

Narada face crumpled and his wrinkles deepened. 'Don't you understand, my lady? I'm innocent …' and before he could complete, Holika smashed his head against the table, breaking his nose as he began to bleed and groan. 'You … shouldn't have …' he was close to tears of pain, 'done that.'

'I can kill you right now or I can set you free,' Holika said casually. 'Or I can make you weep from pain for the rest of your life. I like the last option, don't you?'

Suddenly, Narada's brows cleared. The tears stopped, and he looked at her with a smile. Instead of being frightened, he chuckled. 'Tsk, tsk.'

Holika was confused by the sudden change in his behaviour. 'What?' she asked.

'You pretend you are so brave, but you've forgotten, haven't you? Oh well, you probably haven't.' He leaned back in his chair. 'After all, how does one forget what happens when you lose a child … twice?'

Holika gritted her teeth.

He's bringing up my past.

'Losing once is hard, losing *twice*, oh dear, that must have been terrible, mustn't it?' He chuckled through his bloody nose. 'Tell me, how does it feel to have miscarriages that finally lead to being abandoned by your husband? And now, to spite him, you are hurting innocent men like me. I mean, how does it feel doing that?'

Holika suddenly felt like she was back in that horrible time of her life. Those initial days when she'd been so weak, so exhausted. Always in bed.

'I can't be here. I need some air,' he said. 'I have to leave for Pataal. Coming here, it was not right for us. We were never right.'

She was in the bed, tears in her eyes. 'Please don't. I need you.'

'Holi.' He knelt beside her bed. 'Don't you understand? I want a child and you can't give me one.' He was a noble himself. Holika knew that if Hiranya found out, he would get her husband killed.

But she would never tell Hiranya the truth.

Because she loved her husband.

Narada was in the background, calmly listening to everything. He was her doctor, her guide who helped her through her problems.

'I'm your wife. You can't just leave me like this,' she whined, even though she knew that, as per Asura law, a man had every

right to leave a woman if she was unable to bring forth offspring, for procreation in Asura culture is of utmost importance.

'That doesn't mean I don't love you. We have tried twice and failed. Each time, as hard as it is for you, it's hard for me too. I'm sorry. I need some space,' he said, kissing her on the head. 'I need to think straight. I'll return. I promise.'

But he never did. Hiranya asked multiple times about him, but Holika had kept what happened to herself.

With a cry, she returned to the present and threw her chair back, grabbing Narada by the throat. 'You don't have the right to comment on my life, vermin. My pitiful brother brought you here to the capital, even though you were a believer, out of guilt for the crime he committed against your Gurukul. To be honest, I don't care what happened to those children,' she lied. She had indeed cried for the children, and had raged at Hiranya, but Narada didn't need to know that. 'All I care about is you telling me the truth. Where are your men?'

'Does it matter?' he shrugged. 'If I tell you, you kill me and then go and kill them. If I don't tell you, you kill me but you don't get to kill them.'

'So you are a part of the Vishnusena?'

He nodded, a manic grin on his face. 'Spearhead it, in fact, and believe me when I say this … there's much more that we are yet to do, much more than what we've already done. This is just the beginning.'

Holika flared her nostrils. She grabbed one of her twin swords and was ready to swipe it right across the old man's throat when she heard it – an explosion!

Holika turned to see her guards, who were as astonished as she was. Holika threw an inquisitive glance at Narada, who looked confused himself. She hurried out, gesturing to one of her guards to stay behind with Narada to make sure he didn't escape.

As she moved along the cells, the other prisoners began to yell, scream and spit at her.

Just then another explosion ripped through the air.

Holika came to a standstill when she saw that before her, a fire was raging and black, thick smoke rose from it. From the smoke, she saw black-cloaked figures emerging, their swords drawn. All of them were marked by a lotus symbol on their chest.

The Vishnusena! They are behind this!

Holika didn't wait. She instantly sprinted forward, her twin swords drawn. She slammed her body against one of the Vishnusena followers, plunging her blades inside him.

Another appeared but she deflected his sword with hers as she kicked him on the chest and he fell against the cell doors.

Everything was in chaos as Holika entered the smoke and two blades came out of nowhere. Using her twin swords, she deflected them, but her guard couldn't, taking the blow and falling to the ground, dead.

Holika closed her eyes and focused on the next attack. For a few minutes, she swiped her blades and cut through her enemies.

When she was done, she came out of the smoke to find a line of corpses of her men. One of them coughed. He was still alive, though barely.

Holika knelt next to him and leaned forward. 'How did they enter?' she asked him.

'The … the prison guards were called for an urgent meeting by the king.' Her guard coughed blood and went on. 'There was an assassination rumour, so his highness wanted as many soldiers at his disposal as he could.'

That's too much of a coincidence!

Holika waited till he closed his eyes and stopped breathing, and then stood and walked on. When she reached the end of the corridor, she finally saw that the entire prison fort was overrun by black-cloaked men with lotus symbols on their chest.

There are too many. It's good I didn't have too many of my men here.

Holika had to be smart about it. She couldn't stay here. She turned and walked rapidly to the other end of the fort, where a field led downwards to the stream. She was on the first floor, since Narada's cell was on that floor.

But what if they open all the cells and let the prisoners out? No. That won't be the Vishnusena's way of living. No matter how bad we are, the prisoners we keep – they won't be freed.

Holika took a deep breath, relaxed her body as she saw the plain over which she had to jump. She sheathed her twin blades at the back and stood on the ledge.

And then she jumped.

She felt her body fly through the air and then land on the ground. She rolled to her side and jumped up on her feet, letting the pain shoot through her. She took another deep breath, letting it subside, and then she looked up. There were sirens, fire blazers, and horns being blown. She had to get her army and clear the prison of all the Vishnusena terrorists.

But they won! They bloody won!

Gritting her teeth, Holika couldn't believe she had been this close to killing the terrorists' leader, but no! And now Narada was free and back with his gang.

As she walked to the main gates of the capital, only one thing troubled her – *why had half of the guards been called away by Prahlad?*

She was loathe to think it, but she also knew that her instincts never lied.

Could he be ... could he actually be a part of this?

28
NARASIMHA

Ravens were being sent to Andhaka. A truce had apparently been declared.

Surprisingly, Bhairav had listened to Nara about this. But even Bhairav knew, deep down, that it was the right thing to do. Another raven was to be sent to Indra, informing him about the burning down of the Pashupatastra and the probable outcome of this – the end of the war with Andhaka.

To commemorate the truce, there was a small celebration organized – people danced, flutes played in the background, a bonfire was lit, around which all of the people in the fort gathered to celebrate.

Nara stayed back, his arms wrapped around himself to beat the cold. He was content – he felt like he had achieved what he set out to do and that was the greatest feeling ever. And then he touched his chest to see whether a symbol had finally appeared on him, the symbol of Vishnu —

It hasn't. I saved people without becoming the Avatar.

He breathed in relief. He didn't want to be the chosen one for this age. He closed his eyes, recalling what Rudra had said to him …

'He doesn't know himself,' Rudra had said about Indra, coughing as he spoke. 'But I know. I met one of the rishis. They told me ... this Yug, this Age, it is different than the previous ones, more twisted than the rest.'

'What are you saying?' Nara asked.

'You can't be the hero who saves this age. You need to delay it as much as you can, to the point … to the point that it's too late. So that the prophecy has no scope of coming to fruition.'

'What are you thinking about?' a voice came from behind him.

Nara turned to see Chenchen. There was such peace and calm on her beautiful face. He felt the guilt of hurting her parents, of killing them, rise within him again. Even after all that she'd suffered, she had so much strength, more than any of those people out there; she had the strength to forgive Nara. 'I don't know,' he lied. 'I am just happy, I guess.'

'You should be. Have the ravens been sent to Andhaka?'

'Tomorrow morning,' Nara said. 'They are also being sent to Indra.'

'Indra is going to be so angry,' she chuckled, like the idea of troubling Indra delighted her. She stood next to him and looked at him, as light, melodious music played in the background. 'So what now?'

'I don't know.' Nara arched his brows and then he turned to see Chenchen. 'Are you married?'

Chenchen was taken aback. 'Where are you going with this?' she said, and then a smile came on her face.

'No, I'm just uh …' He scratched the back of his neck nervously. 'I'm just asking.'

'No, I am not. Though I used to be,' she said.

He looked at her questioningly.

'Widowed,' she explained shortly. 'He was killed.'

Once again, Nara was horrified by all that she had lost, and in such a short span of time. 'By?' he asked.

'A bunch of Mlecchas,' she said, shaking her head. 'They worked with the Asuras.'

'I'm sorry.' Nara wanted to ask more, but felt like it would have been inappropriate to probe.

'It's all right,' she said. 'His death brought me here, where I thought I would be able to heal people.'

'You have lost a lot of people in your life.'

Chenchen nodded. 'I wish things could have been different, but they are what they are. I have to live with it. I have decided to stop being close to people now.'

'Of course, I understand.'

'I feel like it's a curse to be with me. Whoever I get close to meets with a terrible fate.'

'No, it isn't. It's a privilege,' Nara said softly.

She looked up. 'You say that now, but I'm a fire that'll burn you.'

Nara stepped closer to her but didn't touch her. 'Do you see me burn?'

She sighed, as she leaned her head forward. He leaned forward too, their foreheads touching each other. 'I'm glad we met,' she said.

'Perhaps fate made us meet.'

'We almost dictated fate,' she said.

'You are good with words, aren't you?'

'I'm a writer. I'm supposed to be.'

He pulled his head back. 'Really? Would I have read anything you've written?'

'Only if you've managed to sneak into my room.'

Nara laughed. 'Can I hug you?'

'You always ask before you do. Why?'

'I believe consent is important.'

And she smiled as she came forward, embracing him tightly. He hugged her back. 'What is your weakness, Nara?' she asked.

'Mine?' he held on to her and for a moment he wanted to say, *you, you are my weakness*. 'It's ...'

And then they started as they heard a loud noise. The horns were being blown.

'Someone is attacking the front gates!' Chenchen cried.

Nara turned and saw the main gates being rammed from the outside, and finally give in, bursting open. Rakshasas poured through the gates. The archers appeared, slinging and shooting arrows across the horizon.

'Get the children!' Nara told Chenchen, who instantly ran towards the kids, who were standing around the bonfire, looking petrified.

Nara walked to the gate, pulling off his gloves. He lunged towards the Rakshasas, slashing and plunging his claws in them, while also trying to find Chenchen in the crowd. He saw her gathering the children and guiding them to the nearby sheds.

And then Nara saw a single arrow fly past everyone and make its way to where Chenchen stood with the kids. In the same instant, she saw it too, and stepped between the arrow and the children, shielding them from it and taking the blow. The arrow plunged deep into her waist.

'Run!' she cried to the children as they scampered towards the shed. She fell to the ground, and blood began pooling around her.

No!

I can't let that happen.

For Nara, everything was suddenly a blur. The battle being fought around him – the Simhas and Nagas fighting the Rakshasas and the Pishach – everything paled. All he could see was Chenchen, lying on the ground, her blood seeping into the snow.

He saw the Rakshasas spot her too, and move towards her.

And then he couldn't control it – the surge of anger that boiled inside him grew to such an extent that he lunged and in one leap, had scaled the distance between himself and Chenchen. He fought the Rakshasas around Chenchen in a blind fury, roaring so loudly and fiercely that for a second, the Rakshasas fell back, stunned.

One of them came towards Nara with his blade, but Nara deflected the blow with ease, his claws scratching the Rakshas on the face and kicking him in the groin.

More were coming towards him but Nara didn't care. He circled around the bleeding Chenchen, his claws bright with blood as he roared at the enemies, warning them to not come close.

Finally, the Rakshasas retreated, afraid of Nara's fury.

As the enemy fell back, the Simhas finally overpowering them, Nara realized that this was not about defeating Bhairav and his followers; it was about crippling them … again and again and again.

He knelt on the ground, grabbing hold of Chenchen's hand. She looked as pale as the snow around them. 'Are you okay?' he asked, his voice choked with worry.

She smiled. 'I am … I am …' she closed her eyes, clearly in pain.

'Narasimha!' cried Bhairav from the back.

Nara didn't turn, and continued to hold on to Chenchen, lifting her close to his chest as he unsuccessfully tried to stop the bleeding by pressing on her wound.

'You wanted peace! Are you happy with it now?' Bhairav shouted, as he came and stood in front of Nara. 'Now do you see? There is no peace here, not with Andhaka, believe me.'

Nara's eyes were bloodshot, and in his rage, he felt like lunging at the Shiva too, tearing at him with his claws, but he tried to control himself, gripping on to Chenchen.

'We need to fight back! And now we don't even have the Pashupatastra any more,' Bhairav said. 'Do you have a plan?'

Nara couldn't think of one. 'We will figure it out,' he said through gritted teeth.

'You better! Because now, we are going to kill him!' And with that, Bhairav left, leaving Nara with Chenchen. 'Get the nurses!' Bhairav called to someone, and soon, a group of nurses ran up to Chenchen and began to move her away.

Before she was taken inside, Chenchen held Nara's hand, a soft smile on her lips, her eyes half-open. 'I know your weakness now …' she said, coughing blood as she spoke.

Nara didn't say anything. He waited for her to complete.

'I know it,' she paused, and then said, her voice soft. 'It's *anger*.'

29

ANUHRAD

What does Andhaka know that I don't?

Anuhrad shifted on his bed as his mind churned with ideas and thoughts. He couldn't stop thinking about the time he had run away from home. The time he met *her*. It was a few years after his mother's death, and he felt a void within him that no one could fill. And then he met *her* … a Nishad, a forest dweller, away from the caste divides, away from the labels of high-borns and low-borns. The Nishad had no religion. They had no system or an organization. They lived a free and unfettered life.

A life Anuhrad wanted – so much and so badly.

After his mother's death, his father had been tough on him, forced him to be a better fighter, a better warrior – trained him to hurt those who threatened the fabric of their empire.

She was my solace.

Anuhrad opened his eyes and watched the ceiling. He didn't want to remember those tender moments. He didn't want to remember anything about that time. He sat up straight on his bed. His long hair was tied with a strand of rope. He held one end of it, feeling the coarseness.

She gave me this.

Anuhrad jumped to his feet and moved to the corridors, towards Andhaka's room. He had somehow managed to spend the night in his cousin's castle. It was not the ideal place to stay – cold, damp and dark as it was.

Andhaka wants to destroy the Asura Empire.

And he wants my help?

Destruction of the Asura Empire meant the destruction and death of Hiranyakashyap, his father.

I can't let him do that. My father accepted me even when I betrayed him.

Anuhrad reached Andhaka's door and knocked on it. He didn't know why he was there, but it was something Andhaka had said that had drawn him there – *we are both made out of tragedy.*

Anuhrad understood now.

Andhaka's tragedy was abuse.

Mine was loss.

Anuhrad realized that Andhaka's room's door was open, and he went in. He stood next to his cousin's bed, as he snored in his sleep. He wasn't wearing his blindfold.

I wanted to avenge her.

The thought hit Anuhrad with a force that surprised him.

Anuhrad saw the pale-looking Andhaka lying there. He seemed different without his blindfold, in his sleep.

'You think that I would let the empire my father built be destroyed by your revenge against the Asuras? Andhaka, you are not an Asura, and you are weak.'

And I have to end you.

It was a sudden anticipation, a cool desire with which Anuhrad came close to Andhaka and clamped his hand over his cousin's mouth. For a moment, Andhaka remained asleep, and then he opened his eyes and his skin flamed as he tried to move Anuhrad's tough frame out of his way – but he couldn't. Anuhrad's hand was pressed hard over his mouth and nose, not letting him breath.

Tears came into Anuhrad's eyes as he pushed down on Andhaka. He couldn't believe he was going to kill someone who had suffered so much in his life; who had been abused by his own father.

I can't do it.

Suddenly, Anuhrad took his hand off Andhaka's mouth. Andhaka gasped for air and sat up on his bed, but didn't say anything.

Anuhrad closed his eyes, wiping his tears. 'I'm sorry. I don't know what got into me,' he said, but Andhaka didn't respond. Instead, he had turned away from Anuhrad and looked like he was staring at something else … something close to the door.

Isn't he blind?

He looked at his cousin's irises, which looked perfectly fine.

Anuhrad turned his head to look at the door too, and found an odd, familiar person standing at the door – a hunched, bald and blindfolded man who came out of the shadows.

Andhaka!

There were two of them in the same room. One was blind and one wasn't. The one at the door resembled the man Anuhrad had talked to earlier.

Anuhrad didn't say anything, but he understood a little bit. Before he could speak, the man at the door said, 'I am glad you didn't kill me.'

'What is going on?' Anuhrad asked.

'I'm glad you didn't kill me, hmmm. Now I know I can trust you.'

'Trust me with what?'

'With the secret, hmmm.' Andhaka's high-pitched voice brimmed with excitement. 'Come, I shall show you something.'

'Who is he?' Anuhrad asked, pointing to the other Andhaka, still sitting up in the bed.

'That is the secret, hmmm. Come,' Andhaka gestured. 'Forget him. He sleeps there for the assassins if they ever come by, which is now even more necessary, after the attack we launched yesterday.'

Anuhrad couldn't believe what he was witnessing, but he began following Andhaka, who took him downstairs. Anuhrad saw Andhaka using the wall as a way of directing himself.

They soon reached the underground cellar.

'Why wasn't he blind?' Anuhrad asked about the fake Andhaka.

'Because the things I went through, I didn't want other versions of mine to go through them too.'

'Other *versions*? How many of you are there?'

'As many as I want. My enemies must believe that every time they kill me, two of me shall rise.'

The cellar opened to an almost dark room, but of course the darkness meant nothing to Andhaka. 'Take the lamp,' he gestured for Anuhrad to take the torch on the wall.

Anuhrad followed Andhaka into the leaky cellar. He could hear rats scurrying about. But as his eyes adjusted to the darkness, Anuhrad could see that the cellar was full of weapons and armours and … beds.

'Why didn't you kill me?' Andhaka asked. 'You had the opportunity.'

'I pitied you,' Anuhrad responded honestly. 'You have gone through a lot and I just thought it was wrong of me to cause you more pain.'

'What I went through is my fate and it's sealed. Nothing to pity about it now.'

And then, Andhaka stamped his feet. Anuhrad looked around and saw figures appearing out of the darkness. And there was something about them – they were all close to Andhaka's height, pale as the moon and hairless. And they had the same facial structure, even though their faces were all slightly different from Andhaka's. Anuhrad realized that if one put a blindfold on them, they'd look almost identical to his cousin.

'Who are they?' he asked. There were more than a dozen of them, hiding like rats here.

'Me, myself and I,' Andhaka walked around, touching each of them. 'I found my lookalikes. Well, not really. I *made* my lookalikes.'

'Why would you do that?'

'I was burnt to death, hmmm, Anuhrad. By my adoptive father. I could never fight. I knew that …' Andhaka explained gleefully in an urgent whisper. 'I knew I had to find an alternative. That's when I found my doppelganger. He was an albino, like me, and an idea struck me. I would find my duplicates; they didn't have to be exactly like me, but just about similar enough. I'd adopt them and teach them how to fight. And now due to this, whenever there's a war, I send one of myself out to fight in my stead. And when I die in the battlefield, I rise up again … because I never die. I live. I am immortal.' Andhaka laughed, waving his arms to take in his doppelgangers. 'I taught them how to fight, how to master their senses. And how wonderful it has been, how entertaining, to see people terrified of me.'

Anuhrad arched his brows. 'How do you know they won't betray you?'

'Because they are me. They believe in me, in what I stand for. These sacrifices are a part of the bigger picture, where we all will rule and there will be no Devas and no Asuras. It will be so much fun,' Andhaka rubbed his hands in glee.

'If you think you can stop the Asuras, you are wrong. I will stop you.'

'Then you should have killed me!' Andhaka exclaimed. 'But you didn't, hmmm? You know what I know about your lady love, the one who was killed during the Mleccha rampage?

Anuhrad froze. He felt his muscles tense up. 'What?' he asked in a whisper.

'I was the one who hired them, the Melcchas.' Andhaka smiled.

Anuhrad was taken aback. He lunged forward, rage blinding him. He wanted to kill Andhaka, but Andhaka raised his hand and said, 'Hear me out. The reason why we are together right now is because we are who we are out of tragedy and the manipulations of our fathers. I didn't hire the Mlecchas because I wanted to. Your father made me. He wanted you to return.'

No!

'I don't believe you,' Anuhrad said through gritted teeth.

'Search my right pocket.'

Anuhrad did as Andhaka asked and pulled out a paper, curled and yellowed with age.

'I kept it with me for so many years because I knew I would end up showing it to you. I wanted you to learn the truth about our fathers. I wanted this to be the proof. Unfortunately, I never had the proof of Hiranyaksha's abuse, but you do, of your father's wrongdoing.' Andhaka sighed. 'It's a royal decree, which came straight from your father's office when I was in charge of a task force in the Empire,' he said.

Anuhrad began reading the decree, and it was … it *was* his father's writing. It ordered the extermination of the Nishad camp in the forest, the camp *she* had lived in.

And at the end of the decree, Hiranyakashyap had added a postscript. '*I want them dead so I can have my son back. He's destined for greater things, not for a carefree and careless life.*'

'I'm sorry, Anuhrad. He killed your love.' Andhaka lowered his head. 'And now I believe, it's your opportunity to kill what he loves most – his empire. Join me.'

Anuhrad felt weak, his knees almost buckling under the weight of the revelation. He felt betrayed and wanted to bash his head against the wall for being so stupid.

Of course, it was him. He never wanted me to be with a Nishad.

'I propose now …' Andhaka came forward, keeping his burnt hands on Anuhrad, 'that we join hands, for a greater cause.'

Anuhrad didn't hesitate this time. He felt his anger boil and spill over, as he lifted his head and looked at Andhaka.

'Yes,' he said.

30

PRAHLAD

Prahlad knew he had done the right thing.

By pulling the guards away from the prison, he had given the Vishnusena an opportunity to attack the prison fort. And he was glad about it. They did exactly what they had promised – they didn't free the other prisoners, and didn't hurt any of the other workers there. They only went for the guards, killed them and saved Narada.

The thought of betraying his family terrorized him. He knew if he got caught – he'd be disowned and executed for it.

But for now, he concentrated on the road.

His face was covered almost completely, his body too. He had no guard with him.

The night was young as he walked the quiet lanes of Kashyapuri. He walked towards the underground trenches where the real heroes waited – the heroes he had helped by betraying his capital. Would he be tried for treason? Of course, but he didn't need to think about it just yet.

Prahlad came close to a small lane and saw two urchins standing outside, looking as idle as ever. At the sight of Prahlad, they were alarmed and pulled out small daggers.

And then Prahlad took off the wraps and showed them his face.

One of the urchins said to the other, 'He's expected, aye.'

The other one nodded and told Prahlad to go in and walk straight down till he found an inn.

Prahlad followed his instructions, and soon, he was standing before the darkly lit inn. The building was tall, with arched windows and doors. Prahlad saw that there were people of all ages around the inn, talking among themselves. All of them were dirty and greasy but Prahlad could see that despite that, they looked like they were all from good, decent families.

As Prahlad walked closer, they all quietened down and turned to look at him. Prahlad could tell that they knew who he was, and for some reason, the thought made him feel uncomfortable and self-conscious.

He went to the door and before he could even knock, it opened and a girl jumped out, hugging him tightly.

It was Dhriti.

He was taken aback for a moment, and then returned her embrace.

'You did it!' she grinned, pulling back and, as if realizing what she'd done, blushing furiously. 'Oh, I'm sorry, heh!' Prahlad saw that she'd pinned fresh lavender to her hair, and recalled how she loved flowers. She looked like she was back to her jolly self as she grabbed his hand and led him inside.

Prahlad saw men in black cloaks who pulled away their hoods when they saw him enter. They were sitting and chatting with each other. Some were sharpening their weapons while others were meditating. It was a war camp in itself, a nest. If Holika found this place, she would burn the whole thing down.

'Like this, we also have other hideouts,' Dhriti explained as they climbed the stairs to go on the first floor. 'And we are very good at hiding. The lookouts outside let us know exactly who is coming and we instantly change our guise and make this appear like a regular inn. And no one knows any better.'

Prahlad nodded as they came into the corridor with more people. In some of the rooms, he saw men and women chatting, some even dozing off.

Prahlad and Dhriti came to the last room and then she just gestured for him to enter it.

'You should go in. He's waiting.' She smiled.

Prahlad nodded, but before he could open the door, Dhriti leaned forward and kissed him on the cheek. 'Best of luck!' she said. 'Hope you do well for yourself.'

And then she left.

Prahlad was frozen for a moment and then touched his cheek. It was warm, and he felt a pleasant glow within him.

Still smiling, he walked inside, entering a small room. A small idol stood on one end, and in front of it kneeled Narada, praying. Stacks of books were kept in one corner. Prahlad saw plans displayed on the wall – from blueprints of major Asura structures and large statues of the previous Asura kings, to the majestic gambling dens and the lowliest brothels that Hiranya had sanctioned.

After praying, Narada came to his feet and faced Prahlad. He had colourful beads around his neck, and a bruised, bandaged nose. Without saying a word, he came forward and embraced Prahlad gently. 'Thank you, my child. Dhriti told me what you did for me, for us.'

'Of course,' Prahlad said, his brows furrowing.

'You seem conflicted.'

'I am betraying my father.' Prahlad felt his heart getting heavy as he leaned back on the wall. 'What do you think, Guruji? Shouldn't I be conflicted?'

'I know, and I understand. Truth be told, I see no point in including you in this. My war is not against your race, it's against the people who hold important positions in this capital and exploit their power. It is to bring forth the age of Vishnu again. Don't you agree?'

'Of course.' Prahlad arched his brows.

'Believe me, pray to Lord Vishnu and you shall feel the power, the brilliance of his greatness in you.'

'But I am a demon,' Prahlad couldn't help but feel something surging inside him – an insurmountable amount of grief that had been haunting him for years.

'Lord Vishnu accepts everyone. He only believes in one thing and that is in your karma. If your deeds are pure and justified, he shall accept you.' He gestured to the idol of Vishnu in the room and told Prahlad to sit down before it. 'You shall feel the greatness of him. Just believe in him and forget all your preconceived notions that have been propagated by the atheism your father practises.'

Prahlad sat cross-legged on the ground and closed his eyes. He began to chant Lord Vishnu's name and felt himself relaxing. Everything seemed to stop and he felt a presence, a warmth inside him that seemed to softly brush across his soul.

It feels like home.

For a moment, he felt like he was floating and he smelled a fragrance in the air and a flute playing in his ears. It was as if Lord Vishnu had descended from the heavens for Prahlad.

And then he opened his eyes to see Narada, who was smiling down at him.

'Why do I feel so content?' Prahlad asked.

'For you have found faith, my dear boy,' Narada said. 'Faith in something brings you closer to the love you deserve and need.'

Prahlad got to his feet, smiling brightly. He didn't feel like he was betraying his father any more, because he knew he was doing everything for the right reasons.

'I don't want to take you deeper into this,' Narada said, putting his hand on Prahlad's shoulder. 'I would suggest you leave this city before we burn everything down.'

'But I would like to help.'

'Are you sure?'

I have never been so sure of anything in my life.

'Of course, I am,' Prahlad said, conviction burning in his eyes.

Narada softly smiled as he led Prahlad to a wall that was covered with battle plans. Prahlad saw that Narada was planning to ban wrestling arenas and liquor vendors, and kill every member of the Asura race, whether they belonged to the nobility or the streets, to bring the purist vision of Vishnusena – no Asura would walk through this city again.

And all of it seemed extreme; not required.

'I plan to do something soon, and I will require your assistance,' Narada said.

'Yes,' Prahlad nodded.

Narada pointed to the board where the blueprint of an establishment were drawn. 'I would like you to distract the guards while we burn down the brothel that plagues this city. It's a corrupt institution which funds the pockets of Shand and the treasury,' he said. 'Lord Vishnu would abide it.'

'What about the people inside it?' Narada asked.

Narada didn't flinch. 'They are part of it, aren't they? They have to go down with it too.'

It seemed extreme, and Prahlad didn't like it. The idea of killing so many women and children bothered him.

But this must be Lord Vishnu's way.

But would Lord Vishnu want this?

'I can't let that happen. People will die. You can burn down the buildings but do not harm people in them. Evacuate them. Then I shall help you.'

Narada's face was impassive. There was a strange, manic light in his eyes, but he nodded. 'All right, I promise,' he said.

Prahlad put his hand forward and Narada took it.

The young king smiled. 'So when do we begin?'

31
HIRANYAKASHYAP

Hiranya didn't like this.

Earlier, losing meant going back to his life, but now, it meant death.

As the scene around him changed, his vision began to blur and he felt a kick to his stomach. He opened his eyes to see purplish-blue skies and then suddenly he was there …

In the second Trial!

He could feel his body grow light, almost evaporate, as it adjusted to this new reality. Once again, he had no armour or weapon, and he felt like he was merely a projection of himself. He was not really there, but he was there. It was confusing.

He was standing in the middle of a very dense, dark forest, with light that shone from the skies through the patchy leaves. He could smell tangerine and other fruits. Realizing that he was starving, he picked up a fallen apple, which he ate and realized that it was real after all. There was a sound in the air too – a kind of whistling.

'This trial is of mental awareness,' the voice said, and Hiranya saw the spirit materialize next to him, suspended in air. 'Come, follow us.' It began to glide across the shrubs and the bushes.

Hiranya walked behind it, his brows arched as he took in the beautiful forest, the small river and the mountains around him. The entire scene was a peaceful, pleasant one.

What mental awareness?

Hiranya mused on what the spirit had said as he walked on. In some time, they reached a small clearing with a cottage, around which cows grazed on a well-maintained patch of land. There was a temple close to the river.

Who would live here?

Hiranya got his answer soon enough, as he saw a young woman drawing water from the well. She was nothing short of gorgeous. And he realized that it was her whose whistling he'd heard.

Hiranya was dazzled, but that was it. He had never thought of any woman other than his wife in a lustful way. He had remained loyal, even after her death.

'It's strange,' the spirit cawed.

'What?'

'You don't feel any lust towards her.'

'Why should I?'

The spirit hissed. 'Look at her. It's a surprise that you don't. Are you sure you like women?'

'Behave yourself,' Hiranya said hoarsely, as he watched the fair-skinned woman go about her chores. She was pretty, no doubt, but no one came close to Kayadhu for him. 'Who is she?' Hiranya asked, raising his brows.

'Ahalya.'

Hiranya had heard that name. 'Ah,' he said, a grim smile on his face. 'She's a joke in our empire, hah! She's the one Indra raped and it cost him his manhood. Ha ha!'

The spirit shook its head in disappointment. 'Sometimes you seem wise, Lord Hiranya and then, you reveal how petty you are.'

'What does that mean?'

'Perhaps you shall learn what we mean by the end of this trial.' The spirit floated over to Ahalya.

'Stop! She might see you!'

'Don't worry, she won't. Neither will she see you.'

'I hope I am not playing Indra in this trial. I am not him.'

'But making fun of someone who was raped is fine?' the spirit mocked.

Hiranya fell silent. He had no response, but he just nodded and came forward, and now could see Ahalya up close. He didn't know much about her, only the story about her and Indra. When he was ruling with his brother, years before Kayadhu's death, there was a rumor of Indra losing his manhood after he had raped a local Nishad.

And then Hiranya saw a man emerge from the cottage – her husband; an old man, with a white cloth wrapped around his body. He was quite fat for his age and he seemed an unlikely partner for the beautiful Ahalya. They talked, and then were hugging and kissing.

'A guru,' the spirit explained. 'Ahalya liked him for his wisdom, but of course, he was old and he didn't bring the feistiness that she wanted in bed. His name is Guru Gautam.'

'I know. I remember the name,' Hiranya paused. 'How is this related to the Trial?'

'Hold on,' the spirit added, as it used its hands to shift reality and then present Hiranya with another scene.

Suddenly, Hiranya was standing in front of a valley, and close to it, Ahalya was washing herself, splashing water on her face and her semi-naked body. And on the other side of the river, Hiranya saw Indra kneeling down, watching her, his eyes lustful.

'Wasn't Indra married?'

'He even had a son, Jayant,' the spirit added. 'What a pity!'

And then Hiranya noticed something – Ahalya saw Indra watching her from afar and smiled at him.

So she smiled at him? But of course, a smile was not an invitation to rape her …

Indra gestured for her to pour some water over her neck and she did. Then he told her to do it close to her breasts, and she did. This unspoken flirtation went on for a while – a young woman with a curvaceous body doing the bidding of the strong, fit king of Swarg, under the raging winds of the forest.

'What do you see?' the spirit asked.

'She likes him,' Hiranya declared. 'But then …'

'History is told either by victors … or by rumours.' A glint of happiness came to the spirit's face as it gestured with its hand, slowly changing the reality. They were back in front of the cottage, and Indra was approaching it with his men.

Gautam came out of his house and he saw Indra. 'Lord Devendra, I have heard great things about you. Please, how can I help?' he asked.

'I am on my way to free more people from the clutches of the Asuras,' Indra said, smiling, the Vanars and Simhas behind him standing at attention. 'And I wanted refuge before I leave tomorrow.'

'Of course, my lord. My home is yours. Unfortunately, I won't be able to be there, since I'm going for my penance in the woods.'

Ahalya came out of her house, with a mischievous smile dancing on her lips. Indra was grinning back at her as well.

'Of course, I won't mind,' he said to her husband.

The scene shifted again, and Hiranya was inside the cottage, watching Ahalya sleeping alone in the bed.

Gautam was nowhere to be seen. And the lamp had been put out. It was dark and yet the light of the moon was enough to illuminate her.

'I thought they would bed each other after Gautam left.' Hiranya was very confused as he watched Ahalya sleep.

'Oh well, they didn't. Now see …'

And at that moment, the door to Ahalya's room opened. The owls stopped hooting outside as the creaking of the wooden floor filled the room. Hiranya saw as the naked Indra came and lay beside Ahalya.

'Gautam?' she asked sleepily. Indra didn't respond. 'Is that you?' she asked again.

'Yes, it is,' Indra responded in the darkness, but it was evident that it wasn't Gautam. Ahalya tried to push Indra away, after which he caught her tightly, grabbing on to her arms and legs …

And then the spirit changed the scene to the morning, where in the courtyard in front of the cottage, stood an embarrassed and flustered Indra next to Ahalya, who had her body wrapped in clothes. Before them was Gautam.

'Now,' the spirit said, 'this is where Gautam caught them in bed together and was angry.'

Hiranya saw Gautam's face red with rage. He had a knife in his hand and he pounced at Indra, who was defenceless. They fought on the mud and Gautam attacked Indra on the face, cutting his cheek. Indra pushed him back, trying to calm him down, but Gautam knelt and brought his knife to Indra's groin, stabbing and cutting it.

Indra fell back on the ground with his hands between his legs, blood spraying from his groin. Gautam lunged forward again, but before he could attack, Indra's men appeared – two Vanars who grabbed Gautam and punched him, tossing him down.

'Kill him!' Indra screamed in horrific pain. 'Kill him now! I need a doctor!'

Ahalya ran up to Gautam and stood between him and the guards. She hugged her husband and apologized to him. 'He forced me. Please ... please... I didn't, I promise.'

As the guards pushed her aside and pulled Gautam away, he said to Ahalya, 'You are a whore.'

And instantly the scene dissolved, as Hiranya realized he was back in the cave with the Brahmashastra, standing on the pedestal. The spirit was floating in the air in front of him.

Hiranya felt disoriented, multiple emotions running through him. He shook his head to clear his thoughts and compose himself.

'What is the Trial in this?' he asked the spirit.

The spirit snarled. 'The trial hasn't even started. You were given a scenario. Now the trial is the question. If you answer it correctly, you will pass ...'

'All right, ask your question.'

'Who is the perpetrator in this story?'

It seemed such a simple question, but for some reason, Hiranya felt blindsided. 'Perpetrator? Of course it was ...'

'Remember, you only have one shot to get it right, so answer carefully.' The spirit lifted its fingers. 'Otherwise, you know the repercussion ...'

Hiranya thought for a moment, and he could feel the trickle of sweat drip down his cheeks. The spirit chuckled. 'Is it Indra who raped her, or is it Ahalya who cheated on her husband? Who is it?' it asked again.

'She incited him, didn't she?' Hiranya asked himself. 'She flirted in the beginning but when he tried things with her, she didn't want him.'

'Perhaps she was okay with flirting but not with bedding him,' the spirit laughed. 'So is she wrong? For inciting him?'

Hiranya realized that the answer to the spirit's question was not as straightforward as he'd thought.

On the surface, Indra was at fault. He was the one who forced himself on her. But if one looked more closely, Ahalya could very easily be wrong too, for sending the wrong message to Indra.

But then Hiranya recalled something. 'You don't want me to win this,' he looked at the spirit, his eyes piercing him.

'What do you mean?'

'You always leave out the important part, just like you did in the last Trial. And in this Trial also, you are playing a game with me. You said Ahalya could be at fault and Indra could be at fault, but you didn't say Gautam *could* be at fault,' Hiranya smiled.

'Because, well …' the spirit mumbled, 'We thought that was obvious. He's the victim in this.'

'No, he isn't.' Hiranya thought quickly, piecing the puzzle together. 'You asked who the perpetrator was in this story. Now, the word *perpetrator* was emphasized by you. But all three of them were wrong. Indra for committing a heinous crime against Ahalya, but … Gautam. What was his fault?'

'Yes, you are right. It could be Gautam too, for being jealous and not trusting his wife when she said that she was innocent.'

Hiranya noticed that there was something odd in the way the spirit phrased his sentence.

I am falling into his trap.

Hiranya smiled. 'No.' He shook his head. 'It's Indra, isn't it?'

I cannot fail. For Kayadhu. I need to avenge her. And if I die, it'll be all over.

'Of course it is,' the spirit said.

'But it's not because he raped her,' Hiranya understood now, slowly becoming confident of himself as he saw the spirit's face changing. He continued, 'The answer to your question is not that simple, because the person who is most wrong is Indra after all, but for more reasons than one. He is guilty not only for the act itself but also for the *reason* behind that act. For thinking that just because Ahalya flirted with him, she would want to sleep with him too. She didn't. She fancied him but nothing more, and he treated that as an excuse to rape her.' Hiranya looked at the spirit, who had fallen silent. 'Am I right?' he asked.

The spirit grumbled and nodded. 'You are good, son of Kashyap,' he said. 'Lord Brahma always believed that consent is of supreme importance when it comes to procreation. If a woman or a man objects and it is still forced on her or him, then it is no longer consensual. It is rape.' It paused. 'How did you know?'

'Because of the thing you said in the beginning of the Trial – that I shall learn something about women from it. And I thought from the woman's perspective, coupled with the idea that there must have been a reason why you showed me very specific scenes.' Hiranya smiled. 'Do I pass?'

The spirit shook its head in dismay. 'Your brother lost at this stage. He was not as bright as you.'

'It's not about being bright, but about common sense.' Hiranya said. He was sad about what Ahalya had gone through.

If only people understood consent. If only they understood that flirting was not permission to do something sexual.

'So, what next?' he asked the spirit.

The third pedestal glinted and rose in the air, and there was a strange symbol on it. But before Hiranya could ask what it meant, he asked another question. 'Would this be Indra-centric too?'

'The reason why the previous Trials were around Indra was to identify your enemy, know where he's coming from, what he has gone through.' The spirit shook its head. 'But the third Trial is not about him.' It smiled.

'What is it about?'

The spirit did not answer. Instead, the symbols on the pedestal changed and Hiranya could now tell that they were of a tall man and a small boy. And for some reason, the shapes looked very familiar.

'Who are they?' Hiranya pointed to the pedestal, but even before he heard the answer, he knew it in his heart.

'It's you.' The spirit chuckled. 'And this Trial is about Prahlad.'

32

NARASIMHA

The plan was simple.

Narasimha and Bhairav would meet in the middle of the battlefield with the intention of giving Andhaka the dismantled Pashupatastra and then using the opportunity of a fake win to actually kill Andhaka and flee. But they couldn't do it in Sonitpur, for it was fortified and if they went inside, they would end up being massacred by his army, so it had to be done outside, in the open.

The raven had been sent a day before to Andhaka, to call for a truce. The message claimed that Bhairav was ready to give up Pashupatastra in return for peace. In fact, it was Nara's idea to use the broken Pashupatastra as bait to lure Andhaka and get him to drop his guard in his arrogance.

And while they waited for an answer from his side, Nara spent his time mostly by Chenchen's side, holding her hand while she lay unconscious and pale. Nara would help her drink water, clean her wounds whenever they started bleeding, and make sure she was warm.

The physician in him could see that she seemed out of danger, but he was still afraid for her. The protector in him prodded him to go ahead and give her the Somas from the vessel that Bhairav kept for the Simhas, but he knew it would be wrong. The Somas couldn't be given to everyone, and sometimes, those who took them could experience adverse effects. It also depended on the person's immune system and how it was able to handle the power of the Somas. Most Manavs, especially Nishads who were poor and battled the many diseases around them, couldn't indulge in the Somas; their systems would probably be overwhelmed by the drink.

Nara had come out of the infirmary and was exhausted. He couldn't sleep much, out of stress for Chenchen's health.

Outside, Nara saw Bhairav standing close to the Nandi bull, looking into the distance with his hands clasped behind his back. He walked to the Shiva and patted him on the back. 'What are you thinking?'

'About peace, and when we can finally return to it,' Bhairav chuckled.

'Do you ever?'

'Ah well …' Bhairav shook his head. 'I don't know what peace is any more. Bearing this title, it's frightening. Do you remember Lord Rudra?'

More than you can imagine.

'He was a good man, right?' Bhairav continued. 'Worshipped as a god here, the quintessential Lord Shiva, and here I am, living in his shadow, trying to live up to his image,' Bhairav said glumly.

'You don't have to, right?' Nara arched his brows, emphasizing his words. 'You don't really have to be him. You are great yourself and you should be proud of what you have done.'

He shrugged. 'What have I done? I have a wife who doesn't want to come out and see all of this ...' He pointed at his home, a small dome-like structure where Parvati lived. 'She has stopped socializing ever since we lost our child. She's still in shock and hates me. She blames me for choosing my duties over our son. My people don't respect me. I have you, and you've rebelled against me. I couldn't even protect the weapon I promised to and I am losing a war, proposing a truce and planning an assassination attempt that may fail.'

'It will not, my lord,' Nara said. 'You don't have to worry. Lord Mahadev sees the divine truth in you and he will protect you.'

'Did I ever tell you, I loved to dance?' Bhairav laughed, perhaps distracting himself from the horrors of his failures.

'No, you didn't.'

'I did, once upon a time. I loved to dance. I loved to choreograph the ceremonies that happened in our Tribe. I was an entertainer, you know, until I was chosen for my bravery by Lord Rudra as his successor.'

'What kind of bravery?'

He shrugged. 'In a nearby forest, I was met by a bunch of Mlecchas who wanted to loot our village, but I fought and defeated them. The usual heroic deed, right? Lord Rudra heard of it and loved it.'

'You were always brave.'

'I was foolish. Imagine if I hadn't done that, I wouldn't be here.' He said, 'I have lost my son, and almost lost my life.

And it hurts me every day. Sometimes I wish I hadn't saved the village from the Mlecchas. That I had just walked away.'

'I did that too,' Nara said. 'But then, I came back. If we had stayed away, we wouldn't be heroes.'

'We are not, Nara. We are evil in someone's eyes. I don't want to be a hero if I can't fulfil the duties of a Shiva by protecting my people and defeating Andhaka. Lord Rudra died here, of old age. He was there from the beginning till the end, doing everything in his power until Lord Brahma took him.'

Nara stayed silent, contemplating what Bhairav had said.

'I did something, though,' Bhairav went on, a soft smile on his lips.

'What?'

'You remember the village I sent you to with Chenchen?' he asked.

How can I forget? That trip gave me the reason to rebel.

Nara nodded.

'I was afraid that they would rebel if they knew what I had done with Indra, how I'd let the Pashupatastra harm them. Though it was unintentional, I'd let that village be destroyed.' He shook his head. 'And I didn't even admit to my mistake.'

Nara nodded. He was wondering where Bhairav was going with this.

'Well ...' the Shiva thumped his feet. 'I did send a raven to tell them that it was me who was behind their illnesses and that I would give them anything in return to repent for my actions.' He paused. 'Aside from the fact that we used the weapon, do you know what else we did? We blamed the attack on someone else rather than admitting to it.'

'It wasn't just you, my lord.' He referred to Indra's involvement. 'Chenchen told me.'

Bhairav chuckled. 'Did she? Well, she ratted me and Indra out, but it's all right. Not many knew, only a few people. It doesn't matter. A man should accept his follies, own up to his mistakes. I plan to leave for the village and settle it with them in person once I deal with Andhaka. I plan to redeem myself.' He smiled at Nara. 'I have done too many questionable things. I want to do something now that makes me proud.'

Nara grinned back. He was proud to have a friend like Bhairav.

He finally seems to be showing signs of the true Lord Shiva.

Suddenly, they heard a noise and turned to see a Manav coming up to them. He was holding a letter, which he handed to Bhairav, and then bowed and left. Bhairav opened the letter, read it and then said, 'It's from Andhaka. He sent a raven.'

'What does it say?' At the sound of Andhaka's name, Nara was alert.

'He wants to meet in the Mahakal forest, and has asked us to bring the Pashupatastra as promised,' Bhairav read, and his eyes widened in horror.

Nara noticed that and asked, 'What happened?'

'I have bad memories of those woods.'

'Why?'

Bhairav folded the letter, sighing. 'It's where I lost my son.'

33

HOLIKA

As soon as Holika entered, everyone in the tavern fell silent.

It was her presence perhaps, or the fact that everyone knew her for her cruelty and heartlessness. When they saw her entering, most of the people's attention was diverted. The music stopped playing. The Apsaras and Gandharvs stopped serving food.

There was absolute silence.

And Holika enjoyed the effect she had; it soothed her ego. She began walking around the place, her two guards following her.

After the incident at the prison, everything had grown calm. The Vishnusena had disappeared and no one knew where they were. Holika didn't question Prahlad about it, for she didn't want to alert him. She had a plan.

And she was here to execute it.

She saw Simhika, her arms full of bangles, in one of the booths. She walked up to her and Simhika rose to hug Holika.

In the booth, Holika saw a tall, young man with a sharp jawline and a small scar across his face. He seemed afraid of her.

It was Viparichit.

I have work for you.

He wore his breastplate, pads and gauntlets to show off his position, and as Simhika sat next to Viparichit, Holika noticed the way she looked at the man.

I know that expression. I used to have it, once upon a time.

Holika didn't order anything for herself as she looked at the couple.

'So? You wanted him here, right?' Simhika excitedly said. 'Isn't he cute?'

Viparichit blushed. 'Um, Lady Holika, she embarrasses me but it is lovely meeting you. I suppose we must have met at one of the morning drills.'

Holika had met so many soldiers that she had lost count. 'Yeah, sure. What are your intentions towards Simhika?' she asked bluntly.

'Uh … um …' Viparichit glanced at Simhika, who was just grinning because these questions apparently amused her. 'I like her.'

'You just like me?' Simhika raised her brows.

'You just *like* her?' Holika pressed further. She loved toying with people, having the upper hand in a conversation.

'Uh, no, no of course … I love her, of course …' Viparichit was sweating. 'I shouldn't have worn my armour.'

Simhika burst out laughing as she ran her fingers through his hair. 'It's all right, love. We are just messing with you. Ma likes you because she trusts my choice.'

Holika struggled to smile. 'Yes, I trust Simhika.'

Viparichit was glad, as he sighed with relief. 'I am so … well … all right. I feel good about it, now. Might I ask how you two met?'

'Oh, didn't I tell you?' Simhika asked. 'Of course, I didn't! I don't share the story often. Should I tell him, Ma?' she asked for permission as Holika leaned back and nodded casually. 'All right, so actually, when I was small, I worked at the same brothel I am still with. Like now, even then I just cleaned and washed dishes. You know already that my mother was an escort there. I didn't particularly have a father, since he left us when I was born. Anyhow, the men who came to brothels weren't really the nicest men. And one of them ended up hurting my Ma …' She blinked, remembering. 'Anyway, to cut a long story short, she fell victim to one of the clients and Holika ma was there, investigating the death. She found the man and basically—'

'I gutted him like a pig,' Holika interjected, her eyes cold.

'Not how I would have put it, but yeah.' Simhika shook her head.

Viparichit swallowed a lump. 'Oh dear, that seems harsh.'

'And justified.' Holika raised her brows, shaking her head.

'And after that, Holika ma and I … we got close. I still remember the time I gave her my bangle. I love bangles, I think you already know about my obsession with them, but I gave one to her, because she didn't wear any sort of jewellery for some reason.'

I had stopped dressing up by then.

Simhika pulled Holika's arm forward, showing the one red bangle that Holika was wearing. 'Isn't it nice?'

Viparichit nodded meekly.

Holika fondly recalled that day when she had met Simhika the first time.

Holika had been making sure the women in the brothels were safe, telling them how to defend themselves should the need arise. Holika even offered them weapons, in case something happened. During her work with them, Holika was greeted by a small girl who had a wooden toy with her.

Holika had seen her earlier. She was Simhika or Simmi, the daughter of the poor woman who was attacked by that fiend.

'Aunties around here say you avenged my mother,' the child said.

Holika smiled, kneeling down. 'Those are big words for a small girl like you.'

'I don't care.' She arched her brows. 'Did he get what he deserved?'

Holika recalled how she had slit him from the groin up. Quite poetic. 'Yes, he did.'

'I'm glad. Do you kill only men?'

'Those who deserve it, which is most of them.'

'I hate them.' She pressed the doll tightly to her chest.

'I hate them too. Here, hold my hand.'

And she did. Simmi was cute and Holika felt a warmth in her heart

'What if it happens again, my lady?' the child asked. 'What if there's another man out there who does the same thing?' she asked, widening her gaze. 'And what if I become their next victim?'

'Don't worry. I'll be there for you,' Holika promised.

'Will you be there for sure?' the little girl asked, raising her brows with delight.

'Of course, I was unable to protect your mother, but I shall make sure I protect you. Just holler for me whenever you are in trouble, all right?' Holika smiled.

Simmi nodded childishly.

'Do you have anyone else to look out for you?'

She shook her head, her face twisting before she burst into tears. Holika was dumbstruck. She embraced Simmi and her heart hurt for the child.

'I don't have a mother,' Simmi said.

'It's okay. I'll be there for you. I won't let anyone touch you, all right?' she said. 'It's all right, darling. You know what, you can call me Ma.'

'You sure?' the girl looked up.

'Of course,' Holika smiled.

And that day, Holika had found a daughter and Simhika had found another mother.

Now, watching Viprachit, Holika said, 'Simhika, I want to talk to him in private. Can you get us something?'

Simhika hesitated for a moment, but then she looked at Viparichit and nodded, before getting up and leaving them alone.

As soon as Simhika left, Holika leaned forward. 'I want to ask you something.'

'My lady, I have the truest and most noble feelings towards your daughter …'

'I know that, boy.' Holika shook her head. 'I also know you plan to marry her.'

'How come?' He was shocked. 'I haven't even asked her yet.'

'She knows. We know. Women are intelligent. Shocker, right?' she smiled mockingly. 'Now, I want you to help me. Think of it as a way to get my permission to marry her.'

Viparichit was surprised. Why did a woman like Holika need his help? But he nodded. 'Of course, my lady.'

'I know you are close to Prahlad. I want you to find out whether he has any involvement with the Vishnusena.'

'Oh, um ...' Viparichit chuckled, 'I'm sure he doesn't. He hates them as much as you do.'

'Find out for me, all right?' she asked.

'And then what?'

'If he's guilty,' she sighed, 'bring him to me.'

'Um, my lady, may I ask, what will you do to him?'

Holika remained silent, her face grim.

But Viparichit understood.

Oh, he understood.

34

HIRANYAKASHYAP

'I am growing tired.' Hiranya fell against the wall.

The spirit hovered next to him, maliciously grinning at his predicament. 'We know you are afraid.'

Hiranya didn't say anything, his face impassive. 'How did my brother fare in these situations?'

'He was afraid too, but he was crazy. The Brahmashastra …'

The spirit floated back to the armour, 'It is meant for the right person, not for the crazy ones. We knew he wouldn't be able to pass it. The Trials … they change according to the contender.'

'Bah! You changed them!' Hiranya exclaimed. 'You don't want me to win. You have been constantly trying to make things difficult for me.'

'So that you can be worthy enough to wear this beautiful Kavach. If it was easy, anyone could have it. Don't you think?'

And then the spirit's face changed into one that felt familiar and yet unknown.

'We sense something.' There was fear in the eyes of the spirit. 'Were you followed?'

Hiranya shook his head. He was sure, but he still got up on his feet and made his way outside the caves with the spirit. And in front of him, under the starry night, he saw rows of men standing guard next to the entrance. And in the middle stood the irascible Agni, the so-called god of fire. His smile was wild and horrific. Hiranya could feel the tremors down his spine.

'He must have sent a spy after me. They have been tracking the horses that leave the fort,' Hiranya said, even though he had been careful about making sure no one followed his footsteps, but it looked like he'd not been entirely successful.

'Not many know of this place,' the spirit hissed.

Suddenly, a fireball rose and smouldered in front of Hiranya, who pulled himself back, and lay flat on the ground as the fire engulfed the place he'd been standing seconds before.

Damn!

'The Third Trial is not done. I need to complete it,' he said.

And get the armour so I can kill this god.

Hiranya gritted his teeth. 'Is there any way to stop them?' he asked the spirit. He did not think he'd actually get help, but he was surprised when the spirit ran its fingers across the crevices of the entrance and instantly, rocks from above hammered on the ground, blocking the cave entrance completely.

'That should hold them for a while.'

'I am surprised. I thought you would abandon me to the sharks.'

'You are our challenger. And while you are going through the Trials, we have the responsibility of protecting you, even if we don't want you to win,' the spirit explained. 'But we cannot protect you for long.'

'That's unfortunate. For a moment I thought you liked me,' Hiranya grinned.

The spirit just shrugged. 'Let's continue since you don't have much time. Their catapults will get through the entrance soon, and if they find you in between the Trials, it's easy for them to kill you since you will be in a trance.'

Hiranya knew he didn't have time and ran back to the pedestal.

He saw the pedestal had a new symbol, which showed a big man and a small boy sitting next to each other, close to a cliff.

Hiranya sighed. 'All right. Let's do this.'

35

NARASIMHA

They waited.

With their army of hairy Vanars, blue-eyed Nagas, the Manavs and the Simhas, Bhairav and Nara waited in the Mahakal Forest that was to the south of Mandara Hills, where the snow was fresh and lush green plants and shrubs were abundant. Many of the soldiers wore thick warm clothes under their dirty, greasy battle armour. Their axes, spears swords and bows were ready in anticipation of an attack.

Nara turned his head to look at the Pashupatastra, which looked absolutely fine, but instead of the bolders made of Mohini's ashes, this one had just ordinary rocks next to it.

The idea was to get Andhaka out of his fortress and once and for all, end him.

'What if it happens again?' Nara asked. He was on his stallion next to Bhairav, who was wearing his leopard skin tightly around his body, his hair matted and the Rudraksh on his arms. 'What if we kill Andhaka, and another sprouts out of nowhere.'

'I can't beat sorcery, Nara. We don't have Vidhyadharas at our disposal,' Bhairav responded. 'But I have a feeling that the promise of the Pashupatastra will bring out the real Andhaka. He'll want to see it for himself. Winning strokes this Asura's ego.'

Let's hope you are right.

Nara didn't want to discourage the Shiva.

'Something funny happened, you know,' Bhairav said. 'Parvati said she wants to try to have a child again.'

Nara beamed. 'That is wonderful.' And he looked at the forest. 'And isn't this such a wonderful time to tell me?' he chuckled.

'I just couldn't believe she said it, Nara. I mean, she wouldn't even let me touch her before this. But perhaps seeing me stand against the ideas of Indra and destroying the Pashupatastra made her believe in me again. Or perhaps she has found forgiveness in her heart.' Bhairav was smiling, genuine happiness on his face. 'And I don't want to lose this second chance. I'll stick to it. From now on, it's her and our future baby above everything else.'

Nara patted his friend on the back. 'Once we end the blind prince's reign here, let's drink to that and celebrate, shall we?'

'I was wondering when you would ask me that. Cheers!'

And then they heard it. The soldiers on the lookout had blown their trumpet, signaling the approach of the enemy. Nara looked around and saw the army of Rakshasas, Pishach and Manavs approaching. And behind them came the Asuras, golden-eyed, broad and handsome. Nara knew that the Asuras and Devas had similar physical traits because they apparently came from one father – Dyaus. But not many believed that myth, and very few talked about it.

Right in the front stood the blind prince – the red blindfold across his face, pale, brow-less and hairless, clad in a jet-black uniform. Next to him stood a young man, his face scarred and his long hair tied back.

He seems familiar.

'It's so strange. I killed him with my bare hands. And now he's standing in front of me again,' Nara said, referring to Andhaka.

'Does it matter?' Bhairav asked. 'He's here, and he's clearly not dead.'

'What should we do?' Nara asked.

Bhairav didn't speak, but gestured for his men to bring the Pashupatastra to the front.

Nara saw the young Asura whispering something to Andhaka, who nodded and then they walked towards the Pashupatastra, alone, without any guards or soldiers.

As Andhaka reached the weapon, he touched it and smiled.

'Is it all right?' Bhairav asked Andhaka.

Andhaka looked up, his face white.

'Creepy bastard,' one of the guards behind Nara said, 'they say he only drinks blood, gods forbid.'

Nara asked Bhairav, 'What should we do? Should we attack? He's defenceless.'

Bhairav was frozen, considering his options. Nara studied his expression and before he could ask him anything,

Andhaka began, 'It's the wrong one, hmmm,' he said, his voice shrill and weak. Nara saw how fragile and bony he looked. Nara remembered the Andhaka he had killed – he had been tougher, built more like a warrior.

'What do you mean?' Bhairav asked.

'I'm blind. But I can smell. I was told the weapon would have sulphur … hmmm,' Andhaka responded. 'No smell of sulphur, why, hmmm? I only smell rocks, dirty ones from your fort. You think I'm a fool, don't you, Shiva?'

Nara couldn't believe Andhaka had caught on to their trick. And just because they had missed one small detail. He cursed under his breath.

'Attack him,' Nara whispered.

Bhairav didn't. He remained frozen.

'Why do you betray people, Shiva, hmmm?' Andhaka came forward, leaving the ponytailed boy behind. 'You shouldn't betray people. You shouldn't leave them behind too.'

Nara felt a chill run down him.

Leave them behind? How does he know?

'I knew you would trick me. We knew.' He pointed to the boy behind him. 'And yet we came, because we are not like you. We still hope, even while you try to manipulate us, hmmm. Again and again,' he said, ripping off his blindfold and opening his eyes.

Nara saw his burnt, brutally scarred eyes, as if someone had put coals directly inside his eyes and surprisingly made him live through it.

'He wouldn't let me die,' Andhaka said in almost a whine. 'He would grill me, stab me, hurt me, and whenever I was close to death, he would give me the Somas so that I lived through it. He got them from somewhere, perhaps from a stock he spent a fortune on. I don't know. I don't care. But he didn't let me die. And after so much pain, I learnt what it meant to be alive. And all that time, you allowed me to be taken away. You didn't return for me.'

Nara was frozen. He stole a glance at Bhairav. He couldn't imagine what he was going through as he stood there, dumbfounded.

'I waited there, hiding in the shadows until the Asura king came for me. He saw me. He did. And he took me away. And I was never the same again.'

'Bhringi?'

Bhairav jumped off his horse, Nara watching as Bhairav tripped, his legs growing weak.

'Don't go!' Nara called out to the Shiva, but he didn't listen and kept walking.

'Bhringi, my child. Is it you?' he cried again.

And everyone was silent on both sides of the battle as Bhairav came close to Andhaka, who also put his arms out.

'You should have told me it was you,' Bhairav said. 'I am sorry. You have no idea how sorry I am. Every waking moment, I regret it. I thought you died. I thought he killed you.'

Andhaka didn't say anything as he embraced his father. It was a poignant moment, and Nara couldn't help but feel tears trickling from his eyes.

'I wanted to kill you, father,' Andhaka said, holding Bhairav. 'But I can't, hmmm. I'm too weak. I thought that I'd grown strong after so much suffering, but no. I still hoped for you to love me.'

'It's okay, I understand. I'm sorry too,' Bhairav said. 'Please forgive me. I want to make it right, Bhringi.'

Andhaka nodded. 'You shall. Do you know that you are correct?'

'About what?' the Shiva asked.

'He *did* kill me that night,' Andhaka said, pulling back. 'Bhringi died the day you left him there. He's no more.'

'No, my son,' Bhairav pleaded. 'You are here. We can be together again.'

'It's only Andhaka now.' The blind prince shook his head. 'Hmmm, I'm sorry.'

'For what?' Bhairav asked.

And then Andhaka pulled a dagger from his sheath and cut the Shiva's throat. Blood spurted as the Shiva fell to his knees …

He was no longer the Shiva. He was just Bhairav – the corpse of a failed father.

For a moment, Nara was too shocked to move. The entire army watched as their leader was slaughtered in front of them, too stunned to do anything.

And then Andhaka gestured to his army … *Attack.*

Nara woke from his spell and then yelled to his army, 'Go!'

The battle had begun.

36

NARASIMHA

There was chaos all around them.

Nara couldn't keep track of everything going on. As the battle raged, Nara couldn't breathe for the dust in the air, and was surrounded by the dirty snow. Rain fell and the ground turned to slush as the blood was spilled.

Nara focused on what he had to find.

Bhairav's body!

The Shiva had to be cremated the right way. He couldn't just lie there like one of the hundreds of other casualties.

Nara's heart was heavy as he looked for the Shiva's corpse. He felt crushed by Bhairav's sudden death, by the fact that a pure soul like him had suffered a fate so cruel.

But the world is *cruel.*

As Nara continued his futile search, a Pishach appeared behind him and slashed his back. Nara groaned and instantly turned on the Pishach, using his claws to attack, puncturing its lung and pulling out its intestines. He was angry. As angry as he'd been when Chenchen had been hurt.

That's why I don't like getting close to people.

Nara turned just as a Rakshas appeared before him. He saw his men around him, fighting the others from the Asura army. The Rakshas before him charged at Nara and threw and tossed him on the ground. He began to punch Nara and then pulled out his dagger, with which he stabbed Nara on the shoulder. Blood spurted as Nara pulled the dagger out and sliced it right across the Rakshas's eyes. The Rakshas fell back, crying loudly as Nara got to his feet.

Where are you, Bhairav?

Nara felt his eyes welling up with tears, but in the rain, no one could tell.

Even Andhaka had vanished. As Nara's army had regrouped and charged, Andhaka and his ponytailed friend had mounted their horses and escaped.

Nara wanted to kill Andhaka, but right now was not the time to exact revenge. It was time to find Bhairav's body and escape, so that he could be cremated.

Someone pushed Nara to the ground and as he turned, he saw it was an Asura – large and beautiful, towering over him with a blade in his hand. The Asura began to use the blade against Nara, struggling to stab him, but Nara sprang from his position and rolled forward, deflecting the attack.

Grabbing the nearest weapon, Nara used it to block the Asura's blows, and then kicked him between the legs.

The Asura fell back and Nara leapt from his position, the weapon in his hand as he swiped it right across the Asura's chest. The blade plunged inside the Asura and he fell to the ground.

Nara plunged the blade deeper, and then realized what the weapon he was holding was – a trident.

A trishul!

A religious weapon of sorts for the Shiva, first wielded by Lord Nataraj when the Gana tribe was just formed, the trident could only be used by a true hero – a born leader.

He pulled the trident out as the Asura took his last breath. Nara knew that if the trident had been near him, Bhairav's body couldn't be far away. And sure enough, a few yards away was Bhairav. His face was almost unrecognizable, and his throat was bloody. The pool of water around him had seeped in, and he looked so … *bloated*.

Nara carried the Shiva's body on his back, a trident in his hand as he made his way back to his camp.

He sprinted as fast as he could, his lungs burning, his feet cold and painful, his eyes brimming with tears.

And as he reached the camp, he whistled for the nearest stallion. He realized the camp had been destroyed. But his men were fighting diligently and by the looks of it, they were winning. Most of the Rakshasas and the Asuras had been killed.

A horse appeared, neighing.

He mounted it and, securing the body in front of him, turned to leave. But before he could ride away, he caught sight of Veerbhadra and called out to him. 'General! I'm taking Lord Bhairav away from here.'

Veerbhadra was engaged in a fight, which he ended by plunging his blade into the Rakshas, before turning to Nara and nodding.

Nara rode away from the battle and, as he came close to the edge of the Mahakal forest, looked back. The large forest was drenched with the blood of the men who fought on either side. They looked like ants from where Nara stood, and he realized that he had become a part of everything he hated by participating in this futile war.

I thought that by destroying the Pashupatastra, I had saved innocents.

Nara accepted the hard truth. As long as there was rage in this world, there would be war.

And before he could ride further, a searing pain pulled him back and threw him off the horse.

He didn't know where it came from and as his blurred vision got a little clearer, he saw it was a sword that had been plunged into his chest. He could feel the blade inside him, draining him of his blood, his life.

I need to get to the Somas.

He wanted to pull the sword out, but also needed to get to the vial. Before he could, he felt the blade digging deeper. Someone was pushing down on it, driving it inside him.

It was Andhaka.

He was wearing his blindfold and his feet were on top of Nara's blade.

'See what one can do with just sound? I don't need eyes to swing my sword at you.' He paused. 'You can't take his body. He deserves to stay there, in the middle of that mayhem.' The blind prince chuckled.

Behind him, the young boy stood, visibly shaken.

Nara was growing paler by the minute. He felt exhausted, weak.

'Take the body,' Andhaka said to the ponytailed boy, who grabbed Bhairav's corpse from Nara's horse and proceeded to saddle it to his own. 'I never indulge myself by sticking around in a battle,' Andhaka said, sighing. 'I see no reason for it, hmmm. It hurts me to see the amount of death around us.'

'Then …' Nara coughed, his eyes closing, 'you shouldn't have started it.'

Andhaka only smiled at that, and it was a disturbing smile. His pale, thin lips stretched wide to reveal teeth that looked too big. 'This is just the beginning of it, hmmm. You are the man they brought in to save the good folks from us? Narasimha, I take it?'

Nara didn't say anything. He was holding on to the blade, which was sunk deep into his flesh.

'I heard you were Dharm, hmmm.' Disappointed, Andhaka lowered his head. 'It's a shame; a Dharm is under my feet. I won't lie, I expected more.'

'That's enough,' said the boy. 'Let's leave now. You don't need to torture him.'

Andhaka didn't listen, sniffing calmly as he turned his head towards Nara. 'This is just the beginning, Narasimha. I shall do so many things to this country. I have such ambitious plans. And I don't tell this to anyone but dying men. For …' his voice became a whisper, 'the dead don't speak and are no threat to me.'

'Andhaka!' yelled the boy, coming forward. 'It's over. Let's go. We've got Bhairav.' And he pulled at Andhaka, who slowly took a step back and nodded.

As Andhaka and the boy left, leaving Nara close to death on the battlefield, Nara knew he couldn't let himself die like this.

He pulled the blade from his chest and sighed as he reached for the vial that was in a pouch he carried with him. He drank it and the energy surged inside him, not too much, but enough to let him get up and grab the trident that had fallen to the ground.

He saw Andhaka and the boy at a distance, riding away with Bhairav's body. Nara aimed the trident at Andhaka. His vision was blurry, but he relaxed his breath and threw the trident with all his might.

It met its target. The trident pierced Andhaka's chest and he fell from the horse, hitting the ground with a thud.

Nara looked on with grim satisfaction, and then closed his eyes, his hand clamped on his wound to stop the bleeding.

And then, suddenly, he heard a cry and opened his eyes …

It was Andhaka.

Impossible! Didn't I just kill him?

He looked to the place where Andhaka had fallen and realized his mistake. His blurry vision had made him shoot the young boy, not Andhaka.

Meanwhile, Andhaka had turned his horse and was making a run for it, leaving behind the body of his young friend, as well as Bhairav's corpse, which was tied to the boy's horse.

Very soon, he'd disappeared into the woods.

Nara came forward and stopped next to the body of the boy, who was bleeding profusely. Nara wanted to apologize, but he didn't.

He was part of Andhaka's war.

Nara grabbed Bhairav and put him back on his stallion. Then he went and pulled out the trident from the boy's chest. The boy was pale, panting and counting out his last breath.

'Please …' he said, 'has he gone?'

Nara knelt on the ground, looking at the wounded boy closely. He was an Asura, a royal with golden eyes.

'I shouldn't have trusted him …' the boy sighed.

'Let me help you,' Nara said.

'No,' the boy retorted, 'this is my karma. I know. I have done some horrible things. I shouldn't have listened to Andhaka. I shouldn't have agreed with my father. I lost everything. I lost everyone. I have no one.' His pupils were dilating. 'I am alone. I will die alone.'

Nara shook his head. 'No, I'm here, boy. I'm a physician. Let me see your wound. I'm sorry. I had not meant to hit you.'

'If you ever find him,' determinedly said the boy, 'Andhaka, I mean. Remember … there are many of him.' He coughed and Nara didn't understand what he meant by this. 'But the real one … the real one is the only one who is blind. Remember that.'

Nara didn't understand. 'What's your name?'

'Anuhrad,' he breathed.

'You are Hiranyakashyap's son?' Nara was surprised.

'Yes. I was supposed to have my revenge, but I know now, I can see the light,' he coughed. 'It's not about revenge. It's about forgiveness.' Anuhrad smiled and drew a defeated breath. 'I do have someone who was there for me the last time I was in battle. He's a good boy, though … I … ergh …' He tried to lean back against a log. 'Why didn't it hurt you as much as it did me?'

Nara wished he could explain, but there was no time. Instead, he reached for his vial of the Somas, hoping he could give some to Anuhrad, but the vial was empty. He cursed under his breath.

Damn!

'I'm worried about my brother. He's the only one left I can call family.' Anuhrad had tears in his eyes. 'And I was the only one *he* had. My father can be cruel, and he would easily kill him if he needed to.'

'His name is Prahlad?' Nara asked.

Anuhrad nodded. 'I wish I could be there for him.' His eyes locked with Nara's. 'I wish *someone* could be there for him.'

And the boy's eyes closed.

Nara felt immense guilt wash over him. And he knew exactly why. He had thought that by destroying the Pashupatastra, he'd ended the war. But he realized now that once again, he had ended up killing one of the good guys.

Inside him, there was fury, so much of it. He looked in the direction where Andhaka had ridden.

He's going to Sonitpur.

And Nara knew what he had to do.

I'm coming for you, Andhaka.

37

HIRANYAKASHYAP

Hiranya didn't know where he was until he fell back.

His reality had been shaped and changed by the spirit into a familiar landscape, and he saw it was Kashyapuri – more vibrant, less smoky, and reverberating with loud music. The people around seemed happy and content, and as Hiranya walked the crowded markets and the beautiful buildings without his armour, he looked around in surprise. The spirit stayed suspended next to him.

'Why is everyone so happy?' Hiranya asked.

'It's the Golden Age. Peaceful times,' the spirit explained. 'We are excited for you to react to this.'

'Why do you keep saying "we"?' Hiranya said, irritated.

The spirit didn't acknowledge the question. They walked further and reached a dome-like structure, with the symbol of a lotus in the middle of it. It stood in the centre of Kashyapuri, where once Hiranya had put the statue of Harigriva.

'What is this?' Hiranya came forward, touching the structure. 'This is not right,' he cried to the spirit, who just disapprovingly shook his head.

'This is Lord Vishnu's temple.'

'Vishnu? *Vishnu*?' Hiranya snarled. 'His soldier murdered my brother and his temple rests in my city?'

The spirit scoffed. 'Who says it's still your city, Lord Hiranya?' he mocked and a surge of anger made Hiranya want to punch him.

'What is this? This is not a Trial. What are you showing me?' Hiranya asked.

'This is one of the Trials, but the meaning of it shall be revealed in the end,' the spirit explained.

Hiranya clenched his teeth and punched the temple's wall with his fist. Then he moved back … only to see the temple was not affected at all. 'What is going on? I don't understand.'

'Lord Hiranya, this is not real. Have you forgotten? This is all a projection.'

'Yes, of course.' Hiranya lowered his head, calming his anger. 'Why are you showing me this?'

'Just wait.'

The spirit then gestured to the temple gates, which opened and from it emerged …

Prahlad.

He had a garland around his neck and a tika on his head. His guards followed him and he looked older.

'My son is coming out of a Deva temple. That's impossible.' Hiranya shook his head. 'This projection is wrong.'

'The Trials of Brahma manifest according to the challenger. This could be wrong, but this is a manifestation of your worst fears – your son turning against you,' the spirit explained. 'It's betrayal that you fear. You can't stand the fact that your son has the capability of *turning into a man of faith*.'

Hiranya didn't even know that, deep down, this was exactly what he had been afraid of. He felt a kind of calmness at finally confronting his fear.

'But why do you feel that?' the spirit asked. 'Why do you feel your son would turn against you?'

Hiranya ran a hand through his hair. He had never shared what was a forgotten memory now. 'Because he's not like me,' he answered briefly, and then asked, 'So you are saying this golden period, this is also real?'

'It's a projection, a probable future if your son chooses the way of Vishnu,' the spirit responded. 'Which is when the golden period will start.'

And the Asura period will end.

'And what if he chooses my path?' Hiranya asked with fear in his heart.

The spirit nodded, changing the scenario – the entire landscape shifted and before them now was a new scene. The sky was red, the buildings burnt to shells, and tall statues of the Asuras stood towering over the landscape. And in the middle of everything stood Prahlad with his hair long and pulled back and sporting a moustache similar to Hiranya's. He was lashing a Manav with his whip.

'The darkest period Illavarti will ever see,' the spirit said. 'Dear, dear, we are afraid.'

'He can't be this evil.' Hiranya shook his head. 'I'm not this evil. How can my son do this?'

'Because a man never sees the actions he commits as something evil, however wrong they might be.' The spirit smiled.

He's right.

Hiranya knew that the spirit was right. There had been times that his mind had avoided thinking about the unlawful things he had done, rationalizing them as being necessary.

'Which path would you want your son to take?' the spirit asked.

'Of course, the latter,' Hiranya answered, without even blinking. 'He needs to carry forward the Asura tradition.'

The spirit had no words, but changed the scene again and this time Hiranya found himself close to the cliff, under the purplish starry night. Birds chirped and the wind blew over his face. And beyond the cliff, he saw darkness. But close to the cliff, sitting on the edge, was a small boy.

Prahlad.

Hiranya's first instinct was to pull his son back from the cliff, but he told himself that this was just a projection, an illusion.

The spirit appeared next to him. 'The Trial is simple. Your last trial, and the toughest of them all.'

'What is it?'

'You have to kill your son.'

Hiranya froze. 'Why?'

'You chose the latter scenario, didn't you? You want him to carry the Asura name. But what if he doesn't? What if he chooses to follow Vishnu, and thus ends the Asura empire, becoming a Deva king? What would you do? The Trial considers that possibility and wants you to take action, be it killing him or sparing him, to see whether you are worthy of the Brahmshastra or not.'

'But what if he doesn't? What if he becomes like me?' Hiranya asked.

'The Trials do not favour that possibility.'

'That's not possible. All of this is hypothetical,' Hiranya protested.

'The Trials are never hypothetical,' the spirit snarled. 'They are part of the Chakras, the atoms that run in the air of Illavarti. Whatever you see, there is a reason for it, and this Trial, there is a reason for it too. The Trial wants you to decide whether your son is more important to you, or the Asura empire.'

'You mean to say there is a possibility my son would turn to Vishnu?'

'The Trial can see the future, the past and the present. So we don't know or we know. Anything is possible.'

'So what does the Trial gain from killing my son?'

'The confirmation that if a need arose in the future, you'd be ready to kill your son again. Remember, the Brahmashastra armour and the weapon is for the worthy. And the worthy have to be ready to do *anything* in the process of getting the weapon.'

Hiranya sighed. He walked up to Prahlad, and this time Prahlad was younger, perhaps seven or eight.

Hiranya sat down next to him.

'Father,' Prahlad said, turning to Hiranya. He looked so real; not at all like an illusion, which made it worse for

Hiranya. 'Look at what I have.' The boy put out his fists and opened them to reveal fireflies in his palms. 'How beautiful they are, aren't they? What should I do?'

Hiranya couldn't speak. He was trying hard not to weep, and he put his hand on Prahlad's head, patting him.

'I'll just free them!' And then the boy opened his palms, letting the fireflies fly into the night. 'Do you remember you told me one of the stars is my mother?'

Hiranya looked up and saw that there was just one bright, shining star in the sky.

'Yes.'

'Whenever that one star would appear, you would say that Mom was watching us, watching me.'

'Yes, I did.' Hiranya felt tears falling down his cheeks. 'She's watching us tonight too.'

'It makes me happy that I have my parents. One up there and one here.' Prahlad hugged Hiranya.

He's so sweet. But what if he grows up to be Vishnu's follower?

Hiranya thought of that possibility.

Would I spare him because he's my son, or would I kill him for betraying my race?

He recalled what the spirit had said. That he has to take the action right now, otherwise – otherwise Prahlad would grow up to be a follower of Vishnu, and end the Asura race.

This is not real. But what if it happens in reality? Would I be able to kill him then?

Hiranya kissed Prahlad on the top of his head.

'Why are you crying, Daddy?' the boy asked.

'Because your daddy is a bad man,' Hiranya said through gritted teeth, fighting back more tears. 'Prahlad ... You are my son. But if there is the slightest chance that you will end up betraying what we stand for, I will do what is necessary.'

'And what is necessary?' Prahlad asked.

Hiranya closed his eyes and placed his hand on Prahlad's back. With a shove, he pushed the boy off the cliff. When he opened his eyes, he looked up at the lone star in the sky. Prahlad was gone.

And Hiranya was all alone.

38
PRAHLAD

Prahlad was standing in his balcony. His city spread in front of him, under the dusky, dark skies. He was lost in thought, his mind going over everything that had happened, and all that was going to happen.

Am I doing the right thing now? I hope I am.

He trusted Narada, but the old man had a penchant for doing what he thought Lord Vishnu wanted, with no care for whom he might hurt in the process.

I'm sure Lord Vishnu wouldn't want that.

Prahlad had borrowed books on Lord Vishnu from Narada; books about his early years with Lord Brahma and the first Shiva, his end at Vaikuntha, how he gave the power of lions to humans, creating the Simha hybrid, and how on his death, he extended the promise to Illavarti that he would send his soldier, the chosen one, in every Age to fight Adharm.

Prahlad found these stories inspiring and heroic, and above all … so important, for they gave people hope that even in darkness, there would be a hero to free them from tyranny.

But unfortunately, I'm part of that darkness.

He also realized, reading these stories and exploring them, that Narada was an extremist, and that he was wrong. In the name of religion, one must preach and spread peace, not violence. Perhaps Narada thirsted for revenge after losing his students and his Gurukul, and that anger was manifesting into extremism.

After reading so much about Lord Vishnu, Prahlad also knew that his father was not chasing Indra because of his mother. Kayadhu was just an instrument to fuel his anger, his motivation. In the end, Hiranya only wanted power, and by killing Kayadhu, Indra had challenged that power. Now, Hiranya was trying to prove to himself and the others that he was someone. It was pure ego that fuelled him.

But that is just my reasoning. Perhaps I'm wrong.

'My lord,' a voice came from the back and interrupted his thoughts.

Prahlad turned to see Dhriti. She stood with her hands clasped behind her, and a sharp dagger hung from the belt around her waist.

'Don't call me that,' he protested.

'I'm still your servant.'

'Come on,' Prahlad said.

Dhriti walked forward, a smile on her face. She had a flower in her hair, as always.

'I have been meaning to ask, what's bothering you?' she said.

'I've been wondering whether Narada is a good leader or not,' Prahlad said, leaning back on the railing of the balcony.

'Don't mind this. He has formed the Vishnusena, but I wonder if he is the right person to lead it?'

Dhriti was silent for a while, and then said, 'He is a bit … extreme, I understand. But don't we need that?'

'We need balance, Dhriti. Not chaos. We already live in chaos under my father's thumb, and while burning down brothels does deplete the royal treasury, it doesn't hurt the ministers too much. To do that, we have to sack the treasury itself.' he explained.

She grinned. 'That's a great idea. Perhaps after the brothels, we can do that.'

'And piss off Shand and Amarka?' Prahlad chuckled. 'I wouldn't mind that at all. They are both a pain in the ass.'

She laughed.

'I don't like to say anything against Narada,' she said, 'because he really helped me. I was lost. I was an orphan, a thief. I remember how I had no direction and I was working under a slumlord who would call me to his room every night.' She closed her eyes. 'It was horrible.'

'But you are so young!' exclaimed Prahlad, shocked.

'I know. But he didn't care, and there was no law that could protect me.'

Prahlad knew that he had to change the laws of the state to suit the needs of his people better, and not let young girls like Dhriti be a victim of the state.

'I'm so sorry,' he said to her, holding her hand. 'I won't let that happen to you again. We must find that slumlord and punish him.'

'You are so cute,' she smirked. 'I ripped his heart out the day I joined the Vishnusena.'

Prahlad didn't know how to respond.

She didn't need my help. I needed hers, I guess.

'Now you are part of us, and we will die for you, and protect you with our lives,' she said, and her smile was genuine.

Prahlad returned it. 'Thank you.' He looked at her lips and she looked at his. There was silence between them.

'I think I should go,' Dhriti said.

'Yeah, I think you should.'

But neither of them moved. They stood close to each other, very close in fact, and Prahlad could feel his heartbeat and hear hers. He leaned forward and ...

There was a knock on the door of the room.

By the sword of Lord Vishnu, who is it?

Prahlad and Dhriti pulled away, and Dhriti's brows furrowed.

'I should hide. No one can see me here at this time of the night,' she said, hiding behind the long drapes. Prahlad nodded and went to open the door.

It was Viparichit, looking frantic and worried. 'May I speak freely, Prahlad?'

He didn't use his first name often, but when he did, it meant something was wrong. Prahlad didn't want him to enter, but Viparichit did so without asking. 'I apologize, I'm just a little bit flabbergasted,' he said.

'What is wrong?'

'I ... uh ...' Viparichit sighed. 'I was visited by your aunt.'

By the gods ...

'All right, and?'

'She thinks you are betraying the empire.'

Prahlad scoffed. 'What makes her think that?'

'She saw how you conveniently pulled her army from the base just in time for the attack. I am not supposed to tell you all of this because she wanted me to spy on you, but you know … I had to, man. You are my friend.' He shook his head. 'By telling you all of this, I am potentially ruining my chances with Simmi, but I have to tell you, all right?'

Prahlad patted his friend on the shoulder. 'It's all right. Don't worry. She has no proof. She has nothing. It's just coincidences she's basing these allegations on.'

Viparichit gazed at Prahlad and then nodded. 'I know. You are right. You know, I had almost made up my mind to spy on you, but then I recalled how once I'd stolen some food from the royal kitchen and you had seen me do it, but didn't turn me in. You … you are a good man.' He smiled. 'I know you would never side with the Vishnusena.'

Prahlad swallowed a lump. He felt guilty for betraying the trust of his friend.

But I can't tell him.

'It's not in your blood,' Viparichit continued. 'What should we do about Holika?'

'I'll figure out a way. Holika's never liked me, you know,' Prahlad responded. 'She has always … well … she blames me for her inability to have children.'

'What do you mean?' Viparichit arched his brows.

'You know how siblings often marry in our culture,' Prahlad began. 'Holika was not happy when my father didn't marry her. Instead, he married my mother because she was pregnant with Anuhrad. And then later, I was born. My aunt was not happy with that. Ever since then, she's hated me and

Anuhrad. In fact, she always believed that if she had married my father, she would have had a good chance of becoming a mother.'

Viparichit shook his head. 'It's sad that she has these personal biases.' He went over and sat on the bed and glanced at the books. 'I thought you didn't like reading, Prahlad.'

'I was just casually ...' Prahlad tried to grab the books, but before he could, Viparichit picked up one of them and saw the title.

He came to his feet as he read the underlined pages that Prahlad had marked out. He walked as he read, and came to a stop next to the long drapes behind which Dhriti hid.

'For a boy who says he isn't part of Vishnusena, you read about Vishnu a lot,' Viparichit said to Prahlad, his eyes narrowed.

'It's just to identify the enemy,' Prahlad said weakly.

Viparichit pursed his lips suspiciously as his eyes tried to find answers in Prahlad's meek, troubled face. 'Of course. Did you find out what happened with the red-haired girl?'

'I don't know. Never found her.'

'All right,' Viparichit nodded. 'I think I should leave.'

He knows.

And before he knew what was happening, Dhriti jumped from the drapes, grabbing Viparichit by the throat and holding her knife against him. 'Hold still, my boy.'

'You are ... working ... for them.' Viparichit flared his nostrils.

'It's more complicated than you think,' Prahlad said.

'You liar!' Viparichit yelled.

The words stung, but Prahlad focused on bringing the situation under control. 'Dhriti, leave him.'

'He will tell Holika,' Dhriti screamed back.

'He won't.'

'I will!' Viparichit shouted furiously. 'I have to tell her that a traitorous king rules this city. Everyone has to know.'

Dhriti tried to slash the dagger across Viparichit's neck when he grabbed her by the arm, twisting it so that she dropped the weapon on the ground. Then he flung her across the room and, pulling out his own blade, lunged at her. He pushed her against the wall and then pulled her hair as she screamed and writhed in pain.

'I shall get Holika your head. She will love it.'

Prahlad picked up the dagger that had fallen from Dhriti's hand and ran up to Viparichit, who moved just in time to deflect Prahlad's attack.

'I can't believe you were behind this,' Viparichit said as they stood facing each other. With one arm, he still held Dhriti against the wall.

The next moment, he charged at Prahlad, who sidestepped the attack and jabbed his dagger into Viparichit's spine. The next moment, Viparichit fell heavily to the ground, face down.

Prahlad walked up to Dhriti, who was holding her injured arm. He embraced her and they rested against the wall, staring down at the dead royal guard before them.

I'm sorry, my friend.

Prahlad's hand went up to hold his locket, seeking solace in it.

If Holika learns about his death – she will know it was me.

40

NARASIMHA

Narasimha stood on the bridge that led to the gates of Sonitpur. The trident hung from a belt around his back.

He had left Bhairav's body with one of the Gana soldiers and ordered him to return to the fort with it.

He would use the trident to end Andhaka.

His head was held high. His wounded chest heaved as he watched the setting sun. He was exhausted and hurt, but he didn't care. He felt a surge of power within him.

He knew why he felt this way.

I may not be Dharm, but I know evil when I see it. And I'm going to kill it.

And while it brought him courage, the thought also scared the living daylights out of him. He was afraid he would turn into the Avatar.

Do I care now?

I don't.

I need to avenge my friend.

Tears rolled down his eyes as he walked on. The bridge was deserted. Andhaka's army was nowhere to be seen; perhaps they were hiding. The bridge was long and the icy river churned under it.

And while he could feel the temperature rising, he saw his enemy in front.

It was Andhaka. He was on his horse – the same glistening red blindfold around him and he had a lance in his hand.

And without much ado, Andhaka moved towards him.

For a moment, Nara was taken aback – Andhaka didn't have a lance back when he had seen him and yet now, he had one.

But it didn't matter.

Nara gritted his teeth.

I shall avenge you, my friend.

He sprinted forward, roaring in the process as he came close to the stallion and instead of just clawing the blind prince, he jumped on top of his horse, throwing him off.

Andhaka kneed him and tried to use his lance to pierce his skin, but …

Nara stopped the blow, grabbing the lance by the blade, bleeding as he did. He twisted the blade and broke it from its long leather hilt. And using the same blade, stabbed Andhaka in the face.

Andhaka was dead.

Nara sighed as he stood there. Had he actually killed the real Andhaka?

But he soon had his answer. Just at the end of the bridge, another Andhaka stood, and next to him, was yet another! In fact, there were three of them.

Three Andhakas!

Nara couldn't believe his eyes. The three men were slightly different in build, but had the same dress code, the same look – hairless and pale with red blindfolds on.

I killed one, and three more have risen.

How many of them were there?

Before he could move, the Andhakas came forward with their lances and lunged at Nara.

Nara began to deflect each attack with his claws as he tried to figure out – who was the real Andhaka among them?

Each Andhaka fought with precision, even with the blindfold on.

The blindfolds! Something Anuhrad had said clicked into place.

Nara ripped at the red cloth, looking into their wide eyes, and realizing something in the process …

They could see.

But Andhaka was blind.

They are all imposters! The real Andhaka is blind. The only one who is blind.

And that could only mean one thing – Andhaka was using lookalikes.

Nara rolled over and from the back, plunged his claws into one of the Andhaka's backs, breaking his spine, and then went for the other one, clawing his throat, ripping it out. The third Andhaka used his lance and jumped at Nara—

Instead of attacking him, Narasimha roared with all his might.

The Andhaka's eyes widened in fright at the sound, and he hesitated. Nara roared again and in the light of the sun that shone from between the dark clouds, his skin glinted. Suddenly, his face was no longer visible. It was only the lion that shone.

Only the beast was visible.

Nara turned his head and he could see that he was surrounded by more Andhakas – six of them.

The real one is sending them to keep me occupied while he escapes.

Instead of attacking them, Nara sprinted forward as tendrils of pain shot down his feet. He broke the barrier of the six Andhakas, pushing them aside and running through the city gates. Behind him, the six Andhakas followed.

Nara looked at the city – the poor, starving civilians had come out and were looking at him in horror.

'Where is he?' Nara asked. Behind him, the Andhakas were gaining ground, about to reach him.

The civilians were confused. They looked at the Simha, and then at the multiple Andhakas.

Before anyone could reply, the Andhakas had surrounded Nara, circling him as he stood in the middle, watching each of them intently.

As each came forward, Nara slashed his blindfold methodically and saw the eyes … normal, healthy eyes, the irises perfect.

And as they lifted their lances and jutted them forward, Nara jumped in the air like a lion, and the lances of the Andhakas slashed each other.

They ended up stabbing themselves.

'It's over, animal,' a high-pitched voice called from behind.

Nara turned to see a feeble-looking Andhaka, walking alone, unarmed. He was rubbing his arms like he was cold. Nara sensed that he was frightened.

'It's over,' the old man said again. 'I have no army left. They were all killed, hmmm,' Andhaka said, shaking his head. The civilians watched them from afar. 'I have troubled them. I have troubled you. I even ended up letting my dear friend Anuhrad die. I had grand plans for him, hmmm.' He knelt on the snow, defeated. Then he gestured towards his lookalikes. 'These men believed in me … they are gone too.'

Nara looked on, grim. He would not waste his pity on a monster.

'And I killed my father.' Andhaka shook his head. 'I thought I could run …' he shrugged, 'but I then I realized, hmmm, what's the point? I have lost. I have nowhere to go. No door that will open to welcome me.' He began to cry, and then the sobs turned into a snarl of rage. 'Do you know how it feels, hmmm, to plan everything and lose it?'

Nara knew what he meant.

I have felt this way so many times.

'Kill me,' Andhaka said. 'I don't want to live any more in this cruel world, hmmm. Please.'

Nara walked closer to Andhaka and pulled his blindfold off, revealing two gaping, burnt holes instead of eyes.

He's the real one.

'It's me,' Andhaka nodded. 'You got me, finally.'

'I didn't think you would give up like this.'

'A man should know when to give up,' Andhaka said. 'Are you familiar with that feeling, you animal?' he asked Nara.

Was he?

He had been running away from being Dharm all his life. He had given up, but he had been brought back here … to this moment. He was born to do this; to destroy evil. And by running away, he had just let evil grow.

'A man should know his responsibilities. Because when you are chosen for greatness,' Nara said, thoughtfully musing about the moment he had learnt he would be Dharm, 'you have to embrace it instead of running away from it.' He smiled. Then he looked at the blind man with a vicious smile. 'Don't think for a moment that I will take pity on you,' he said.

'I know you won't. I'm ashamed to be killed by a Simha,' Andhaka said.

Nara pulled the trident out and aimed it at Andhaka's throat.

'No. You won't be killed by a Simha,' Nara responded, plunging the trident into Andhaka's throat, watching the blood spurt all over the white snow.

He didn't have the symbol of Vishnu to justify what he was going to say. But it didn't matter.

He *believed* in the words that came from him, words that were more important than the symbol itself.

'You will die at the hands of an avatar of Vishnu.'

41

HIRANYAKASHYAP

'You have passed,' said the spirit.

Hiranyakashyap's energy was completely depleted, and for a moment, he felt like he didn't even care for the Brahmshastra any more. It was all too much now, what he had gone through.

'You may get the armour and the weapon now.'

Hiranya nodded as he unstrapped his armour and tossed it on the ground. He removed his gauntlets and his shoulder pads, along with his golden, horned crown – which closely resembled the horns of a bull and represented strength. The horns were created to symbolize the strength and valour of the Asura empire, but the Devas had used them against the Asuras, making the public connect the horns to the idea of demons and evil.

Hiranya went up to the Brahmshastra. The blue beam protecting the armour vanished as soon as he put his hand through it to grab the suspended armour.

As Hiranya began to put on the armour, he realized that it had a life of its own. It latched on to his body tightly, fitting him with ease. It used no straps or buckles, but a strange, liquid that quickly covered his entire body in armour of gold and platinum. The gauntlets were like simple gloves and his legs too were covered by the golden armour.

And as soon as he had finished wearing it, there was a surge of power inside him, giving him absolute strength.

'I feel so good,' he murmured under his breath.

'You are supposed to. Don't forget your sword,' the spirit instructed.

Hiranya nodded, picking up the weapon in his hand. As soon as he did, a golden sheath formed around his hand. Hiranya studied the sword. It had golden inscriptions that glinted and reflected light. He felt so proud, and he hoped that his brother was watching from the spirit world, applauding Hiranya's success.

'The Brahmshastra disappears when you don't need it and when you need it, you can chant Lord Brahma's name to receive it,' the spirit explained.

'This is all magic?'

'Everything is.' The spirit was grinning now as Hiranya sheathed his blade. 'But remember, there are a few rules. The Brahmshastra can only be summoned outside or inside, but never in between. It can be summoned in the morning or night, but never at twilight. It can be summoned on the ground or in the sky, but never in between.'

'That's too specific.'

'There's always a loophole in Lord Brahma's boons,' the spirit said. 'It's a boon he left for mankind, but a demon lord has got it. That means no one was capable of it except you.'

Hiranya felt proud. 'Why did you never want me to have this? Because I'm considered a demon? It's false propaganda.'

'We know.' The spirit nodded. 'We discourage the worthy challenger, to see whether the discouragement stops him, but it didn't stop you. You still kept going.'

Hiranya smiled and made a move to leave, but then stopped and asked the spirit with his final question. 'Why the "we"?'

The spirit was silent. Then it said, 'Because there are four of us.'

'Four of whom?' Hiranya arched his brows. 'I see only one.'

And then, before he could say anything more, there was a bright light and the spirit in front of him transformed into a long, lanky man whose face was invisible due to the fact that it was illuminated. Hiranya blinked and his vision cleared to reveal that there were four men who stood before him now, in multicoloured robes.

'Who is this?' Hiranya grunted, squinting in the light.

'The man whose weapon you wear,' all four of them said at the same time.

Instantly, Hiranya fell to the ground, kneeling with his head bowed. 'Lord Brahma!'

'Yes, my warrior.'

'How is it possible that you are alive?'

'I'm alive only here, in the first temple that was made for me,' the voices said at the same time. 'I'm just a spirit, just the way you saw me since the beginning.'

'My lord, I'm honoured being in your presence,' Hiranya said.

'Use my weapon wisely or else Lord Vishnu's Avatar will find you,' Lord Brahma warned.

'But he cannot win. Your boon doesn't allow him to. I'm indestructible as long as I don't take this armour off.'

'And I hope you won't, but if you do, remember to not do it in front of an Avatar.'

Hiranya nodded, and then asked another question that was running through his mind. 'My lord, may I ask why there are four of you?'

'Because the Brahma is a composite of four men – Vedanta, Gyaneswar, Chaturmukha and Svayambhu,' Lord Brahma explained. 'We were the first men to lead the first civilization. All four of us were buried here and we all were then termed Lord Brahma and worshipped as one instead of four,' Lord Brahma said. 'Farewell, champion. I hope you choose your path well.'

'Yes, my lord.' Hiranya bowed his head. He couldn't believe he was seeing a god in front of him and he felt his faith in his country's religion being restored.

As the light died, Hiranya looked up to see that the figures had disappeared. He still had the golden armour on him. With a smirk, he moved to the entrance of the cave, blocked by the rocks.

He brought the sword in front of the rocks, and it began to radiate, expelling so much energy and light that the rocks flew apart, landing a good distance away from the cave. Hiranya watched, fascinated. He felt strong, almost as if …

As if he was invincible.

He stepped out of the cave with his sword and his armour and looked at Agni's stunned forces, watching him with horror.

They know …. that now, they are in trouble.

42

HIRANYAKASHYAP

Hiranyakashyap was obliterating Agni's men.

He couldn't believe a sword this big was this light and easy to use. As he swung it right and left, it sliced men like they were fruits. Hiranya felt like he'd wielded it for years, and didn't even have to put any strength into his attacks.

He plunged the blade through the ribcage of a soldier and then twisted it until a light began to emit from the blade and …

The soldier exploded into pieces!

A fire rock landed close to him and with one swinging move, Hiranya blocked it with his golden gauntlets. It exploded, but his armour instantly deflected the attack, letting the fire subside.

Hiranya walked through the fire, letting the remaining men come to him while he avoided their attacks and then sliced them all up with one gigantic swing.

As a Naga approached him, Hiranya stabbed him in the throat and pulled the head off with ease, tossing it at the other soldier, who was knocked off his feet.

There was so much bloodshed that the sand turned red, like it was bleeding too.

Hiranya could see Agni's face turning pale. No more did he have that overconfident smile. Instead, his brows arched, and he looked helpless.

Agni's archers shot arrows at Hiranya from a distance, but when they hit him, he didn't feel even a prick, and the arrows broke apart upon touching the armour.

He could feel its power – it was so majestic and magical. He never wanted to take it off. The battle felt like a sport rather than a task now.

Hiranya ran towards Agni and his archers, using his shoulders to push them aside. He first attacked the archers, using their own bows to hit them on the head. Then he saw Agni escaping with his horse, having no men left to aid him. Hiranya pointed his blade at Agni and then ... *He swung it.*

The blade behaved as if it knew where it had to land, and plunged through Agni's spine, stabbing him in the back as he fell on the ground, bawling in pain.

Hiranya looked at Agni as he lay there, writhing in agony.

He was pompous. He shouldn't have come here. But then, he thought I would be alone, easy to defeat.

And then Hiranya realized it. He *was* alone. He'd single-handedly destroyed Agni and his men.

I don't need anyone else any more.

Hiranya walked closer to Agni, who was shivering and panting as he lay on the hot sand. Hiranya pulled out the blade and Agni screamed in pain. Hiranya knelt down next to the god of fire and smiled. 'It's a shame. They used to think you are a god and, well, here you are, lying at my feet, awaiting my mercy. A god at my mercy. Heh.' And there was elation in his voice.

Agni faced the Asura king, his skin white and ghastly. 'How did you do this?'

'How does it matter to a dying man?'

Agni grimaced. 'You are … right.'

'What you should know is that now, I'm going to destroy your brother while your body rots in this desert.' Hiranya laughed. 'And no one will know where Agni went – has he died? Is he alive? Where is our god of fire? No one will know what happened to you, and that's a death you deserve. Yes, it feels right after what you all did to my wife.'

Agni shook his head. 'No …'

'What?' Hiranya cocked his head forward.

'It was not us.' He lay his head on the sand and looked at the stars. 'We attacked the city, yes, but it was not …' He coughed and spat blood, 'it was not us. We didn't kill your wife. Yes, it was … Indra's responsibility, but the man who actually executed her … was someone else.'

Hiranya arched his brows. 'Who?'

'Indra told me about it. He wanted to scare K-Kayadhu, not kill her.' Agni coughed again. 'But Kayadhu attacked him and his guard, and ...'

Hiranya grabbed hold of Agni and pulled him up, but Agni's life was fading.

'No … no …' Hiranya slapped Agni on the face, 'Who was it? Who was the guard? What is his name? Tell me!'

Agni opened his eyes, a triumphant smirk dancing on his cruel lips, as he said his final word—

'Narasimha.'

43

NARASIMHA

The war was over.

Or perhaps it's just beginning.

And no one had won. Andhaka was dead. Sonitpur was free from the Asuras. Word was out and everyone knew now that the Pashupatastra had been dismantled and destroyed.

Bhairav's army had partially won, but he had lost his life in the process – at the hands of his own son.

Nara watched Bhairav's body burn on the pyre as Chenchen stood next to him, holding his hand. Nara saw Parvati in the front, her arms wrapped around her body. She was a beautiful woman – exhausted, but extremely beautiful. There was a saying that if one saw her, one would fall in love with her. He wanted to speak to her, but refrained from it.

Later, she turned her head towards Nara, and walked up to him. Nara bowed a little out of respect. When he saw her, he noticed that her eyes were dead – no remorse, no anger.

'Is Bhringi alive?' she asked.

'No, my lady. I killed him. He was not Bhringi any more. He was Andhaka.'

Nara saw she wasn't disappointed.

'The karma of Bhairav ended here at the hands of his son,' Parvati sighed. 'But it's a new beginning for me.' She arched her brows. 'Will you help me rebuild this place?'

But I have other plans.

'My lady, I need to leave. But my Simhas will be at your service.' Nara turned his head to look at his Pride. 'Virsimha can guide you. I have appointed him the new leader of the Pride.' The Pride wasn't happy about this, since Nara had replaced their previous leader and was now escaping his responsibilities again, but Nara had explained to them that he was never supposed to lead them. He was supposed to guide them towards their next leader, a worthy one, and Virsimha displayed all the right qualities.

Parvati clenched her jaw at his response. 'But what about you?'

Nara exchanged glances with Chenchen. 'I have somewhere to go.' He paused, a sad smile on his lips. 'And, let's be honest: I was not going to be around here forever.'

Parvati nodded. 'A raven came in this morning – Indra is coming to the fort. He's furious we destroyed the Pashupatastra.'

'Of course he is.' Nara grinned. 'But I don't plan to stay here till he comes. I have no respect for him … not any more.'

She smiled. 'Likewise. Veerbhadra will handle it.' She looked at the lieutenant, the man who was going to be the next Shiva for the Gana tribe.

'And I wish Lord Vishnu is with you in your mission,' he said.

'You too.'

'I have Lord Bhairav's trident. Should I give it to you or Veerbhadra?' Nara asked.

She shook her head. 'Keep it. I'm sure he would have wanted you to have it.'

The cremation ended and Nara walked with Chenchen to his cabin. He was without his skin and wore a dhoti and a soft muffler. He began packing for his journey. Chenchen was standing behind him, her hands clasped behind her. 'I didn't know you were leaving.'

'I thought you didn't want to know,' Nara said as he began to put medicines, weapons and his skin inside the bag. 'You belong here, Chenchen.'

There was a long silence and then she came on his side and put her hand on his. 'You don't get to tell me where I belong and where I do not.'

Nara smiled, looking at her. 'All right. What do you plan to do then?'

'I want to stay with you, Nara. You need me as much as I need you,' she said.

'What about the villages you were saving?'

'My nurses are still here, aren't they?'

Nara shook his head. 'You are getting carried away, Chenchen. You have to stay here and serve the purpose you have decided for yourself.'

She kept her head on his shoulder and he wrapped his arms around her waist. 'You are right. I was just … being emotional, heh,' she said.

'Of course. I will return, if our fates desire it. And then we will do something about your marriage.'

They both chuckled at that.

'Where do you plan to go?' she asked.

Nara had been thinking about it for a lot of time. 'Kashyapuri,' he responded. 'I have to meet Prahlad.'

'Why?' she pulled back. 'The demon prince?'

'I have to protect him,' Nara said. The prophecy might not be fulfilled and the secret of Lord Rudra, the secret of this Yug, would remain with him.

Perhaps I have changed my destiny. I thought I would become the Avatar after killing Andhaka … but I still haven't received the symbol.

Am I really the Dharm?

But he was going out in the world and there was a risk … of him receiving it after all.

But I have to take that risk. I have to save the boy. I have to embrace my destiny.

I'm not afraid any more.

'I don't understand, why?' Chenchen asked.

Nara glanced at Chenchen.

If only she could understand.

'I killed his brother.'

'But you didn't know any better.'

'I didn't. But I have a responsibility. I have to save him. He has no one except his father and his father is not a good man,' Nara replied.

'I still don't understand,' she was pulling away from him. 'You had no role to play in his fate, and if you killed his brother, it was a mistake, one that happened during a battle.'

Nara sighed. He recalled the battle at Kashyapuri – the time Hiranya had left for Pataal and Nara had gone to his palace with Indra. They had sacked the city and killed Hiranya's wife.

'I do actually,' he began. 'You see, the reason he is under the malicious thumb of his father is because of me.'

'How?' Chenchen asked.

Nara recalled the horrible day it had happened. It was one of the many reasons he had left the war. 'It's not only his brother I killed,' he said.

'Then?'

'It was his mother too.' The fire crackled in the grate as he spoke. 'To save Indra on the day of his crusade to Kashyapuri, I murdered Kayadhu and her blood is on my hands. And his brother's blood is on my hands now …' he paused, 'I'll make sure Prahlad's blood is not spilled. His safety is my responsibility now. I won't let anything happen to him,' he sighed. 'This is my redemption. *He* is my redemption.'

44

HOLIKA

Holika knew something was going wrong.

At the very onset, the weather itself was an issue, and the air was troubling. There was something brewing, something sinister, as if the shadow of the Vishnusena was growing day by day. Narada was nowhere to be seen. He had just vanished, as if he had never existed in the first place, and even the ministers had been questioned on his whereabouts.

I have to stop them.

She touched her bangle and wondered whether Simhika was safe.

Perhaps I should take her away from here, at least until the Vishnusena is brought to its end.

Prahlad ruled the city, but she didn't trust him. It wasn't just the fact that she considered Kayadhu's boys weaklings, but also because she'd always thought that there was something about those boys that was not quite right.

But most of all, she had to find out what was going on with Viparichit. He hadn't got back to her and it had been days since she'd given him his instructions.

Holika sat in her study, close to the burning lamp. She had sent her guard to look for Viparichit. When the guard returned, he knocked on the door, and she looked up, expecting a positive response.

'My lady, he has disappeared. No one has seen him,' the guard said.

'That's impossible.' Holika shook her head.

The guard shrugged. 'Even his father is worried about him.'

Holika hummed, thoughtfully musing over this.

Is he even alive?

She was getting a bad feeling about this. 'Where do we send the unclaimed corpses to every week?' she asked.

'We either hand them off to the Pishach at the border,' he said, referring to the flesh-eating Tribe, 'Or we just burn or bury them. Some of them are also thrown into the sea.'

'Show me the next set of bodies that are going to the Pishach,' Holika said.

The guard nodded. 'You can come now. A cart is leaving as we speak.'

Holika grabbed her twin swords and sheathed them. She followed the guards with a heavy heart.

Let's hope Viparichit … Let's hope. Simmi really loved him.

She didn't want Simmi to lose Viparichit. No matter how hard a time she gave the poor guy, he had seemed good for Simmi, who was quite stubborn.

They made their way to the cart. The gravedigger, as fat and greasy as anyone could be, saw Holika and froze in fear. As she approached him, he bowed to her.

The cart was large and flies swarmed over it. Holika's guards pulled off the long sheet that covered the corpses. They began to examine the bodies while clamping one hand on their noses.

Let's hope he's not here. Let's hope.

'Have any corpses also been sent for mass burial this week?' Holika asked.

'Not in the last few days,' the guard replied. 'These, which you see in front, are all the unclaimed corpses in the past week.'

'I have a feeling we won't …' Holika began when she heard something.

A clink.

Her eyes darted to where the sound came from and she knelt to the ground and picked up a shiny object. It was a ring.

No.

Holika then went forward, inspecting the corpses herself, looking for the body the ring had belonged to, and finally, under the greasy, smelly bodies, she saw him.

No!

It was Viparichit, still in his armour.

Holika's heart sank.

Prahlad has done it. He has done it, that bloody vermin!

'What should we do, my lady?' asked her guard.

She thought for a moment. 'Don't give him to the Pishach. Bury him but don't let anyone know,' Holika said. She didn't want Simmi to find out.

The guard nodded, directing the grave digger to remove Viparichit's body from the cart.

Feeling uneasy, Holika moved away from the cart and stumbled across the lonely street. She had never felt so horrible and guilty for a death. She knew it was because this time, it was related to Simmi. And Simmi was very close to her.

As the cart pulled away, a guard walked up to Holika. She noticed that he was not part of her recent entourage, but a messenger guard who had come running up to them. 'My lady, I have just received word. The Vishnusena were seen near the brothels close to the fort, piling explosives around them. By the time we reached there, the fire was already lit. We reached late because all of us had been called to a meeting by King Prahlad.'

That puny child!

Then suddenly, the full meaning of his words hit Holika.

The brothel near the fort? But that's where Simmi is ... No!

Instead of asking for her horse, Holika began running in the direction of the brothel, passing through the lanes and coming to the main street only to be met by civilians who were standing around watching the raging flames in horror.

Holika's eyes darted around, and finally rested on the brothel where Simmi worked. It was going up in smoke, the flames licking the air. Other brothels close to it were on fire too, and the effect was horrific, like the entire city was going up in flames.

'Try to evacuate the establishments,' she told some of her guards who had sprinted to her side.

Holika tried to locate Simmi among the people who had managed to escape the burning buildings and were now tending to their injuries with the help of the other civilians. There was no sign of her.

There was no sign of the Vishnusena anywhere either.

Holika grabbed the nearest guard. 'Have you seen Simhika?' she asked him. He shook his head.

Is she still inside? By the heavens, I hope not!

Holika tore a piece of cloth from her tunic and wrapped it around her face to keep the smoke out of her lungs, and then she entered the burning brothel. She fought through the collapsing building, breaking the doors as she heard the shouts of her guards calling out to her.

She began to frantically search for Simmi, looking everywhere, paying no heed to the flames burning her arms and legs.

'Simhika!' she shouted.

Holika saw a few burnt bodies lying on the ground. She was horrified by what the Vishnusena had done.

'Simhika!' she cried out again, but her voice was weaker, as she had inhaled too much smoke despite the makeshift wrap, and her lungs were giving up.

Holika knew where Simmi's room was, and as she made her way up to it, a wooden beam collapsed and landed in front of her and she narrowly avoided it.

She leapt over the beam, feeling the unbearable heat on her skin. She opened the door that belonged to Simmi's room. Before her, on the floor of the room, lay a girl with arms covered in bangles, a flaming log on top of her. Holika gasped. She needed to remove the burning log before it completely consumed Simmi.

Using her bare arms, Holika pulled the log up, her hands buzzing from the searing pain that shot through her body.

She screamed in agony as she tossed the log in the corner, and sighing, she picked Simmi up, patting her on the face. But before she could do anything else, she realized that the flames were closing in, and the floor was cracking under her feet.

I need to get out.

She looked at the window and without even giving it a second thought, took Simmi on her back and jumped from it, her eyes closed. She landed on her feet, her legs buckling just as an explosion behind her ripped through the building.

Holika laid Simmi on the ground and knelt beside her. The guards came to her with blankets, but Holika didn't care.

She was watching Simmi, whose eyes were still closed.

'Baby, it's all right. Wake up, you are fine. I saved you, okay,' she smiled as tears filled her eyes. 'Come on, Simmi. I know you are fine. Let's do it. Please, wake up.' She leaned forward and hugged her daughter, and then listened for a heartbeat.

But she heard none.

Holika's heart sank.

No.

This can't happen. I can't lose another one. I just can't. Not again.

'You were supposed to holler for me, baby. Why didn't you, eh? *Why didn't you*?' she said, her throat choked with tears.

Holika could feel the anger boiling inside her. So much of it. And as the fire blazed behind her, her golden irises shimmered with tears. She had never felt such hatred before.

She felt a pang, and noticed that her arm was bleeding. She looked at it and saw that the bangle she wore, the bangle Simmi had given her, had broken and pierced her skin.

I'm coming for you, Prahlad. I'm coming for you now.

45

PRAHLAD

Prahlad could see the fires from his balcony.

And he knew trouble was on the way.

But before he could do anything about it, someone rushed inside. He moved to grab his weapon, but he found it was Narada who entered the room, panting and in haste.

'They have done it, haven't they?' Narada smiled, as he walked close to the balcony. 'A wonderful sight!'

'I am getting reports,' Prahlad began, 'that people have died in the fire. You promised that you would evacuate them.'

'I told my men to do it.' Narada shrugged. 'If it wasn't feasible for them, I can't do anything.'

Prahlad clenched his fist and without even thinking twice, grabbed hold of Narada and pushed him to the edge of the balcony. 'I didn't want this. How are you better than my father?'

'Calm down, son.' Narada's voice sounded like the guruji who used to teach Prahlad in his formative years. 'You need to think straight. Your father had built this capital on violence and only through violence will it be able to end.'

'But does that mean good people need to die?'

'Good people don't go to brothels. They are sinful places. Please, son, understand,' Narada pleaded.

Prahlad moved back, the respect he felt for Narada preventing him from doing anything more. He ran his hand through his hair. 'You can't be seen around here. Holika knows about your involvement,' he told the older man.

'I know the secrets of this palace better than you do. I knew where to come from and where to go.'

'And why are you here?'

'To warn you,' Narada said.

'About what?'

'She has released them. But it's all right. You have your own army to defend you.'

The ground shook suddenly, and chills ran down Prahlad's spine. He turned and looked out from the balcony, and watched the silhouette of the massive and malignant figures against the sky, walking towards the palace.

Danavs.

'Where did she get them from?'

'Some were stationed in the outskirts of the city. She summoned them. And she is coming for you. We need to leave for the inn,' Narada said.

'But what about this palace?'

'You are not part of it any more, son.' Narada's hands cupped Prahlad's face. 'You are more than this. You are part of Lord Vishnu. Please, come with me.'

Prahlad saw from his balcony that his Asura guards were heading towards the major gates, holding spears and shields, javelins and swords, unaware that they were getting ready to defend the interim king who had betrayed them. Archers were lining up along the towers. Trumpets were being blown; vultures circled overhead. Everything was in chaos.

Prahlad's guards entered and Narada hid behind the door.

'My lord, Lady Holika is closing in. You must be sent to the underground tunnels.'

'Yes, of course,' Prahlad nodded. 'I'll go myself. You worry about fending them off. Protect my father's kingdom by defending this palace.'

'But my lord, why is Lady Holika attacking us?'

Prahlad had no words. 'Because ... it's a misunderstanding.'

'Please, my lord, we beg you to stop her by going to the palace front and talking to her,' the guard said.

'All right, I'll see.'

The guards nodded and went back for the gate. Prahlad turned to see the destruction the Danavs were doing, breaking the walls of the palace gates, tearing them apart as arrows from Prahlad's side hit their faces.

'You need to leave,' Narada said. 'Don't you understand? You cannot surrender and talk to her. She's angry.'

But the fate of my people rests in my hands. Can I run from my responsibilities?

'You leave,' Prahlad said. 'I cannot go.'

'Why? You choose your people over us?'

'No, I choose to stop this chaos. I'm sure that's what Lord Vishnu would have wanted,' Prahlad said. 'And, for your information, he would have never wanted unnecessary deaths, which you have caused in his name.'

'Will I ever see you again?' Narada asked. His face was twisted, as if Prahlad's words had stung him.

'I don't know.' Prahlad sighed. 'Give my wishes to Dhriti. Keep her safe.'

Narada watched Prahlad for a moment, and then left his room. Running a hand through his hair, Prahlad thought of what he was about to do.

I'm going to die. There's no other way out of it.

He looked down at his guards and called out to them. 'Surrender. And tell Lady Holika I'm waiting for her inside.'

The guards from downstairs nodded and blew their horns.

Prahlad put on his black tunic and got ready.

This is it. I'm about to die.

46

PRAHLAD

He waited.

He was in front of the main gates of his palace. And he waited for his aunt to come and take him away. The violence had stopped. The Danavs were not causing the quakes any more. Everything was silent and for that, Prahlad was grateful. He had at last achieved peace.

At least, I shall die a Vishnu bhakt.

Prahlad had a dozen guards on each side. They weren't there to kill Holika, but to protect him if things went wrong. He still hoped he would find a way to calm her down.

Anger is an evil feeling. It corrupts those who are weak.

The door flew open and Holika dashed out, clad in her heavy set of armour. She had her twin swords in her hands.

And she was furious. Her nostrils were flared, her brows were arched and she was frowning with terrible horror. He recalled how afraid he used to be of this look when he was a child. He remembered also how his aunt would often eye him and shake her head, clearly because she considered him a disappointment to the Asura race.

'Prahlad!' she screamed and instantly, without even saying anything, she slashed her sword at him.

He used his shield to deflect the attack.

She isn't ready for peace.

'Prahlad, you are a dead man.'

'I want to make peace. That's why I've come to surrender.'

'With your men around you? That's not surrender, boy. That's cowardice,' she spat and then lunged forward, attacking Prahlad, but his guards came between them.

And no matter how much Prahlad wanted to stop this bloodshed, he couldn't, as Holika slashed and swung her sword at the guards, stabbing and slicing and severing their heads. She was so quick and agile that it was hard to even follow her movements.

'It's a shame I have to kill men of my race,' she said, as she was done with the last guard. 'Because your stupidity, your betrayal, so many of us have died. We have lost so many lives because of you. If only you hadn't involved yourself with the Vishnusena …'

'I tried to stop them.'

But Holika didn't listen.

She grabbed Prahlad by the hair and put the blade to his throat. 'You didn't stop them. Why did you betray your kind, Prahlad? *Why*?' she snarled.

Prahlad was tearing up. He was in pain. 'Because I was unhappy where I was. And I wanted something to look up to.'

Holika didn't say anything. She kept glaring at him. 'You are a stupid, stupid boy.'

And then she brought the blade down —

Suddenly, there was a scream.

She let go of him. He fell to the ground and saw how she turned quickly to deflect an attack which came out of nowhere.

She instantly jabbed the weapon inside the assailant's stomach, giving him a fatal wound. There was a loud cry from the assailant and Prahlad saw it was none other than Narada.

Holika twisted the blade inside his guruji, and he fell to the ground, blood flowing from the wound.

No.

Prahlad got to his feet, staggering as he saw Narada, who smiled at Prahlad.

'Remember … to … lead them wisely,' he paused. 'Unlike me.' And then his eyes closed.

No.

Holika pulled the blade out and kicked Narada and turned to Prahlad, who was pale, his face streaked with tears.

'You cry for this monster?' Holika shook her head.

'Kill me and be done with it.' Prahlad closed his eyes, ready for his execution.

'You know what, a petty boy like you who weeps for a traitor doesn't deserve such a death, where no one gets to see the crimes you have committed,' Holika replied.

And Prahlad opened his eyes at that.

No.

'What do you mean?'

She knelt close to him, her eyes dark and angry. 'You need to be publicly shamed and … *publicly executed.*'

47

PRAHLAD

He had been confined for days now.

He could smell his own filth. He was hungry and parched, but they had given him nothing to eat or drink.

This is worse than a public execution.

Prahlad was shackled in a corner, watching the sunlight shining through the barred window that was close to the ceiling. He tried to smell the air of Kashyapuri, but couldn't. He was stuck here and every moment, he hated himself, but he never second guessed his decision to turn towards Lord Vishnu.

I believe he shall come and see me.

'And what if he doesn't?' a voice said, as if someone had read his mind.

Prahlad looked up to see a woman – a curly-haired lady with a beautiful, familiar smile. She looked exactly like the portrait that his father kept in his study.

It was his mother.

'What if he doesn't come, son?' Kayadhu asked, coming forward, and she felt so real.

Am I beginning to hallucinate?

'He will. I believe in him,' Prahlad responded, but his voice was weak.

'You've been here for three days now. You are about to give in to darkness and yet you believe in him. Why is your faith so strong, son?'

Prahlad sighed, shaking his head.

She's just a product of my own fears.

'Because I have nothing else, and when there's nothing else, there is Lord Vishnu. And there's faith. Sometimes, you need to blindly follow it, to be guided to the light.'

Kayadhu's eyes softened as she placed her palms across Prahlad's cheeks, caressing them. 'I hope you are right, son. I died for this empire. And you are going to die for your faith. I don't know which one is worse.'

Prahlad had no answer for that, since they were interrupted by a loud clattering of the gates opening and Kayadhu disappeared. He could feel his heart tug tightly, but he remained quiet. He looked at the gates and saw Holika enter with two of her guards. Prahlad saw that her eyes were bloodshot and she looked tired and weary.

'Today is the day, boy,' Holika managed a smile. 'Are you ready?'

Prahlad nodded.

'Good. I have another surprise for you. The raven's message has arrived. Your brother is dead,' she said.

His heart sank.

'Killed in the war,' she chuckled. 'Isn't that funny? The two boys of Hiranya get what they deserve.'

'My father will kill you for this.'

'You know him better than I do, Prahlad. He will applaud me for killing a traitor, not berate me for killing his son.' Holika shook her head. 'He always thought of you as his rightful successor and you betrayed him. I have sent a raven to inform him of your actions and I told him your execution cannot wait any more. You will face the consequences of your actions. Get him,' she told her guards.

The guards pulled Prahlad up and pushed him outside, their spears prodding him on the back. He was in a long tunic that covered his entire frame and he began to follow Holika out of the prison.

He couldn't think about anything except Anuhrad.

Dead. No.

His heart was sinking, heavy with hatred for the world.

As soon as he left the prison, he saw a long passageway on either side of which were people shouting and spitting at him, holding hoardings that read, 'FALSE KING'.

'You might ask why I took three days for your execution,' Holika said, grinning. 'To make sure they all knew what you did. To make them all angry. To make them hate you as much I hate you.'

'Why do you hate me so much, Aunty?' Prahlad asked. The sunlight was gleaming on his face, almost blinding him. He felt so exposed. It was over.

The entire city hated him.

'Is it because of my mother?' he pressed.

'No, you fool. I liked your mother,' Holika growled. 'It is because your actions have led to the death of someone very close to me.'

Prahlad's eyes widened. He hadn't thought of it from that perspective.

'And once you are executed, I will be hunting down the rest of your mates for what they did to my Simmi.'

'I apologize deeply. I didn't … I didn't know,' Prahlad said. 'If I had known …'

'You wouldn't have cared, boy,' Holika snapped at him. 'I never had a child of my own, but when I found one, you stole her from me.'

Prahlad felt so much guilt that he wanted to express, but he was short of words. Then he saw where he was being taken. There was a large river that ran close to the southern gates of the capital – and it was deep. The civillians were forbidden from entering it, since they were sure to be drowned by its powerful current.

'I thought my head was being cut off,' Prahlad said, laughing at his fate.

'Death by drowning suits a traitor like you more,' Holika shrugged.

Prahlad nodded as he heard the people jeer. He wanted to have one last look at Anuhrad, at Dhriti, at Narad and even at Kayadhu, his mother. He came close to the river, beyond which were the dark woods.

Prahlad turned back to see all the civilians who had come to watch the execution of the interim king. They stood there, waiting for the entertainment to start. He even saw the ogre-like Danavs watching from afar, silently gazing at the spectacle.

A guard pulled off his chains before tying his legs up with ropes, at the ends of which were two rocks.

'Any last words?' Holika asked.

'May the virtue and blessings of Lord Vishnu be with me.'

Holika laughed. 'All right.'

The guard pushed Prahlad to the edge of the river. And then he picked up the rock which was tied to Prahlad's leg and threw it into the water.

There was a jerk, but not enough to pull him in. He could feel his heart thumping hard, as he clasped his hands together in the name of his god.

The guard then picked up the second rock, tossing it into the river.

And instantly Prahlad's feet jerked forward, dragging him into the water.

All he saw was darkness. The sound of people died down. Everything around him was water, devoid of life.

And the rocks pulled him in deep ...

EPILOGUE

ANDHAKA

Did everyone think I would die so easily?

Andhaka had a smile as he was taken away in a caravan, fifty miles away from Sonitpur. He had his army of Rakshasas, Pishach and his surviving soldiers … all together as they marched into the sunset, away from the snow and towards the greener side of the land.

But Andhaka couldn't see … he could only smell the scent of rainwater drying, the smell of leaves. He could hear the sparrows.

He knew Narasimha was behind him and he had to be stopped, so that Andhaka could save what was left of his army and escape with his own life. And thus, the decoy had been placed, for an easy surrender in front of Narasimha. It had been one of his doppelgangers that Nara had killed – the only one Andhaka had blinded out of desperation, so that he'd be more convincing.

He hadn't wanted to, but it was necessary.

There was also another purpose for letting the decoy out. Now that Narasimha had killed him and the word was out that he was no more, he could work patiently on his grand plan.

I will take everything from the Asuras and the Devas. They took my childhood. Their petty wars took my life. And now, I will take their empires.

He couldn't help but grin.

'Where to, my lord?' asked Kalanemi, his humble servant.

Andhaka breathed deeply, and his grin widened.

'Kashyapuri.'

Will Prahlad be saved?
Will Narasimha find redemption?
What is the secret Lord Rudra told Narasimha?
Will Hiranyakashyap be able to kill Indra?
What are the details of Andhaka's grand plans?
Find out in Book 2!

TO BE CONTINUED IN …

THE MAHAVATAR TRILOGY BOOK 2

HIRANYAKASHYAP

ACKNOWLEDGEMENTS

So many people think that a book is created just by the writer. But there's really an army of people behind every book's making.

Let's start with my parents – Jyotsna and Leslie Missal. They have been a rock in my life and I'm so grateful for that.

Also, my agent, Anuj Bahri of Red Ink Literary Agency. He's my guide in an industry which has so many doors, so many paths that it's easy for someone like me, a 22-year-old, to get lost. Mr Bahri didn't let that happen.

I also want to thank my awesome publishers. They have been just so enthusiastic about this book that I have to pinch myself to make sure it's really happening.

Starting with Swati Daftuar, who commissioned this book and listened to all my questions. Thanks. I can be a real bother, but you were quite patient with me.

Prerna Gill, who copy-edited my book so deftly. Percy Bharucha, who planned my marketing strategy. He calls me 'bro'– a good change from the usual 'sir'.

I am especially grateful to Jitendra and his team at Arthat Studio. I realised I don't thank them enough. They create such amazing cover art for my books and display such professionalism. And I also want to thank Bonita Vaz-Shimray from HarperCollins India, who used her artistic superpowers and made this cover even more awesome than it was already.

I want to thank Bijit Sinha, who edited the first draft of this book. He's the most awesome guy I've met.

A big thank you to my first beta reader for this book – Shivangi Saha. You were my first reader and you made this book better by telling me about all the flaws. This won't have been possible without you.

I want to thank my family too –my cousin Ryan and my aunt and uncle, all of whom are so close to me and were always by my side during this journey. One should never forget the people who made you who you are today.

Thank you to Prakhar Bhargava and his team for creating the book trailer, and to Vishal Bawa for acting in it. Shubham Ghatge for creating the clips that I promote on social media. Hitesh for doing crazy character designs used for promotions.

I also want to thank my friends – Ragini Raghuram, Chetan Sharma and Ayush Dogra. I discuss my ideas about my books with and they had been always enthusiastic and patient with me.

And finally, I want to thank Somya Sharma.

She always has such cool ideas about marketing the book. Don't ever think that your ideas go unnoticed.